How Sweet the Sound

How Sweet the Sound

Ann Tonnell

Desert Palm Press

How Sweet the Sound

By Ann Tonnell

©2022 Ann Tonnell
A
ISBN (book) 9781954213340
ISBN (epub) 9781954213357

Desert Palm Press
1961 Main Street, Suite 220
Watsonville, California 95076
www.desertpalmpress.com

Editor: Toni Kelley
Cover Design: Michele Bordeur - eebooWORX

Printed in the United States of America
First Edition June 2022

Acknowledgements

A special thanks to Lee Fitzsimmons and Desert Palm Press for taking a chance on this novice writer. Lee and editor, Toni Kelley, were great working companions. They were extraordinarily patient with delays due to my broken humerus. Toni's guidance through the first novel perils was invaluable.

This book would not have been possible without the Golden Crown Literary Society and the Cate Culpepper Mentorship Program. It was an honor to be mentored by Nat Burns for my second novel, *Not Sorry*. It helped me shape *How Sweet* into a much tighter offering.

A thank you is not nearly enough for the help provided by Beta readers G.L. Irwin, Lori Fournier, and my avid reader-wife, DL. Speaking of my wife, I must bow to DL for her support in the effort to tell my stories. The trips, the campground discussions and visits, the bike tour, and more.

Last but not at all least, heaps of praise to Christina Wood-Martinez. Not only did she guide me and correct me, she supported the validity of the story. I could never have submitted this to DPP without her. If one could insert emojis into a paragraph such as this, there would be one of those COVID-safe yellow faces hugging the red heart tightly.

I dedicate this book to my mother. She taught me love is love. She taught me unconditional love is unconditional. In her last two years she told me several times she wanted to read my book as I typed across the table from her. I told her she could after it was published. MKDB – 1931-2020

Prologue

"I never said it would be easy, I only said it would be worth it."
—*Mae West*

VAL SCOTT LOOKED AROUND her aunt's living room for the last time. With the rest of the estate settled, selling the large colonial on Martha's Vineyard marked the completion of her executor duties. The finality was not as freeing as she expected. Instead, she felt the enormity of what was ahead. She sat for a moment on what had been Aunt Grace's favorite overstuffed, leather armchair by the living room fireplace and remembered the last discussion she had with her aunt.

"Just picture it, Val—" Grace's hearty, guttural laugh interrupted mid-sentence. "Just imagine driving by that big, lighted casino gate in the middle of rural Georgia!" She waved her hand in an arc through the air as her laugh was replaced with a raspy cough.

"You okay? Here, this'll help." Val smiled as she brought over a glass of whiskey. "It'll definitely be something to see."

"Come on now, Val. Surely you can picture this happening."

"I hope so." Val's grin was accompanied with a nod and a chuckle. "How can it not succeed? I mean, if we get it through the legislature." The grin settled into a serious countenance as she set her jaw. Almost as quickly, the grin returned. "Who's going to argue with helping their church? The Lord does work in mysterious ways, eh?" Val chuckled.

"I'm depending on you to carry this out, you know. It's a hefty chore to leave you," Grace said as she swirled her Irish whiskey through the ice with her index finger. She looked between Val and the roaring fire. "Well. That's a pensive look. What are you thinking?"

"I agree there'll be some hard work, for sure, but let's think of it as good trouble. Shall we go through it again?" Val tapped her pen on the legal pad in her lap.

Val and Grace had originally hatched the plan, loosely, over drinks by the Vineyard home's fireplace one winter. Throughout the years, even though they joked about it, it had become a viable prospect.

"I know it started as a joke for us, but I can see the project's feasibility now. All those times you joined me at Connecticut casinos, it just became clearer...and doable. I wish we had kept track of all the time we've spent honing the concepts and structure since that original discussion. Don't you?" Grace asked.

"It's definitely been a long time coming," Val replied. After reviewing the plan one last time with Grace, Val stood and poked the fire.

"I think that does it. I know it's not long now. I feel it," Grace said softly before taking another sip of her whiskey. "I feel ready, and the estate is in order."

"Not sure I am, though, Grace....Ready, I mean." Val sighed and blew out a breath.

"I wish your mom had seen what a fine woman you've become. You know, she'd be proud of you...of your willingness to attempt such an endeavor."

"The endowment for this project is an incredible legacy, Grace. I hope it's successful."

"I'm afraid it's time for this old lady to hit the hay," Grace said as she struggled to stand. Val assisted her to the bedroom and into her large feather bed. As she pulled the blanket over her shoulder, she said, "Remember my Mae West quote when it gets tough."

"Yeah, I know. It'll be worth it." Val leaned and kissed Grace's forehead. She turned off her bedside lamp, and pulled the door halfway closed. She sunk into that favorite overstuffed chair and watched as the fire became embers. She thought about Grace's life and what a remarkable force she had been.

Grace had been a successful real estate broker in Boston. After Val's mom died, Grace had become more of a close friend than an aunt. Val accompanied Grace to numerous political and charity fund-raisers as well as high social celebrations.

Grace was well educated, well spoken, well respected, and beautiful—perhaps even more so as she aged. Val had been the light of Grace's life, the only child between the two sisters.

With her aunt's estate providing significant seed money, their planned organization would not need immediate outside financial support. Val thought of no better way to memorialize her aunt than the non-profit casino they had envisioned—Amazing Grace.

Now here she was in that same chair—the chair where she likely was sitting when her aunt left the world in her sleep. The room was cold without a fire.

Time to head to Georgia and roll the dice! Val thought as she returned the key to the lockbox.

Chapter One

VAL GENERATED INTEREST AS she backed her '95 classic silver camper into site fifteen. None of the sites were as private as she had hoped, with only a few trees at the edge of her site near the water. She leveled and stabilized her temporary home just twenty feet from the lake.

Luckily, only a few of the campsites were occupied. She looked around at the other rigs and nodded to those who were looking at hers.

She walked around the perimeter of the trailer and patted the metal manufacturer's tag three times. This was a camping ritual. *Good ol' Bambi*, Val thought.

Val noticed one site in particular looked to be long-term campers, perhaps full-timers—those who made state parks their home. While only two tents are allowed per site, these campers had huge tarps connecting the tents serving as an apparent great room. A small refrigerator and a single kitchen base cabinet with a simple laminate surface were situated on an open, flatbed trailer that was pulled under the great room tent. An elaborate system of camp stoves circled the fire pit grate. Steam escaped from a large cast iron pot on the grate's center. One man appeared to be preparing vegetables on the grill. Three other men were sitting at the picnic table deep in discussion, but they all looked across and nodded in greeting. She wondered if these were folks down on their luck. *Just another facet of society who might benefit from our plan, Grace,* she thought as she looked at the cloudy sky.

***

That evening after her sandwich supper, Val looked at an area map to prepare for the week's explorations. She had a lot of ground to cover to find the perfect acreage for Amazing Grace.

Chapter Two

SO FAR, HAMBURG PARK seemed an ideal setting. The area had plenty of back roads for cycling–her respite and workout component as well. The park sat on some seven hundred plus acres in Washington County, Georgia, not far from the town of Marshall in Hancock County. This allowed her easy accessibility to the places she'd need to visit to get a real feel for the area.

First things first, though, she thought. *Gotta get into town to check it out.* After coffee and a banana, she headed toward the library, a usual spot for free internet access. A computer screen made it so much easier to see land tracts and satellite views. After researching some available land tracts online and making notes, her stomach growled.

The Pizza Joint, a place she'd spotted on the main drag, seemed to be a good prospect for both food and info. A cute young woman, holding a boxed pizza and on her way out the door, almost ran Val down as she entered.

"Woah!" Val stood back with her arms raised.

"Sorry. Sorry. I'm running so late." The woman smiled as she rushed out to her running red pickup truck.

"I see that," Val said with a smile as she turned her head and watched the woman drive off. *Oh yeah,* she thought. *Now she's one of those people I'd like to meet.*

As Val waited on her order, she nosed around a bulletin board with business cards push-pinned among the social and church flyers and business discount coupons. She took a card for a local realtor, Sandy Ann Smithfield, whose picture looked just as one might expect in rural Georgia. Big styled blonde hair, a pearly white smile, and a gold chain necklace matching the bracelet that adorned the wrist of the hand whose index finger pointed to her tilted chin. Val filled her plastic cup with water and took a seat at a red cafe table in the corner.

Val overheard the two employees, who filled the roles of cashier, cook, and server, dishing out local gossip to the customers as they slid pies onto and off of the oven's belt. When her pizza rolled off, it was swiftly cut into slices and delivered right to Val's table.

"Here you go, hon. Normally, I'd call out your name, but since this is your first time in, I decided to bring it to your table. I'm Peggy," she said, as she pointed to her name tag. Peggy was likely Val's age, or close to it. She wore a plain gray, neatly pressed uniform dress. Her hair was pulled back and covered with a hairnet.

"Nice to meet you, Peggy. Val," she replied. "In town for a couple of weeks. I'm staying out at Hamburg."

"My ex-husband loves it out there. It's beautiful. He used to spend more time at the park than he did at home. I hope you have a great time. We sure appreciate your business."

"Well, thanks. I appreciate your bringing my pizza to the table. Hey, you know anything about Sandy Ann Smithfield?" Val held up the card.

"Oh, lordy. I've known her for years. We went to school together. Well, everybody in Marshall went to school with everybody else here." Val and Peggy both laughed. "But Sandy Ann is a real doll. She really wants to match a person to a house. So, you're looking to move here?" Peggy asked as if Val had lost her mind.

"I'm looking for some property. More of a commercial acreage venture."

"Oh, my! Well, there is plenty of that around here. Nothing but land. It's either planted for timber, belongs to the Little Ogeechee flood plain, or it's clear-cut for all of the subdivisions needed to house all of the people who are *not* moving here. You shouldn't have any problems finding land. Though Lord only knows why anyone would move here. Mind you, I love it here, but I was born and raised in Marshall. My family is here. I understand the beauty and rich history. Most outside folk don't see that, but if anybody can find you land or a house or a big ol' building out in the middle of nowhere, it's Sandy Ann. She's a real gem. A doll."

"Well Peggy, that's just the sort of recommendation I needed. I'll give her a call."

"Nice to meet you, Val. Come back now." Peggy placed an empty, smaller pizza box on the table next to the pie for any leftovers. "And good luck."

"Yeah. Thanks, Peggy. I'm sure I'll be back."

Val studied her property list as she ate. Once she was back in her truck, she called Sandy Ann, whose voicemail message sounded as perky as she looked. She would get back to Val "faster'n a hot knife through butter" her voice message advised. As Val pulled into the library's lot just down the street, the phone rang. She answered with a hello and a smile. Grace had always said that people are more receptive to your voice while you're smiling, and Val had adopted the practice.

"Is this Val? This is Sandy Ann Smithfield, your Home Town Realtor. What can I help you with?"

"Thanks for returning my call so quickly. I'm new to the area, and I've been looking online at land around Marshall for a couple of days. Several tracts look interesting." After outlining size and rough location, Val explained she wanted a face-to-face meeting for additional information, especially tract layouts and dimensions. Sandy Ann answered that tomorrow would work and they agreed on a time.

Val could hardly wait until morning. Land hunting tomorrow was going to change her biking plans, but she could walk or hike later in the day when it was warmer. She would be able to mull over the newly acquired real estate details as she walked. She compared her land tract findings with online descriptions for a couple of hours at the library to help her organize tomorrow's meeting needs.

***

It was a mild afternoon, and Val sat at her site's outdoor picnic table. The fleece helped cut the chill of the light breeze. The squatters were seated around their fire pit drinking from coffee cups. The usual nods were exchanged. She noticed shiny silver filets arranged on the blackened grate. *The boys have been busy fishing. Looks like a feast this evening.*

As the sun dropped below the tall pine tree line, she heard a barred owl's "who cooks for you?" Val realized she should probably get a bite to eat before she bedded down.

Val loved the glow of the low light in the camper. Bambi was sixteen feet long, with a bed, a dinette and kitchen area, and a separate bathroom with a shower. Small but convenient. Cozy. She snuggled into the covers and read herself to sleep.

At times during the night she could hear the distant yaps, calls, and howls of a pack of coyotes. She pictured them coming up on a field of deer and feasting on the weakest of the group. Even with that image, forest sounds were typically comforting. Well, comforting as long as she was in a hard-shell camper.

Val considered how her project might interfere with the solitude of places like the park. As she drifted back to sleep, she remembered

Grace's challenge to preserve as much natural habitat as could be managed.

***

Sandy Ann opened her office's front door and stepped out onto the deck as Val drove up.

"You must be Valerie. I'm Sandy Ann," she said, extending her hand as Val walked up the steps. "Welcome." Sandy Ann motioned for Val to sit on one of the upholstered chairs in the lobby, and Sandy Ann sat in one of the chairs turned toward Val. "Let's hear some more about what I can do for you."

"First, please call me Val," she said, smiling warmly.

"Sure! Val it is," Sandy Ann replied, returning her business card's smile.

"As I mentioned, I need more info on these tracts, and perhaps even go walk around some of them," Val said, tapping on her legal pad.

"If you can give me an idea of the land's usage, we can talk zoning, although you've probably figured out there isn't too much zoning around here," she said, chuckling. Sandy Ann was much more professional than Val had expected based on her picture. The adage about judging a book by its cover passed through her mind.

"I'm not quite ready to reveal any details at this point. Any discussions we have are to be kept confidential. This is a sensitive matter for many reasons." Val wondered as she spoke if Sandy Ann would be open to the changes that this type of project would mean for the community. Could it mesh with the area's political climate? Such ventures were often met with mistrust in the South. Many attempts throughout the Carolinas had been raided and shut down by those citing religious objections and area blue laws. Val hoped appealing to the people's economic interests and social consciences could help push her project through.

"Well now, Val. That's quite intriguing. I can help you, regardless. Obviously, the more I know, the more I can steer you toward properties that might be better suited. But I'll give this a go. Let's see what you've got, and we'll look at it on an area map," she said, motioning Val to her desk.

After looking at prices, road frontage, terrain, and tract layouts, Val chose her top two. These two tracts were both under her expected maximum acreage, had what appeared to be ample road frontage, and were within a twenty to thirty-mile radius.

Riding around to the sites in Sandy Ann's car, Val learned details of Sandy Ann's family. She married her high school sweetheart, now the high school principal. Their boy was a third grader, and their girl was in the sixth. Sandy Ann invited Val to the New Canaan Methodist's Sunday service.

"Well, I appreciate that offer. Not much of a church-goer, and if I'm up on weekend mornings I'm usually riding my bike."

"Oh goodness. I see folks out riding around here. I couldn't ride two miles," Sandy Ann said with a laugh.

"I sure don't recommend you ride without training for whatever distance you do ride. It takes a while to get used to sitting on a saddle. And you do have to have some muscles, but I've been riding for years. I look forward to seeing some of these same roads from the saddle. You really get a sense of the land when you're that close to it."

"Never thought of it that way, but I guess you're right."

"I couldn't do what you do, that's for sure. I'm not a big talker in general. I tend to keep to myself most of the time. I wouldn't call myself reclusive or private, though. Probably a lot of people think I'm snooty. I'll be civil, but it takes me a while to warm up to folks."

"You're right. That wouldn't work for this job." Sandy Ann chuckled.

"I like this property we're headed to now. From the satellite map, it seems like it has the sort of layout and frontage I've been looking for." Val tried to change the subject.

"So, speaking of frontage, that usually means something in particular in the business world...that, and that you want accessibility to the major transportation arteries."

"I can tell you there will be at least two large buildings and huge parking areas," Val offered.

Sandy Ann raised her eyebrows and sported a sheepish grin. "That sounds like retail space to me. Outlet mall, shipping business, maybe? You definitely are looking for something that will handle commercial construction."

"You could say that, certainly."

Val had to give it to Sandy Ann. She nailed the best location based on Val's list—a sweeping four-hundred-acre tract that would have little residential impact.

During the next week, Sandy Ann handled the usual back and forth between the seller and Val to come up with the best deal. Because it was a cash sale, by Monday afternoon, papers would be signed, money would be transferred, and Val would be a property owner in Hancock and Washington Counties. The tract included almost fifty abutting acres in Washington County, and this section could potentially accommodate the solar farm.

-

Chapter Three

VAL'S HEAD WAS SPINNING, and she thought she might explode if she didn't get a bike ride in. She drove back to the park and quickly readied for a ride to de-clutter and de-stress. *Overcast and cool. Perfect.*

After eighteen miles, Val felt a light misty rain. It broke her meditative cadence, and she realized that in her haste, she had not checked the forecast. She had not biked a mile into her shortcut before her rear wheel started hissing. *Not a flat. No, no, no.* By now it was pouring, but she was able to find a flat spot, not too muddy. Typically, she carried a spare tube, but the ride was going to be short, and she hadn't counted on rain. Val was skilled in repairing a tire, but rain does not make for an easy patch seal. She hovered over the tube to block the rain and dried it with one little corner of her bandana.

It was four-thirty by the time she reached the park. She was covered with grease, she was drenched, and she had the hallmark cyclist's rain and road grime streak down the center of her backside. *These clothes are going to need more than the usual handwashing,* Val thought as she grabbed the rest of her dirty clothes and headed out for the laundromat she had seen on Main Street.

"Shit," she cursed. "Shit."

What if they're not open? What if they don't have somewhere for me to change? What happened to your planning skills, Scott? Oh yeah. No change and no soap either. She was lucky she had changed out of her bike cleats and into sneakers. Val rushed through the front door just as the attendant was closing the top part of the hinged office door. *Great, just great. I look like a greasy dork right now,* she thought as she realized it was the cute woman who had run into her at the pizza place. *Just remember, you hoped you'd see her again. Yeah, Scott, but not like this!* "Excuse me. Hi. Could you please change a ten before you leave?" Val called plaintively as she pulled her basket through. When the attendant reopened the top part of the door, she laughed.

"I'm sorry, but you need that change! Sure. Of course. That's the least I can do for you, right?"

"Yeah, thanks. I had a flat on my bike ride...just as it started raining," Val replied.

"I knew something had happened. I couldn't have guessed what, but I gathered it was on a bicycle." She looked at Val's clothes.

"Ha. I guess so." Val nodded as she looked down at her own outfit—Carolina blue jersey and typical lycra shorts with a saturated pad. She frowned and shook her head.

"Hey, I remember you. Sorry I stabbed you with my pizza box the other day." The woman smiled as she spoke.

"It's nice to meet the dragon slayer," Val said, returning the smile. "I'm Val Scott. I'm staying at Hamburg for a while."

"I'm Nicki. You'll hear some people call me Lucky, though. My nickname. I was born on Saint Patrick's Day. Chief Cook and Bottle Washer of Marshall Coin-op Laundry." She extended her hand for a shake. "Look, I tell you what. Get your clothes in the washer. The soap is on me today. New customer special. Normally, I close early on Wednesday. Not officially, but no one comes in Wednesday evening. They're all in church...or pretending to be."

"Oh. I don't want to keep you. I'll—"

"Don't worry about that," Nicki interrupted. "But here's a proposition for you. You look reliable enough. I'm going to lock up and leave you in here. I mean, you'll sort of be locked in. Use the back door through the office in an emergency." She reached in a cabinet, pulled out some clothes, and placed them on the counter of the bottom part of the office door.

"And here is a shirt, a pair of pants and socks—way too big—that someone left years ago. Change into those so you can wash those nasty bike clothes." She showed Val the office and the door to the back of the building. "I'm going to go grab a few things at the store and grab something for dinner. I'll come back. If you finish before I get back, feel free to shower and clean up in the back room. No sense getting your clean clothes all greasy."

"Wow. This is not the service one gets in a big city."

"You'll find most people around here are pretty friendly, especially once they get to know you."

"All right, Nicki. You've saved my life. I owe you one." Val tried to ignore the warmth between her legs as she completed the handshake. *What a smile!* Val could feel her cheeks redden as she withdrew her hand.

"Oh, don't worry—I'll collect." Nicki jumped off the table, grabbed her purse and ran out the front door, flipping the sign to *closed.* As she locked the door, she raised her eyebrows and cast Val a devilish smile.

Did that just happen? She was flirting, wasn't she? She was. Val shivered with goosebumps. *And it's been a long time since I've been lucky. She's adorable. Lucky, huh? Yeah, I want to get Lucky. Every pun intended.*

She was wearing a royal blue sweatshirt and a white collared shirt. She had on small silver-colored hoop earrings with one stud in the top left ear. Jeans. Not too tight, but not baggy. Leather Keens. Nicki was probably two inches taller than Val, thinner, and appeared to be toned. *Youth versus exercise?* Val wondered. She was quite happy with her life, and she had no regrets with how her body was "progressing," as she called it.

As she looked around, Val saw it was as she expected—a simple, coin-op place. The office door sign displayed attendant hours. The restroom was clean. A faded wallpaper border depicting clothes pinned and drying on a line outlined the walls. The border's clothes were being blown as if on a windy day. Blue, hard plastic chairs with metal legs, fused together in threes, were placed in strategic spots. Metal laundry transport carts with racks for hanging clothes were parked under the edges of the folding tables.

Laundry had always been one of Val's favorite chores, especially in her adult life. She found it relaxing. With unbridled access, she took the opportunity to check out the cleaning products in the shower and above the sink as her clothes agitated in the wash cycle. To her surprise, tubs of Goo Gone and GoJo lined the shelf above the sink in the office.

Val grabbed a cleaning cloth from the stack next to the tubs and used it to begin removing the bike chain's greasy deposits from her hands, arms and legs. This would make a shower unnecessary until she was home. Val chuckled to herself as she realized how long it took to clean herself up. The wash cycle had completed in the short time it took her to remove the grease. *Might as well have showered!*

A neatly made full-size bed, bistro table, two chairs, base cabinet with microwave, toaster oven, induction burner, coffee pot and an apartment-sized refrigerator rounded out the furniture in the office. All that and the desk and chair, sink and shower. *Someone could live back there. Definitely could have a nice time,* she thought as she folded the last of her dry clothes.

The back door opened and startled her. Val had not seen the car drive around from the storefront window. The clock on the wall revealed an hour and a half had passed. *Wow. Time flies.*

"I'm *baaack*," shouted Nicki.

"You must have a secret getaway alley back there."

"Something like that. If I stay overnight here, I don't want the car up front. It's not that it's completely hidden, but most people wouldn't notice someone is here." Nicki unloaded a few items into the refrigerator and base cabinet. She sat a bottle of wine on the bistro table and pulled two glasses out of the cabinet.

"Want some?"

"I would, but I haven't had any water or anything to eat. That could be a dangerous combination. Especially since I have to drive back to Hamburg. You're kind to offer, though. I'd like to take you up on that sometime."

Nicki handed Val a bottled water from the refrigerator and smiled. "Okay. I'll drink alone. Hey, want half of my sub? It's a veggie. I never eat more than half. No need to starve."

"Sure. I could eat a horse. Well, if I ate land animals I could. I *already* owe you."

"You do. As I said, I *will* call in my favors," Nicki said as she flashed her devilish smile. "How 'bout dinner Friday night? At your place. Tent or camper?"

"Sure, again. Small camper. The classic, silver one. And I'd be honored to have you. My first friend in Marshall!" *Jeez, is this happening? Honored? Scott, come on.*

"Do you mean Sandy Ann didn't friend you up?"

Val looked puzzled.

"Come on." Nicki chuckled as she spoke. "You thought word of a new person coming here to Marshall looking for a realtor wouldn't get around town?" She smiled at Val and looked directly into her eyes.

"Well, I just didn't think about it, I guess. So, you didn't talk to Sandy Ann?"

"Oh no. This was restaurant talk. Attractive woman came in looking for a realtor. I knew that had to be you as soon as I remembered seeing you the other day."

"Well, thanks for that compliment." Val smiled.

"You cleaned up, eh?"

"Yes. No shower, but I still need to wash that rag and these clothes for you," Val said, pointing to the dirty rag on the edge of the shower stall.

"I'll put them in the bucket under the sink. When we have to work on the machines, we generate quite a few of these. We clean them when we have a full load of them."

"We?" *Surely the girl doesn't flirt like that if she's attached.*

"Don't worry. I'm single." Nicki beamed, winked, and quickly flashed that devilish smile again. "John Henry is *the* most important person to this laundromat, including me. He can fix any mechanical thing in this world, I'm convinced. Between the vending and the coin slots, we can generate some grime!"

"I see." Val finished eating her sandwich and drinking her water. "I'll get out of your hair so you can go home," Val offered.

"Oh, you're no bother. I'm serious. I planned to stay here tonight anyway. I have to be back at seven in the morning. John Henry is coming by to look at the change machine. It has been sticking some, and I don't want to go into the weekend that way. I wish you would have a glass of wine with me."

"Friday evening, remember. What time do you close?"

"I leave at five most days. I don't close up the laundry until nine, but on Fridays, John Henry does that for me. He stays overnight on Friday and opens up on Saturdays."

"Now *that's* a gift!"

"You're right. It is." Nicki looked away for a few seconds as if contemplating the thought, then smiled and returned her gaze to Val. "I can be at your place by six, I think. Will that work?"

"Perfect. I know you like merlot, but are you opposed to pinot noir? I have a nice bottle from a friend in Oregon I'll share with you...as a thank you."

"I love it all. We don't get many opportunities for fine wines here, unless we're invited to some fancy Chamber of Commerce shindig. And my business isn't always thought of as 'Chamber' material, even though I am a member."

"Hmm." Val felt annoyed by that notion. "Any food allergies or restrictions?"

"I don't eat meat. And raw onions don't agree with me. Other than that, I'm open. What should I bring?" Nicki asked.

"Nothing except yourself and your open palate. I'll come up with something to go with pinot. See you at six Friday evening."

"It's a date. A *date*." Nicki smiled and looked away quickly to conceal it. Val hadn't known Nicki long enough to understand if she were joking or flirting. *Come on, Scott. Sure seems like she's flirting. You have entertained a lady or two in your life. Don't seem so shocked. But someone that much younger? Benefits to that, I guess. Mm-mm.*

At five feet and four inches tall, Val weighed in between one hundred forty-five and one hundred fifty pounds on any given day. She considered herself more muscular than fat. She kept fit by lifting free weights, cycling, and holding a daily two-minute plank. Nothing special. At fifty-five, she knew she couldn't take her body for granted. Her wavy gray hair was often stark and short. Wavy became curly when it was longer. Sometimes she would allow a curl in front, so she resembled Longfellow's "little girl" of rhyme fame. At least that's what her mother had always said when she had been naughty. Her hair would never grow past her ears, though. Many would call hers a boy's cut, but she instructed stylists she wanted an Ellen DeGeneres hairdo. Her blue eyes and fair complexion with scattered freckles were mere vestiges of her formerly red-headed self.

It had been two years since her decades-long relationship had ended. It was an amicable split, but it still hurt. She learned there was nothing like facing the prospect of dating when you're considered older. She was approaching senior citizenship according to the mail she was receiving. *Great. Just great. Well, it does feel nice, Scott. Yeah, but it's the let-down I worry about.*

All the way home, Val considered what she could prepare and what might transpire. *A date?* She questioned if she could have misread Nicki's meaning. *Why would Nicki be bashful after seeming so forward?* Val realized she and Nicki hadn't exchanged phone numbers. She didn't eat meat, but Val wondered if Nicki ate seafood. She assumed by the cheese on the sub that she must eat dairy. Val would make something vegetarian, but not vegan. She would go to the grocery in Milledgeville, where the selection was wider than the local stores. They all were within an easy drive of Hamburg. And Val had nothing but time on her hands for the near future.

Val enjoyed her shower back at the park. She was tired, and she slipped into bed much earlier than usual. She found herself picturing Nicki. She could use a friend more than she could use a lover. Grace was gone. She had other friends, but they weren't here. *And talking to yourself isn't always the best way to work on problems, now is it?* Again, thoughts of the age difference floated through. *Lover? Why are you even thinking that?* Nicki might simply have a flirtatious style. *You need to get this shit out of your head.* Regardless, Val was truly thrilled and nervous at the same time, no matter what her brain was telling her heart...or other parts of her body.

Val woke to rain on the camper's metal shell. She loved that sound. It was either early or so overcast with the rain that it seemed darker. She found her watch. Seven-thirty. Val didn't think she dreamed or even moved all night, her mind exhausted.

***

It was Thursday, and Val had lots to accomplish. She spotted the ranger's truck at the bath house and ran up the hill to catch him.

"Hi, I'm in fifteen...Val Scott."

"Yes, I remember. Good morning."

"I know most parks enforce the fourteen-day stay. I see I need to be here a while longer."

"That is the intent of the rule, Ms. Scott, but it's not a busy season for us. I don't need to enforce it to the letter. If you're willing to pick another site, I'll extend the stay."

"That'd be great."

"Yeah, the guys over there are doing the same thing. They have quite a complicated set up. I hate that they have to move it all. They're interested in your site. I'm trying to make it work for everyone."

"Sure."

"Check back with me in an hour or so and I can let you know what's available. I need to make sure someone hasn't reserved a place online."

"Fair enough. Now, I'm going to leave you to it, and I'm going to have my breakfast and get my day started."

"Have a nice day, and I'll check that reservation as soon as I get back to the office."

***

Val had already visited the website for Thumbprint Tiny Homes. Their products were well known from their television presence. She looked through a brochure downloaded onto her laptop to write down specifics in advance of calling to arrange for her tiny house purchase. Bambi had been her home for the past six months, again thanks to Grace, but she wanted more space. A tiny house seemed a perfect choice—permanent enough if desired but mobile enough to relocate if needed.

When she arrived at the library, she pulled into the parking lot to use the internet and make her calls in the privacy of the truck. With

Thumbprint, she chose a sale model with all of the upgrades. With a huge sigh, she clicked the submit order button.

"Thank you again, Aunt Grace," she said, eyes on the clouds and blowing a kiss to the sky. Her new home would begin its trek from Colorado in a month to her new land tract. She would have to arrange for septic, electric, and a well. After an hour on the phone, she found who to call for new installations and services, what could be required, and cost estimates, and she made a reservation to relocate at another site in the park.

To her surprise, the electric company now had fiber optic internet lines that could run to her new tract since it was within the maximum distance of the main road. That was some of the best news of the day. After Monday, she would be able to secure an official street address with the post office. She would have to find someone to erect a box. Maybe her new friend would know if John Henry could do such a thing. She blew out a loud sigh. *After all that, it's grocery time!*

The Milledgeville trip proved fruitful, literally, given the great selection of fresh fruit at the grocery today. This would be a perfect dessert with some dark chocolates on the side. Val settled on a spinach and mushroom quiche. With a homemade crust it would be rich enough for a red, but not so strong as to overpower the pinot.

She found herself thinking of Nicki again. Val didn't even know Nicki's surname. How jumbled her mind was the past few days. *What should I wear? Oh, quit worrying. She was flirting with you when you were covered in grease and dirt! What would Nicki wear? How should I set the table?* Seemingly never-ending stream of concern. *You are nervous, Val Scott!*

Chapter Four

AS IF KNOWING VAL needed calm, a cold front had pushed the rain out, and the sky was clear. The light breeze brought an enveloping chill. Val needed a long-sleeve jersey and a windbreaker today. The barely visible ripples running across the lake reminded Val that all was not settled. The tall pines surrounding the lake swayed very gently. *Look at that. You couldn't ask for a more perfect spot. This view should be a textbook example of serenity. If that's true, why is my stomach turning upside down?* The heaviness accompanying a low weather system may have headed out, but she felt plenty of pressure. *A date. Yeah, a date.* It seemed as if it had been a lifetime ago since her last date. This day would be a long one. She knew a bike ride would help burn some of her nervous energy.

After her ride, Val tried to stay busy tidying Bambi, making a crust, cutting vegetables and fruit, and preparing ingredients for easier assembly later. Using the park's comfort station shower prevented excess humidity in the small trailer. And it successfully washed away the kitchen and cycling odors from her body. Only three hours to wait. *Just relax.*

Val drifted into a luscious nap, the sun streaming across her bed. She woke up an hour later. It was years since she had napped so deeply. No cares. Comfortable. Warm. Content even. Maybe all of the tension had floated out with a dream's end.

At five-thirty, Val illuminated the awning rope lights, readied firewood in the pit and arranged two chairs with a camp table beside the pit. Inside, she decanted the wine. The dinette table was set, albeit with travel-ware. Val dressed in a gray T-shirt under a white cotton Oxford shirt, both tucked into her jeans—her favorite go-to comfort outfit. Her hair was somewhat spiked, but curly. She was ready, if a bit anxious.

Val had not given Nicki her site number, but she figured Nicki would just look for the white pickup truck and her silver camper once she was in the park. Even being a weekend night, only six campsites were occupied. It was dark enough for the awning to illuminate the camper and pickup, and Nicki slowly pulled in behind it. *Here goes,*

Scott. She took a deep breath and blew out a sigh just before opening the door of the trailer.

"Welcome," she said, waving Nicki inside.

"This is so cute. I've always wanted to look inside of one of these. This is an Airstream?" Nicki was wearing tight black jeans—not too tight to look trashy though. A simple, white, princess neckline, cotton T-shirt, untucked, a black leather motorcycle-looking jacket, and what looked to be motorcycle boots. She was one of those women who could be breathtaking in the simplest of outfits. Or was that just Val's perception clouded by a crush?

"It's only a three-step tour. The dinette and the kitchen." Val pointed with the sweep of an arm. "Step one. The refrigerator and the bathroom. Step two, the bedroom. Step three, back to the kitchen."

"I love it. I mean, I *love* it. I could live in this myself," Nicki said. Val motioned for Nicki to sit at the dinette bench, and Nicki slid in and leaned against the side wall.

"Correct. You could live in it by your*self.* It would be small for two. Unless you were crazy in the first year of young love," Val offered.

"Oh, I think you're right. Two people should have space to get away from one another."

"Agreed. Wine?" Val poured as she smiled at Nicki, not waiting for her answer.

"Please." Nicki nodded and returned the smile. "Something smells delicious."

"I wish I had a regular oven, but I think I've finally mastered this convection microwave. What you smell is a quiche with one of Valerie Scott's famous flaky crusts. Although it won't be as flaky as it would have been from a real oven. Cheers."

They toasted. After the first sip, Nicki quickly darted her eyes to Val's and raised her brows.

"This is delicious. Oh my god. We just don't get this quality around here. Oh, my. I hope you have your *own* bottle." Nicki laughed out loud.

Val smiled. "Thought you'd enjoy it. I have another case stored in a friend's basement in Athens. I'll share." Val slid into the dinette across from Nicki.

"I'll take it, but seriously, can I order this?" Nicki asked.

"Not sure. I don't think so, unless you do that when you're at the winery in Oregon for a tasting, but I might be wrong."

"Don't make me sad." Nicki pouted as she spoke.

"I'm trying to say 'thank you,' so I hope not to make you sad."

"I'm still focused on the sharing part. I assume you mean the wine."

"You are a tease, and yes, that's what I meant," Val replied, smiling behind the rim of her wine glass. "After dinner, we can sit by a fire at the pit if you'd like."

"Sure. But you know, I'm not sure I need a fire to warm up." Nicki gazed directly into Val's eyes and flashed another smile.

"Hmm," Val said with a chuckle. She leaned forward. "I realized I didn't even know your last name, nor did I have a number to call you."

"Ahh. Jennifer Nicole Williams Harris, but I'm a Nicki, not Jennifer or Jenn. I'll put your number in my phone. That'll give me a reason to call you." She smiled at Val. That same smile with the raised eyebrows. *Devilish smile. Big flirt. I like it.*

"Ha, ha. You don't need a reason. Just call. And Harris, a married name?" *Just great. Your first date in years is married.* Val could feel her shoulders sinking, carrying her heart with it.

"I was married. We were kids. My husband died several years ago. Long story. Let's not."

"Oh, I'm sorry. We'll drop it." Val turned to the microwave, eyes looking up. *Whew*, she thought as she blew out a silent breath.

"You look great tonight, by the way," Nicki said as Val served the quiche. "I thought you looked good Wednesday. Well, let me tell you. You look great now."

Val swung around and put a plate with quiche and a small fruit salad on the table.

"Thank you," Val replied, blushing. The blush was felt somewhere other than on her cheeks. She gathered herself enough to continue. "This is a simple meal. We have some chocolates and more fruit for dessert later if you're interested."

"Yum. This looks gorgeous, Val. Thank you." Nicki raised her glass and they toasted again.

Nicki was the perfect guest for boosting one's ego. And what a flirt! Val wasn't used to that. It may have caught her off guard but she certainly enjoyed it.

"This is delicious. You are right to brag on your crust. Buttery...melt in your mouth. Mushrooms and spinach. Oh my, this is good. By the way, you've probably noticed I dive right in...and I'm not just talking about eating, you know."

"I have noticed that. It doesn't frighten me, though." Val smiled. "I like it, actually."

"So Val, what are you doing buying property in the middle of Nowhere, Georgia?" Nicki asked bluntly.

"Well, what are you doing living in the middle of Nowhere, Georgia?"

"Touché, my friend. If I start, we'll end up talking about my husband. Can we wait until I have more wine to take my turn?" Nicki was smiling, but it wasn't what Val would have called a happy smile.

"Sure. Fair enough," Val replied. "I'll give you some information, but if I told you everything..."

"Yeah, yeah. You'd have to kill me," Nicki said. "Top secret operation." They both laughed.

"I've been looking for a large tract of land within close proximity to the major highways and roads linking Atlanta, Augusta, Macon, and Savannah. It's a large project, and I hope it will bring substantial resources into the area. I know the economic stats here, and maybe this can help provide jobs. Honestly, I want to involve some local residents in the planning. Who knows, maybe you'd be interested. I know this is vague, but..." Val sized up Nicki's countenance for some hint of a reaction.

"Of course, we could use an economic boost. And I'd love a real full time job with benefits. I know plenty of people who would say the same thing. We keep losing people to nearby towns for jobs. I have a social work bachelor's and am in the final year of an MBA. Doing it online. Seems like I've been in school forever...going part time, you know. I'd love to sit down with you and talk about your project."

"You are a fount of surprises, Ms. Nicki Williams Harris." Val shook her head in disbelief. "Wow."

"Just Nicki Williams now," Nicki replied. "And you?"

"I'm retired. Early retirement," Val said. "Hence the leisurely days of cycling and camping. Prior to that, I practiced as a registered nurse, and then at the nurse executive level. Nurses always say it's a calling. We typically go into it to help people. To make a difference. That's what I want with my project. I'd been living in Maine, but I moved back down here after my ex and I broke up.

"I'll be honest, here, but I prefer others not necessarily know all of my history. I don't usually share stuff like that. Anyway, my Aunt Grace was a big real estate broker in Boston. She and I became quite close after mom died, and I inherited her estate. Grace made it possible for me to begin this journey."

They moved outside after the fruit course, and Val started the fire. The night was clear and the stars were twinkling. They didn't talk for a few minutes as the fire grew, just stared at the sky above the lake. Occasionally, Val poked the fire or shifted the logs.

As Val poured them both more wine, Nicki popped one of the chocolates in her mouth. As cliché as it seemed, Val was fascinated by the chocolate passing from Nicki's fingers, resting briefly on her bottom lip, and sliding seamlessly into her mouth. Nicki caught Val's gaze and smiled. She puckered her lips as if to blow Val a little kiss. Val felt another warm stirring between her legs. *Oh no, no, no. Don't go there. Just relax.* She wondered if she could handle a relationship right now. She didn't want to destroy what might be a close friendship with sex. *Sure, you can have both, but how often does that happen in life? Then is she going to decide to leave because I'm no longer exciting enough? Too much of an age difference. Jeez, Val, you haven't even kissed. What's with all the worry?* Again, the usual brain chatter. A few minutes passed as they looked at the fire. Nicki cleared her throat.

"Okay. Here goes. I was in high school and was taking several advanced placement classes. Our high school also had an arrangement with the university to take college courses in our senior year—2005. I was walking from the university's parking lot to my car, and I passed a group of guys leaning against one of the cars in the lot. I assumed college guys. They were hooting and whistling, the usual doltish kinds of things guys do. Well, nobody messes with Nicki. I walked right across to them and said, 'don't be assholes.' At that point this one guy—tall, dark, almost black hair and the greenest eyes—said, 'I'm sorry. We're just admiring you.' He was a total package. I suppose some sort of Darwinian force took control, but I tell you now just as I thought back then, that he was the most beautiful man I have ever seen. Anyway, it was only a matter of time before we were dating.

"That March I turned eighteen and graduated high school in June. I was queasy sick the entire time from a couple of weeks after my birthday until after graduation. I thought it was the stress of projects, the advanced courses, and preparing for exams, but I decided to check, and sure enough, I was pregnant." Nicki wiped a couple of tears from her cheeks.

"Shit, Nicki."

"We got married. Very small wedding. And he went crazy. Not abusive to me, but he was all survivalist. He was a motorcycle rider and went to hang out with his buddies in the mountains of northern Georgia and North Carolina on weekends. He never invited me. A guy thing...plus, I was sick a lot. I guess they talked him into the survivalist thing. He wanted us to live off of the land, and he could hunt while I cared for the baby, tended the garden and canned stuff. You know, frontier life kind of thing. I was in love with him, and he wanted to take care of us—me and the baby, when it arrived. It was just easier to go along with it. One of the guys he rode with had close to twenty acres north of Dahlonega in a tiny community. The guy had a little shack there and told Mike we could live in it if Mike would oversee the land, keep the fences up, make repairs and do some renovations to the house. Mike had a horticulture degree. He had just finished, and here he wanted to go right away and live off the land. At the time I was overwhelmed. I thought that would be fine...just whatever he wanted. I was young enough to pick up school later. You know, I was getting ready to be a mother. Anyway, we had a baby girl that December." By this point Nicki was crying.

"Hold on a sec," Val said as she excused herself and quickly retrieved a box of tissues from inside. "Nicki. This is intense." She pulled her chair closer to Nicki.

"What on earth am I doing?" Nicki asked. "I have no idea why I'm so emotional. Other than the wine." She smiled through her tears. "I realize I haven't grieved since her birthday this year. I must be comfortable with you because very few people have seen me cry. I usually just lash out in anger." She wiped her nose and blew it.

"I'm honored, Nicki. I can't even imagine that experience. And to know you lost your husband and your child. I'm so sorry." Val teared up herself. "What was your daughter's name, if you don't mind talking about it?" Val was hesitant to ask. At the same time, she recognized the power of catharsis.

"Jordan Trahlyta. Harris, of course. We called her Trolly most of the time. She was named for the daughter of a Chief of the Cherokee Nation. There is a stack of stones in the roundabout intersection of Georgia 60 and US 19, north of Dahlonega that is said to mark Trahlyta's grave. They call her a princess on the historical marker, but I'm pretty sure princess is not a PC description." She shook her head and wiped her forearm across her eyes.

Val had driven by that stack of stones many times on her way to visit a friend's cabin in the town of Suches, and she wondered if that is where Nicki and Mike had lived. Nicki continued to describe her life with Mike as newlyweds and new parents.

23

"Mike was all into government plots by that point. I was still overwhelmed and simply couldn't deal with it. I just went along and tried to be the best mom I could. Mike would hunt or fish. He would trade some of his catches for home-canned vegetables from friends. I was able to get assistance through WIC for fruit, fresh vegetables, and milk. Of course, baby food, too. Mike had insisted that Trolly not be vaccinated. I fought this as much as I could, but I went along with him. I was so young. So unprepared. I'd known other families on that anti-vaccination path, and they all seemed to be doing okay. He would swear that Trolly would become autistic or have some sort of strange allegiance to the 'establishment.' I swore to him though, if anything happened to Trolly because of his and his buddies' paranoia, I was leaving." She sat back and sighed.

Mostly, Val listened. She had poured her final glass of wine. Nicki reached and took the bottle, emptying the remainder into her glass.

"I'll need more of this if you want me to continue." She pointed to the wine as she raised the glass.

"It's a horrifying story, Nicki, but it seems to be good for you to talk."

"I think it is. I've only talked about this in group therapy at the VA. After Mike's death. Around here, most everyone probably knows my story. Not from me, though. I was close to my aunt, too. She was a church goer. But the group is what really helped me through this. Don't get me wrong. People were so nice to me. Still are, really."

Val nodded in understanding. *Good to know community support is available.*

The fire was out. It was getting late. They moved into Bambi and sat at the dinette. As Nicki sat, Val retrieved a wine half-bottle, opened it, and headed to the seat across from Nicki. Nicki took her hand and said, "Please come sit beside me." Val nodded. It was a tighter fit than she would have liked, and she couldn't look directly at Nicki this way, but she had to admit, the closeness was nice.

"Trolly was eighteen months. I was visiting residents at a personal care home periodically. Trolly and I, both. Residents loved the visits. They enjoyed seeing little kids. And Trolly was so good. Not afraid of their hands touching her head or cheek, you know. We encountered some children visitors who had come by to see one of the ladies I normally visited. The kids' mom seemed at the end of her rope because the children—a girl and a boy—were crying. Their faces were so red, I thought they must have a fever. The mom said they had been fussy all night. She thought getting them out of the house might perk them up since they always loved visiting 'big gramma.' They didn't even seem interested in the horse that lived behind the building. I told the mom that maybe we could all have a playdate sometime soon. We exchanged phone numbers. Later that same day, she called me and said she'd taken the kids to the emergency room and found out they had the measles."

"Oh shit." Val knew how childhood diseases spread like wildfire.

"Sure enough, within a couple of weeks, Trolly had seemed fussy all day. No fever, and it didn't seem to be any of the other typical causes. In the middle of the night, Trolly woke us up with a shrill cry that caused us to jump out of our skins. She was on fire. We knew we had to get her to an emergency room quickly. Before we left, Mike put baggies of ice under Trolly's armpits and closed her coat around her so she couldn't knock them off. We sped to Blairsville, thirty minutes away. Trolly had what looked to be two seizures on the way. The staff didn't make us wait; they took her straight away. She had to be airlifted to the children's hospital in Atlanta. By the next day, she was brain-dead. It was horrible. We had to...remove her from life support." She sobbed, head in her hands on the table. Val rested her hand on Nicki's shoulder. When Nicki regained her composure, she continued.

"It was several days before I could function. I packed my suitcases and called a friend to take me to my great aunt's place here in Marshall. My folks died when I was a kid. My aunt Mae and my grandparents raised me. Mike knew he better not call me. I was devastated. Not just from Trolly's death, but from our split, too. Mostly I was furious with myself for having listened to Mike's nonsense. Of course, I was mad at him, too. I couldn't even consider having to talk with him or see him if we were to begin a divorce or mediation."

"Oh my god, Nicki. I'm so sorry. You know, though, you don't have to continue if it's too much."

"It's okay. I prefer to get it all out."

"Of course." Val rested her hand on Nicki's forearm.

"Mike, in his typical fashion, made a one-eighty. He called me two months later and told me he was joining the service. He had already signed the paperwork. Once basic training was completed, Mike was sent to Afghanistan. He wrote a few times. I could read the hate he had for himself, even if it was between the lines. He was torn up by Trolly's death, too.

"It was approaching his two-year mark in-country when I heard a knock on my door. I knew as soon as I saw the uniforms. Mike was on a recon mission as an explosives expert. The men also gave me a letter. It was addressed to me in Mike's handwriting. They said it was found on top of his gear as if he were intending to mail it when he returned. It hadn't been opened, and I didn't open it then. They gave me VA contact information and said a liaison would be reaching out within a few weeks. When Mike's body, or what was left of it, was returned, he was buried in the Andersonville National Cemetery."

Val slid out long enough to grab a glass of water for Nicki. She drank a few swallows and then continued.

"One of his unit buddies called on me a month after his death. He said he was pretty sure Mike had a death wish. That he volunteered for any risky mission that came the company's way, but he wanted me to know how significant I was to Mike. Even more, he wanted me to know how important *Trolly* was to him. He said Mike would entertain the men for hours telling stories of Trolly and me. How we all used to dance around. Mike would sing at the top of his lungs, dancing like 'little Trolly.' The guys would laugh and laugh. That was so clearly Mike that I believed every word. After his buddy left, I pulled that letter out of my chest of drawers. That was the first time I opened it. He had written some lyrics from the Natasha Bedingfield song, "Unwritten." All the times we danced around the cabin singing it. Trolly loved it and would sing what words she could, mostly nonsensical sounding words, but occasionally a 'you,' or a 'boo' for 'book,' or an 'ain' for 'rain.' We would laugh and laugh and laugh. Laughter is what I missed the most." Nicki wiped her tears again.

Val now understood why Nicki was such a jokester. Laughter seemed to be Nicki's centering activity. She assumed Nicki had seen so many sad things, laughter helped balance the scale for her.

Nicki leaned on Val's shoulder. They were quiet for what seemed to be hours. Val noticed Nicki had fallen asleep, exhausted. She gently jostled Nicki's shoulder and led her into the bed and tucked her in. Val made the dinette into a bed and she, too, fell asleep.

Val woke with the morning sun. Nicki was still asleep. Val made coffee and reassembled the dinette as quietly as she could. She guessed it had been close to three when they finally went to sleep. Val was glad Nicki didn't have to rush into the laundry this morning. She clearly needed the rest.

As Val sipped her coffee, she studied Nicki's shape in her bed. Val felt the familiar stirring again. *Come on, Val. Buck up. Let this thing, if it is anything, evolve in its own time.* Val knew having a good friend was much more important than having sex. Even though an intimate encounter sure would be fun. She frowned. *Nicki may just consider you more of a big sister figure.* She frowned again. *No fun. Even if it is charming.*

Nicki began moving around. She turned and squinted.

"Ugh. I have a bit of a headache. I don't even think it was the wine. I might be dehydrated from tear spillage." Nicki smiled her devilish smile again.

Don't keep doing that. You're killing me. That smile sure doesn't look like I'm your big sister. Val put some coffee and water on the table. Nicki looked down at her clothes, shook her head, and slid into the dinette seat. Val made cheese toast for the two of them.

"You know, you're a nice person, Val Scott," Nicki said, reaching across the dinette to place her hand on Val's forearm. "I want to apologize, just this once. Something makes me think that'll be sufficient."

"You're right, but you don't need to apologize for anything." Val smiled at her.

"You know the neighbors might talk with your having an overnight guest." Nicki nodded her head at the squatters' place.

"Let 'em. I'm sure everybody thinks I'm a bitch, anyway. I nod. An occasional smile. But I don't usually speak to anyone if I don't already know them."

"Me too. I'm nice to customers, but I usually keep a hard exterior so guys don't try to come on to me," Nicki replied. "I much prefer a lady's smile these days."

Val sighed, evidently audibly.

"Oh, I'm sorry. And that's an apology for something different," Nicki said. "I realize I'm flirting with someone who may not be up for that."

"Ha, ha, miss missy. I've taken on the best of 'em," Val teased. "You're fine. It's fun."

Nicki tossed back the rest of her coffee, then apologized for eating and running.

"I need to run by my house, change clothes, and get to the laundromat to relieve John Henry."

"Sure. I get it. Thanks for coming."

"Oh wait," Nicki said as she was leaving. "Give me your number so I can call you." She leaned and gave Val a peck on the cheek. As she closed the door, she leaned her head in and gave Val that smile again.

Val shook her head back and forth, frowning, as Nicki drove off. *That settles it. She is definitely trying to kill me. And that was definitely flirting.* Val could think of nothing else *but* Nicki now. *She'll probably never call, will she?* She smiled to herself. *No time to dawdle like a love-struck kid, Scott. You've got some moving to do.*

Today was the day she had to move to campsite twenty-one. It was another site directly on the water. The lake's dock was nearly part of the site, which made it especially appealing. She had an hour to move. Val hated having to put everything back together only to drive a few sites down the circle, but she could picture items falling as Bambi rocked back and forth from the potholes as she backed in. *Just do it, Scott. Git 'er done.* At least it would only be another fourteen days or so at the campsite. She would then move permanently to Amazing Grace if all went well.

***

As Nicki rushed into her house to change, she looked around. She considered her space to be perfect for her. It was fine with her aunt there, but she welcomed the closeness at that point of her life. After having been at Val's, she recognized the luxury of having space.

She plopped onto her bed and shifted herself to the center. She spread her arms and legs as if creating a snow angel. She wondered if she would be comfortable sharing her space now. She glanced at the wall clock.

"Oh god. I really need to get ready," she said aloud, and she sat up hesitantly. "Let's go, girl."

In the shower, Nicki thought briefly about Val. About how attentive Val had been. The almost instant connection. Her phone's daily chime alerted her to twenty-minute travel time.

Chapter Five

WITH BAMBI SETTLED IN at site twenty-one, Val decided to walk around the park's trail system for a little sunshine, fresh air, and a dose of forest bathing. She had read the practice of simply taking in the sights, sounds, and smells of the forest could lower stress hormones and help one's immune system. Years ago, when she volunteered at a nature center in Athens, Val was convinced dragonflies would come sit with her near one of the center's ponds. If a dragonfly did not light on her, it would often fly suspended, wings beating quickly as if its blue or green needle-like body were being held in place by some invisible thread. This evoked calm, and she relished that feeling. Back then, she didn't even know what forest bathing was, but Val had developed the practice across the years. She felt justified when she learned what she, and probably millions, had been doing for years was now recognized as a thing.

By the time Val returned from her walk, the sun was low in the sky. The orange-ish glow of the western sky was intense enough for Val to pull the shades on that side of the camper. As she enjoyed her soup, she found her thoughts had drifted back to Nicki.

What a heartbreaking story. Marshall had become a safe haven for Nicki. Val was familiar with the routine of putting one foot in front of the other in a structured life to help one recover from such an emotional assault. She wondered when, or if, she would hear from Nicki.

Val didn't even light the awning as night fell. She simply closed everything up and crawled into her bed. *Oh, how I missed you.* Sometimes her own bed was the most comforting place in the world. Because she had not had enough of her usual beauty sleep, she was ready to fall asleep almost right away. She read a few paragraphs before turning out the light. As if on cue, her phone rang. Nicki. She smiled.

"Hello."

"Val. It's Nicki. I should have called you earlier. Did I wake you?"

"Not at all. Though I'm not long for the world. I can't believe the call came through; the service is so bad here. How are you feeling today?" Val asked.

"Oh, I made it through okay. I was dragging until noon. Just foggy headed. John Henry brought me a milkshake. It perked me up. Once I closed up, I felt as if I had run into a brick wall. I'm staying here at the laundry tonight."

"Sounds like a good idea if you're as worn out as I am. I'm glad you called. I was thinking about you."

"Same here." Nicki sounded somewhat down.

"But you're okay, right? You sound a little down, Nicki. I shouldn't worry, should I?"

"No. Not at all. I'm tired. Sunday is always a mixed bag here. I wish I knew it was going to be slow. Sometimes Sundays drag and drag. Other times, especially after church, the place is crazy busy until closing." A beat passed. "Could we get together Monday?" Nicki's voice had lowered an octave.

"Well, that depends. I'm closing on the property on Monday."

"That's right. Let's celebrate then. At my place. Not with half a bottle of wine and the world's saddest story, though." Nicki's voice was much lighter. Val could picture her smile. That devilish one.

"Nice. After closing, then. Should have everything wrapped up by four. I'll swing by the laundromat after Sandy Ann's."

"Great. I can't promise as nice a dinner as last night's, but I'll figure something out."

"Looking forward to it. See you then." *Oh my. Oh my. You're on!*

***

Val didn't typically ride on weekends, especially Sundays, since afternoon traffic worried her. Instead, she decided to go out and drive around the property a final time before she signed the papers. The day was nice, but overcast and cool. It was quiet when she drove up the main road. She noticed what appeared to be a couple of vehicles near the back at the edge of one of the clear-cut areas, close to where she expected Bambi to be parked.

Someone had erected two primitive deer stands, close to twenty yards apart and facing the de-forested acreage. Two men stood in each one, with trucks below. She opened her truck door. A man's voice boomed from one of the stands. "What the hell are you doing here?" The men began climbing out of the stands. Val tensed, but tried to portray a relaxed stance and smile.

"Funny thing, I'm buying this land tomorrow," Val replied. "I wanted to drive around one more time before it's officially mine. Are you the owners? I'd love to—"

"We might as well be. We've been hunting out here for years," the man interrupted. She heard agreements from the others. As they narrowed their eyes and tightly gripped their firearms, her stomach sank and she clenched her jaw. She attempted to relax her jaw and speak without tension, breathing deeply.

"Just so you know, I will definitely be putting up posted signs. Enjoy yourselves today. I don't want any trouble. Your stands weren't here when I was here the other day with Sandy Ann." She thought the name dropping might increase her cred.

"You're probably going to have some problems if you don't let folks hunt out here, no matter who you know." What seemed to be the ringleader walked alarmingly close, invading her personal space.

Val resisted the urge to tell them she would be living there in a couple of weeks. All of the men walked toward her. Holding their guns, a collection of automatics and shotguns, they invaded her space, circled her, and glared at her.

"We don't want no trouble neither. You ain't from around here, are you?" the same guy sneered. The smell of alcohol was undeniable.

Whoa. This is serious. Stay cool.

"Look. I'm just going to drive back out to the road and leave you to your lives. I'm not looking for trouble," Val said. She ducked out of the group and got in her truck. They followed her to her truck. One of them slammed her door closed once she had cleared it. She was shaking on the inside as she backed around and headed back down the main road. She heard them laughing. By the time she had made it to the highway, she could barely hold the steering wheel she was shaking so hard.

Val was no sissy. She had always been comfortable around her dad or granddad's guns, but they had instilled in her a healthy respect for anyone on the butt end of a barrel. "Never mouth off to that person," was the lesson they taught.

By the time Val arrived at the laundromat, she had calmed some, but she was still shaking. Nicki was in the office, thank god.

"I'm a day early," Val said brusquely.

"Lord, god, Val. Get in here! You look like a deer in the headlights. What on earth?"

Val collapsed, sitting on the desk, legs quivering. As she relayed her encounter, she managed not to cry, but it wasn't easy.

"Fucking assholes!" Nicki shouted. Luckily the typical laundry noises drowned out her swearing. "Let's go right now." Nicki was standing, throwing her coat on her shoulder, and grabbing the "Be back in a few" sign to put on the door.

"No. Tomorrow is another day," Val said. "I'll be able to legally put up signs and a gate."

"That's not going to stop them." Nicki sneered angrily. "They'll probably drive through your gate, rip up the signs, find your car and bash it in. Those jerk rednecks. Thank god they don't know you're a lesbian."

Whoa. Val had not even considered that scenario when she posited the cons and roadblocks to Amazing Grace. She anticipated discussions with evangelical Christians who were opposed to gambling. She had considered large crime organizations who might be threatened by any gaming competition in the state they did not control. She considered the other larger gaming chains that might want a Georgia stronghold. But she never thought a group of hayseeds would want her land for their own private hunt club. Nor had she considered being a lesbian would be a big factor. Live and let live. She didn't flaunt it. She didn't hide it. *I've been in Maine and Athens too long, I guess.*

When she worked in Athens, her staff and hospital administrators knew she was a lesbian. Everyone welcomed her partner at the time. In Maine, when she was gravely ill and hospitalized for three weeks, staff would discuss anything regarding her with Gail. Her hematologist would find Gail in one of the waiting areas and fill her in on the day's plans. It didn't matter if Val was conscious or not, her partner was as important to the healthcare team as Val was as the patient. That was the way it should be—honor one's important relationships.

Nicki offered to ask John Henry to help Val with increased security. Val looked forward to his ideas.

"I'm so sorry you've had such a horrible experience. Most people around here don't act that way. They may be rednecks and hicks, but they aren't mean."

"I'm not sure the alcohol wasn't giving them additional courage they might not normally have."

"Oh great! *Drunk* assholes with guns. What a nice welcoming committee." Nicki snorted.

"At least I'm not shaking anymore. I was scared," Val confessed.

By now, the laundromat had completely emptied out. Nicki pulled a bottle of Jack Daniel's whiskey from the desk drawer. She grabbed a glass and a couple of pieces of ice.

"Here's one country boy who will help you get better," Nicki said as she passed the glass to Val. "He's got just the thing to settle you."

Sipping good sour mash was a delight. Sweet, smoky heat all the way down. *What a good idea.*

"Thanks, Lucky." Val smiled widely. *God, she is something!*

"You remembered!"

"Of course. But maybe I should adopt the name. Seems like I'm the lucky one in this scenario." Val held the glass to her lips and sipped as she watched Nicki run out to the floor.

Nicki took four baskets of folded clothes out to a customer's car. After the woman drove away, Nicki locked the front door and flipped around the "closed" sign. She turned off the main lights and walked back into the office, pushing the door closed behind her. Val was sitting on the edge of the desk. Nicki walked forward and leaned between Val's legs.

Val's head was spinning, and it had nothing to do with the whiskey. The familiar tingle she felt when seeing Nicki was now a pulsing, roaring ache. Nicki pulled Val to her and brushed her lips against Val's.

"Mm. Jack." Nicki smiled as she obviously smelled the whiskey. Val felt the warmth of Nicki's breath and her tongue as their lips met softly. Nicki sighed a low moan. She pulled back.

"This is nice," Nicki whispered. Val's ache warmly pulsed with each kiss. "Hope this is okay?" Nicki whispered as she moved her hand down Val's neck, around her shoulder, and onto her breast. *How many women has she been with? She definitely knows what she's doing.*

Val quickly lost all thoughts as Nicki reached inside her blouse and under her bra to lightly caress her breast. Val sucked in her breath. Nicki pressed her lips hard against Val's again. Once again, she released, and their lips barely touched. Nicki hovered, eyes closed. Val let herself simply feel Nicki against her. That pressure of soft curves, lips, warm breath. *Intoxicating.* Val noticed the pace of her breathing had increased; she deliberately slowed and deepened it. Nicki relaxed fully against Val's body. She moaned into Nicki's mouth. Nicki reached to unbutton Val's jeans. Val lightly held Nicki's wrist.

"No," Val whispered into Nicki's mouth. "Too fast...I think."

Instead, Nicki pulled Val's shirttail out of her jeans and ran her hand under the shirt and around to the small of Val's back.

"Maybe it isn't.....too fast. Isn't too fast, I mean."

"Oh. Hmm," Nicki replied. "Then will you come to the bed with me...here?" Nicki asked softly as she led Val backward onto the bed. For what must have been three hours, they held one another close. Fully clothed, though disheveled, mouth-to-mouth. Val continued to pulse with arousal. This was a feeling she did not want to end.

"Stay with me tonight. No pressures. Well. Some *pressures*, but nothing against your will." Nicki was extraordinarily persuasive. *In a good way.* Val turned Nicki onto her back, hovered above her and moved to her side. Val's hand slid from the small of Nicki's back, up under her shoulder and around to her breast. She lowered her face to Nicki's breast.

Nicki pushed Val back lightly and whispered to her, "If you need me to slow down, you'll have to stay away from that." Val fell back, smiling.

"Maybe too fast was hasty," Val replied. "And yes, the pun *was* intended."

"Hokey," Nicki whispered as she rolled on top of Val, pressing one thigh between Val's legs. Nicki rocked gently, feeling Val's flesh and her muscles. Nicki dropped her face gently onto Val's neck, and with a soft, warm whisper said, "This is the welcome you deserve."

Val realized she would be unable to stop this progress now. Nor did she want to. They continued kissing as Nicki removed her own clothes and slipped under the covers. Val followed her. When Nicki slid her thigh between Val's legs again, Val shuddered and moaned.

"I would love to discover more of you," Nicki whispered. "But I respect going slowly. You are remarkable. I hope you understand that." Val was speechless, paralyzed. She wanted more, but she wanted to savor the lovemaking. She missed feeling a woman against her, feeling the mouth, the breast.

"Forget the slow," Val whispered. She was powerless to quiet her moans.

Nicki pressed her lips again on Val's and searched for Val's tongue. Val now took Nicki's hand and pressed it to her own groin. Nicki pulled her face back and smiled at Val. Nicki did not insert her fingers, but rather, lightly stroked, brushing fingertips through Val's hair in a teasing manner. Nicki stroked Val's muscular thighs and moved her nails from her thighs up between her legs, then lightly across Val's belly and up to her breast. She leaned into Val's right breast and caressed the nipple with her tongue. She alternated between a light suck and brushing her lips across both breasts. Val was throbbing, burning. Her head was back onto the bed.

"Please," Val whispered as she pulled Nicki back to her mouth.

So much for slowly. It's been more than five years since I've made love. I'm afraid it might be five more, and I don't want to lose this. Val rolled onto her side and slid lower so she could find Nicki's left breast. Nicki was soft in Val's mouth, and her nipple became erect as she ran her tongue along the areola. Nicki sucked air in and blew it out through clenched teeth. Now on her elbows, Val worked her mouth along Nicki's right side toward the right breast. She ran her tongue around the nipple again and lightly sucked just under the nipple. Val slid down Nicki's belly to just above the pubic bone. She lingered and gave a light love bite before moving back to Nicki's left breast. After caressing the nipple and areola with her tongue again, she lightly licked Nicki's left side. Val pulled herself back to Nicki's mouth again. They continued to kiss as they moved their bodies in a light rocking motion. The pressure of the pubic bones, the softness of their mouths, their breasts. Their hands locked together. Val softly moaned into Nicki's mouth. Nicki shuddered. She held Val close, applying more pressure against her soft flesh. Val raised her hips and rocked as she pulsed toward orgasm. Nicki shuddered again, and stifled soft *Oh's* in her throat.

After kissing again, Nicki rested her head just below Val's shoulder on her upper chest. One of Val's arms wrapped around Nicki's back and shoulder, and her other hand's fingers pushed up through Nicki's long sweep of hair and pulled it back down. They fell asleep wound together. Warm. Still.

Chapter Six

"GOOD MORNING, DOLL," NICKI said as she pushed gently on Val's shoulder. Nicki was holding a cup of coffee. Val looked around. Nicki hated to wake Val. She enjoyed watching her sleep, her butt's shape forming the mound at the top of the muscular leg extending from the sheet. Nicki could hear the soft passage of air as Val breathed. If only she could snuggle against Val's back again, even for a few minutes.

"What time is it?" Val asked as she turned to face Nicki. Without a larger window in the room she couldn't tell.

"Six-thirty. In the morning, of course. I know it's early, but I have to open up in a half hour. You're welcome to stay, but I wanted to give you the option before I started my workday. I closed early already one night this week. Don't want to mess up folks' routines."

"Oh, no. Thanks. I'll get out of here." Val grabbed her clothes from the floor. She looked up as Nicki watched her dress. Val smiled and shook her head. "I can't believe this. I mean—"

"I believe it." Nicki raised her eyebrows and smiled back.

"What I meant to say was that I had an unbelievable time. And you know, you have a very devilish smile."

Nicki walked to Val and tilted her head as if to kiss her cheek. Val turned her head and lightly met Nicki's lips with her own.

"Yeah, I know," she whispered.

"Mm. Nice," Val said as she pulled away, smiling. "I gotta go."

"Yeah, you do, but I look forward to another visit soon."

***

In the shower, Nicki imagined Val's wet body pressed against her. She replayed some of last night in her mind, and thought there were worse things than going into a workday feeling horny.

***

Today is a big day! Val thought of all the things she needed for the closing this afternoon as she returned to Hamburg. As she drove in toward Bambi, she saw the group in site fifteen sitting around the picnic table watching her. *Wonder what the squatters think of my being gone all night long?* She was too busy to worry or wonder what gossip they may have heard. She had to run to the bank, get the cashier's check, and verify the money transfer was still on. As she walked in the door, the phone rang. It was Sandy Ann. *Surprise! Not.*

"Good morning!" *Bubbly, bubbly before seven-thirty.* "I know it's early, but I heard you were awake. Look, I don't want what happened to you yesterday to bother you any more than it already has. I hear JH is going to be helping you out, but please let me report this to the sheriff for you. I can't have clients tormented by a bunch of local butts." Sandy Ann barely stopped to breathe in her tirade.

"Dang. Word sure gets around. Look, the cell service here is horrible." Val wasn't sure Sandy Ann even heard what she said. It did appear, however, that the cell signal booster she had bought was helping.

"Honestly, I saw your truck as I took the kids to school this morning. On the way back, it was gone, and I stopped by the laundromat to investigate. Nicki let me know what happened."

"Oh. Yeah. It was scary. I'm not sure we should involve the sheriff...I tell you what, Sandy Ann, let me drink some more coffee. I'll let you know this afternoon."

"That'll work," Sandy Ann replied. "I'll see you at four. Everything still on track? I was afraid you'd back out after yesterday."

"No. I'm pretty tough, Sandy Ann, although that might not be what Lady Laundry told you. I was so grateful to have found a friend. Well, two now." Val smiled and hoped Sandy Ann could hear that.

"You better believe you have new friends! Just like my card says. I *mean* it. And just wait till you meet JH. See you later, *dawg.*" She chuckled as the call ended.

Sandy Ann was Southern with a capital S. That *dawg* just kept on going as if it would have had three syllables. Some was for emphasis, but some she couldn't help. Val had forgotten how some University of Georgia Bulldog fans tended to call friends dawgs as an endearment. She studied Sandy Ann's card. "Start as a client. Leave as a friend." *Yep. Trite, but true...at least in this case.*

***

Sandy Ann's office was crowded. The attorney for the owner's mortgage company, the owner's realtor, the title company's attorney, and Sandy Ann's real estate attorney on Val's behalf—John Elbert, Esquire—filed in around the table next to Val and Sandy Ann. Sandy Ann passed out bottles of water. The title company attorney passed out deep, blue-barreled ballpoint pens with a gold company logo stamped on them. Everyone had a stack of documents in front of them. The mortgage attorney did most of the talking. It was all pretty routine, based on Val's experience. During the signatures, Mr. Elbert turned to her.

"You know, Sandy Ann told me what happened yesterday. I hope you *will* consider calling the sheriff. The sooner the better." His distinguished appearance instilled confidence that, indeed, it would be the thing to do. "I've seen some of these guys at the courthouse. I probably can tell you who did it."

"Yeah. I'll see. You're probably right, though." Val kept signing, but looked up at him and nodded. She knew she should report it. "Hopefully John Henry will have some good ideas for me." Mr. Elbert nodded.

"He's a good man, but don't wait for ideas. Sandy Ann told me you intended to live out on the property as your project is developing. That's not safe right now. Even with ideas. You might want JH to stay on the property a few days before you move yourself. We have a small guest house. You're welcome if you need a place."

Val thanked him. She wasn't sure she wanted her business all across town, but she recognized that as talk circulated, it might induce some peer pressure on the jerks that accosted her. She thought the sheriff was probably a good idea. She'd go by his office tomorrow.

As they broke up from the signing, Sandy Ann handed Val a nice bottle of champagne. Val had never had it, but she was familiar with the vintner. Taped to the bottle was a card.

"Welcome to our community, Val." Sandy Ann hugged Val. As she did, Sandy Ann whispered in Val's ear. "A little birdie told me you liked wine."

Val thanked her profusely. She was humbled, excited, and nervous. Everyone drove away as Val put her papers in her briefcase and stashed it behind the truck's bench seat. She opened the envelope and looked down at the card—a hundred-dollar gift card to the Milledgeville grocery. *That little birdie has been singing quite a bit, but she sure hit the nail on the head, didn't she now?* Val smiled. *Oh my god, I wonder if we're still on for this evening!* She had promised that morning, but had neglected to confirm.

The laundry was still open when Val drove up. Val felt a strange nervousness. A combination of excitement and anticipation. She saw Nicki through the big window. She smiled and felt a pull in her stomach and a wonderful ache elsewhere. Val shook her head again. *Oh my. Here goes.*

"Hi. Are we still on?" Val asked.

"You better believe it. One thing Nicki Williams likes is a party. Especially a party of two!" She beamed at Val. She reached into her front jeans pocket and pulled out a slip of paper with an address. "That's my place. I'll meet you in an hour. That'll give me time to close up the office and take a shower."

"You're on." They fist-bumped with an explosion, both laughing. Val shook her head to herself as she pulled out of the parking lot. When she drove by the squatters back at the campground, she was pretty sure they hadn't moved. She smiled and nodded. They waved. She waved as well. *Wow. A wave. You know, Scott, give people a break.* Yes, she probably hadn't been friendly, but when she began nodding in return and smiling, they had begun doing the same thing. *You know, like neighbors, Scott. Loosen up.*

Val wasted no time preparing for her evening out once she walked through Bambi's door. She looked in the mirror for one last check. Clean. Royal blue mock turtleneck. White Oxford shirt, tucked in. Jeans. Black woven leather belt. Brown L.L. Bean blazer. Small, blue sea glass earrings. *I'll do. I hope she thinks so, too.*

Val wondered where they would go for dinner. She wasn't sure any of the town's restaurants would be celebratory enough. Not to mention none of the places had beverages to her liking. She shrugged at her pickiness.

Her GPS guided her directly to a small bungalow just off Cody Johnson Road. The house was adorable, white with green trim and a gray metal roof. The lawn was well manicured with typical red tip hedges, neatly trimmed. She saw Nicki's red pickup in front of the closed, one-car garage on the back side of the lot. Val turned into the driveway and parked so she could step out directly onto the little path to the front porch. Colorful pansies filled the porch planters. The porch ceiling was painted a typical Southern sky blue.

Val knocked on the front door. As Nicki opened it, she pushed open the screen door. Val worried her knees would buckle. Nicki's mid-thigh, black shirred dress hugged her body. She was gorgeous. Pearl necklace, pearl earrings. And flip-flops. Nicki's stance with her arm opening both doors necessitated Val's passing close to Nicki.

"Oh, my god." Val breathed aloud as the stifled words came out. She kept looking back at Nicki as she entered the house. Nicki just smiled.

"Welcome to my home." Nicki looked down at the bottle of champagne Val had brought in. "You won't need that. Take it back home. We'll have it at your place."

"I thought we could have a glass before going out," Val replied. She noticed, though, that the table was set, just off the small, cozy living room. The glorious aroma of something cooking wafted through.

"We're not going out. I'm cooking. Sort of." Nicki picked up a couple of wine glasses, already filled with a red. "It's merlot. Again. Hope it's okay."

"Of course," Val said. "Something smells delicious, and I'm not one to turn down a home-cooked meal."

"And congratulations," Nicki said as she raised a glass to Val.
They toasted.

"This is nice, Nicki," Val said after her sip. She couldn't stop looking at Nicki. The V at the neckline revealed the top of her cleavage. Val felt weak again.

"You look fantastic. I mean, no-words fantastic."
Nicki smiled and pecked Val's cheek.

"You're sweet to say so. I did try." Devilish smile again. "I hope you eat fish. I didn't call to ask."

"Love it. Is it salmon?" Val asked based on the aroma coming from the kitchen.

"It is! It's an Asian-inspired recipe a friend of mine always makes. Truth is, John Henry prepared it. I'm just heating it up."

Val was amazed. She shook her head in disbelief.

"That John Henry must be the eighth wonder of the world!"

"He is. He learned to cook in the service, but he took a couple of culinary classes with the GI bill before he settled on his degree. A bachelor's in criminology," Nicki explained. "He can do anything, but I think I told you that already."

"Please, don't let that food burn. It smells too good."

"Don't worry. The cooking is foolproof—tried and true. I knew I wouldn't have time to cook. JH went to Milledgeville for me, picked up some fish and veggies, brought it by and did all the prep work. When I came home the packets were in the refrigerator, ready to heat up. The wine was uncorked and the table was set. I can picture JH standing at the table, nodding his head in satisfaction. But where are my manners?" Nicki exclaimed. "Please. Sit." She motioned for Val to sit on the couch.

Val sank into the couch cushion. Nicki sat next to her, pulling her dress down to lay across her thighs. She leaned her shoulder into Val's, and let her head drop onto the back of the couch.

"I'm tired. At least I can just enjoy the meal. And the company."

"On a hunch, Nicki, you don't know if that's a Moosewood recipe, do you? You probably don't even know what Moosewood is, you're so young."

"Oh yes, I do. JH gave me the cookbook with that recipe. I didn't know of it before him, though."

"You will not believe this, but that is my absolute favorite recipe. Not bluffing." Val positioned herself so she could convey a suitable serious countenance to validate her claim. "*Moosewood Cooks at Home*," Val stated confidently.

"You're right," Nicki answered. "I don't believe in coincidences. At least I didn't before." Nicki pulled Val's shoulder back down so theirs could touch. They sat sipping the wine.

Val looked around at Nicki's things. A few charming garden prints on the wall. She noticed a closed-off fireplace behind the couch as they sat down. The couch faced windows, and occasionally, Val saw cars drive by. Eckhart Tolle books mixed with a couple of John Grisham novels lined a small corner bookshelf. On the middle shelf was a black and white picture of Nicki and Trolly. It was a lovely close-up of their smiling faces, heads touching. Trolly's little hand held a daisy, and she touched one of the petals with her right index finger. Nicki's hair was shoulder length, but the smile was the same. Captivating.

"This is a lovely picture, Nicki. Is that Trolly?" As soon as the words left her mouth, Val turned her body toward the photo to hide her grimace. *Foot in mouth, Scott. Great.*

Nicki jumped up and pulled the picture to her lap.

"Yes, it is. She was so sweet." Nicki kissed the picture.

Val leaned over and kissed Nicki, then silently blew out a breath of relief.

"You're pretty sweet yourself. Trolly obviously would have come by that naturally."

"And you're pretty hokey, but thank you." Nicki smiled, continuing to look at the picture. She wiped tears from her eyes. The kitchen timer beeped.

"Please be seated at the table, Ms. Scott. I'll join you in a second." Nicki declined Val's offer for help.

Val heard rustling of foil and the clink of china. Nicki reappeared from the swinging door to the kitchen with two fine china plates. She placed one in front of Val and the other at her place. Val poured each of them more wine.

"This looks lovely, Nicki. It's funny to see this plate, too. Kutani Crane. It was my brother's favorite. He died as a young man. I was still in college. He had been sick for several months—leukemia. It was tough, but luckily, enough time and grief counseling has taken the edge off that. I believe Laura Nyro when she said nothing cures like time and love."

"I'm going to remember that." Nicki smiled. After a beat she explained, pointing to the plate, that she had seen the pink flowers and Asian-inspired crane print in an antique and junk shop when she moved back to Marshall. "I thought Trolly would have loved these. I think of her every time I use them."

Val continued to be amazed by and enthralled with Nicki. *How long will this last? Just stop and enjoy the present.* Mr. Tolle might be pleased with her self-discussions of appreciating what *is*.

"You know, Val, you know practically everything about me now after my breakdown the other night, but I don't know much about you except that you were a nurse, you like wine, you now own property in East Nowheresville, you had a brother, your aunt was significant to you, you live in a camper, cycle, and are gorgeous," Nicki exclaimed with that devilish smile again.

"Still a nurse, Nicki. Once a nurse, always a nurse, they say, but those *are* the high points of my life."

"I saw a photo of you in a nursing cap, holding a candle, when I was at your place."

"My pinning. Nurses graduate, but they also have a pinning ceremony. The candle honors Florence Nightingale's care of Crimean War soldiers by lamplight. It's a big deal.

"Gail, my ex, and I moved from Georgia to Maine for a few years. I worked all the time. Managers don't get days off these days, especially in small hospitals. Gail worked in a doctor's office and had set hours and lots of time off. We began to drift apart.

"Then I got sick. It was right after my mom died. It was a horrible time. I spent twenty-three days in the hospital. Even had a stroke while I was there. Gail was great then, I have to admit. I mean, we had been together a long time. It wasn't like we didn't love one another, you know." She briefly explained her rare blood disorder.

"TT what?" Nicki asked.

"It's called TTP because that's easier to say. Only three or four in a million. I survived, obviously. Had outpatient rehabilitation for the stroke deficits, but I was able to go back to work with no problems. I'm in remission and hope to stay that way." Val shifted position to face Nicki.

"Life is short. We're not promised another minute, but I don't have to tell you that. Anyway, I resigned my position, and I sold most of my own things that Gail didn't want. I kept a few things in storage for a while, and I moved temporarily to Aunt Grace's place on Martha's Vineyard. Beautiful and quiet. Not a bad place to hang out," Val said.

Val changed the subject onto her life as a teen, going to college in the mountains of North Carolina. She loved the mountains. She explained that she came to know the area around Suches where Nicki had lived with Mike and Trolly because an Athens friend had a cabin there.

"Beautiful country. We've hiked from Woody Gap to the cabin more times than I can count," Val added.

Nicki teared up again but smiled. She explained how she and Mike had scattered Trolly's ashes off the overlook point called "Preacher's Rock." She had not been back since.

"That's a beautiful place for a beautiful soul," Val said quietly. She reached across the table for Nicki's hand. They sat quietly.

***

Val dried as Nicki washed up the few remaining dishes. JH had left her an otherwise spotless kitchen. As Nicki was putting a dish into the upper cabinet, her dress hiked up to the top of her thigh. Val walked in behind Nicki and pressed against her. Nicki felt the warmth between her legs.

"Don't make me break my dish." Nicki turned quickly. They kissed. "You are predictable, you know," she continued. "But I don't blame you. I would have done the same thing. Just so you know." Nicki looked up at her clock. Nine o'clock.

"Oh shit! I've got to go close up. You drive." She locked the front door and ran out to Val's truck since it was blocking Nicki's. "No one in town would notice, but that doesn't matter. I know."

"I'm surprised JH didn't close the laundry up for you," Val said as she drove.

"He couldn't. He's got a group at the VA in Milledgeville this evening. He'd never make it back in time."

"I'm really amazed by this John Henry dude. I'm not kidding."

"You should be. He leads a grief rap group for vets and family members who've suffered loss. We met before he became the facilitator. We had both been regulars, two of twelve on any given session. He had quite a bit of experience with loss. He's fifty-eight now, but then, his wife had just died of breast cancer around the same time Trolly died. Two years before Mike died.

"Then that VA liaison contacted me and told me about the group. I drove to that Milledgeville building where the group met four times before I went in. I'd sit in the truck for fifteen or twenty minutes then drive away. When I finally made it in, John Henry welcomed me and sat next to me. He was a rock for me and took me under his wing."

She explained it was then that she found out how handy he was. She loved to be able to give back to John Henry by hiring him for her various odd jobs. He was more than a handyman, though. He was her best friend.

Val waited in the truck the few minutes it took for Nicki to close. On the way home, Nicki looked across and smiled to herself as she noted Val's profile.

"I can't wait for you to meet John Henry. I'm going to find out when he can have dinner with us. He needs to give you some ideas for protecting yourself."

"Yeah, I need some safety ideas. I've ordered a tiny house. It's supposed to be delivered to the property in a month. I plan to live there until the project is completed and self-sufficient."

"Oh no, no, no, you won't," Nicki said. "You'll live here before that!" she vowed as they pulled into her driveway. Val laughed.

"I don't think so." Val looked at her and shook her head.

Nicki had just pulled down her dress again as she hopped out of the truck.

"Come in for some coffee, tea, or dessert. Please."

"Do you have decaf for the old lady?" Val smiled.

As they walked in the door, Nicki locked the deadbolt behind Val. She pushed Val against the front door and pressed against her.

"Nothing old about you." Nicki pulled off her earrings and put them on a small table by the door.

Chapter Seven

VAL WOKE UP IN Nicki's bed. Alone. It was an old metal bed, painted white. The box springs and pillow-top mattress created a significant step down to the floor. Nicki was not in the bathroom, either. The oversized clawfoot tub had a suspended oval ring above it and a curtain, making it also a shower. She hadn't noticed its size before. *Mm. Nice tub.* Nicki had obviously showered this morning. *Too bad I slept through that.* Val looked through the kitchen window and saw the red pickup was gone. Nicki wasn't home. Val looked at the clock. Seven-thirty.

Val noticed a small bunch of dried rosemary on the table with a note.

To put in your camper. See you soon. Don't worry about the deadbolt. Just lock the door behind you as you leave.

Val's keys were next to the note. Her truck was now on Nicki's front lawn rather than blocking the driveway. *Already at the laundry, I suppose. No kiss. My loss.*

***

The squatters smiled and waved this morning. They had changed their positions, but were still holding court at the picnic table, and smoke curled from the fire pit. Val returned the wave and the smile. She wondered if she should make them cookies or something else neighborly. *Maybe next time.*

After cleaning up from a thirty-mile ride, Val drove in to meet with the sheriff. She shook off the dread of recounting the encounter with the hunters, and rolled her shoulders before pushing the door open.

"Can I help you?" came a voice from an office on the far side of the room.

"I'm here to speak with Sheriff Jenkins," she answered as she approached the office door.

"C'mon in. I'm Jenkins."

"Sheriff Jenkins, my name is Val Scott. I've been encouraged by several people to report an incident I had with some hunters on a piece of property I've bought."

"Have a seat. I'm assuming this is in our county."

"Yes. It's the cleared track that was originally to be the Grist Mill subdivision." When Jenkins nodded, she continued. "It's been over a week, but I didn't report it because I didn't want to file an official report. Just didn't want to ruffle feathers, you know...but I wanted to look around again the day before I closed on the property. When I drove in, I saw a couple of trucks and two of those deer stands...they looked temporary, or hastily constructed maybe. Hadn't been there when Sandy Ann and I had looked at the property the first time."

"This doesn't surprise me. It's hard to monitor all of this land—cleared or not. Give me any details you can remember."

"There were three guys, with one being what I would call the ring leader. He had a scruffy beard, brown. They all had on camos. They all had guns. They pretty much came down from the stands as soon as I pulled in. I was frightened, of course, when the main guy started mouthing off, but I tried to just make nice.

"They surrounded me and pretty much told me bad things would happen if I didn't let the land there be open for hunting. I explained it wouldn't be open for hunting. Then they surrounded me...with their guns, though not pointing at me. As I got in my truck, the main guy slammed my door closed. They all smelled like they'd been drinking. Anyway, I'm not asking for an investigation or anything, but I wanted you to be aware."

"You said there were two trucks. Happen to get a plate number?"

"No. I really have tried to remember the trucks. I think I was too focused on the barrels of the rifles, frankly. Well, two rifles and one shotgun, but I think one of them was dark, maybe dark blue. One may have been white...mine is white, so I think that may have triggered me to remember another white truck. I'm so frustrated with myself for not remembering."

"It's perfectly understandable. Are you planning on trying a subdivision?"

"Oh no. I have a commercial-type project in mind, but I do plan to have a tiny house brought onto the land to live in while building is going on."

"I don't advise you to be out there by yourself. Not unless you plan to have a protection dog...and maybe a gun yourself."

"Well, John Henry Evans is supposed to come out and make some recommendations...help me secure things, give me advice, you know."

"John Henry! You should have said that right off the bat," the sheriff exclaimed. "He'll get you squared away, but you still shouldn't stay alone. I'll ask the Highway Patrol and my guys to increase their drive-bys." He scribbled something on a card.

"That is my personal cell. If you have any sort of problem, see something off, or whatever—call me. Someone will be out within five minutes or so. Until a fence is up, one of us will be driving through at least once a day. I think I'll ask the game warden to up their surveillance for illegal hunting in that area too."

"I appreciate your help, Sheriff Jenkins." She looked up from the card he handed her and did a quick visual health assessment—a habit from years of nursing.

Sheriff Jenkins was probably her age, mid-fifties. He was wearing a wedding ring. He also had corneal arcus rings in his eyes, white around the brown, a typical sign of untreated high cholesterol. He surely didn't appear overweight. *Family history?* After inner debate, she opted for a general approach to satisfy her assessment.

"Sheriff Jenkins, do you know of a good family doctor? It's time for a checkup. I need to get established with someone in the area."

"I hear there are some in Milledgeville, but I can't say myself."

As they shook hands and said good-byes, she considered ways to incorporate general health education and promotion into the project's scope.

On the way back home, she swung by the Pizza Joint. Peggy smiled when Val walked in.

"Well, well. If it isn't my good friend Val," Peggy joked. "I heard what happened to you. I'm pretty sure one of those guys was my drunk brother-in-law. He's one of those creeps that makes your hair stand on end. Truth be told, I hate him. I'm sorry he ever married my sister." She explained he hunted deer for years, even off-season, on that land. He bragged about it. "If I see him—"

Val interrupted her.

"Please don't say anything, even though I might appreciate it. I talked with Sheriff Jenkins today."

"Well, good. What'd he say?"

"At first, he said he didn't want me to stay out there by myself, but as soon as I said John Henry is supposed to help me figure out some protection solutions, he was all good. Said I should've started with that!" She chuckled as Peggy nodded.

"Well, you probably shouldn't stay there alone. That's a bad crowd with that damn brother-in-law of mine."

"He told me that he would alert the Highway Patrol and his other colleagues to increase their drive-by traffic. Said someone would drive through at least once a day until a fence is up. And he's going to tell the game warden, since they were illegally hunting."

"He will, but I sure would like a reason to call Ben Linton a dirty, scumbag, drunk to his face." After a beat she added with a smile, "But you didn't come in here for me to get all up in your business, did you? Now, what can I get you, doll? The usual?"

"Sure. Sounds good. Only I want it to go, please." *She remembered what I ordered? This is only the second time I've been here!*

"Oh, I see. You must have some *laundry* to do," Peggy said as she turned away. She turned back around, winked with a smile, and sashayed behind the counter to make the pizza.

Oh my. So it goes. She was again taken aback by how everyone knew everyone else's business. *Small town, Georgia, USA. Guess I better get used to it.* But Peggy was right, in one sense. She did plan to go by the laundry and see if Nicki wanted to eat some pizza with her.

Chapter Eight

THE LAUNDROMAT WAS HOPPING when she arrived. Val noticed an old panel van behind the building next to Nicki's truck. With pizza box in hand, she walked in and up to the half-door.

"Special delivery, ma'am," Val said, knocking on the door. Nicki turned around from her desk and smiled.

"Come in. I'm starving." Nicki waved Val in and jumped up to sit at the bistro table. "Hey, did you see the guy working on the jumbo washer? That's John Henry."

"I didn't notice. Besides, a glowing light radiating from this room led me where I needed to be," Val teased.

"Oh, my god! You are *so* hokey." Nicki leaned and pecked Val right on the mouth. She laughed and looked at the door to check if anyone saw her. "Oops. I'm glad you're here. When JH is done, he'll come give me an update."

"I look forward to meeting him. All I've heard is what a great person he is...from everyone." Val was trying to open the box lid as she talked. Nicki pulled it away, ripped the lid open, and grabbed a slice.

"It seems I haven't eaten in days, but I know I had *plenty* last night." Nicki smiled as she looked directly into Val's eyes. Val looked up and shook her head. Nicki beamed.

"You're an easy target, you know. And thank goodness, you're a good sport. But seriously, JH is a wonderful person," Nicki said. "And he'll be a good friend to you. I hope he'll talk some sense into you about staying on the property alone."

"I have no doubt about his friendship, Nicki. After what he's given you, both spiritually, emotionally, and physically, I already like him. We'll see about the other. Do you mind if I sit in here and make a few phone calls? I have some things I need to arrange at the property."

"I don't mind a bit, but you may want to hold off until you talk to JH. He can probably steer you to good, reliable folks," Nicki offered.

"You're right. I—"

"Speak of the devil!" Nicki exclaimed, interrupting. "John Henry Evans, meet my good friend Valerie Scott...Val."

"Val, it's a pleasure to meet you. Nicki has said lovely things about you. Any friend of Nicki's is a friend of mine." John Henry was not necessarily as Val had pictured. She was expecting more of a country man. John Henry sounded as if he could be a tenured professor. Smooth voice. Well spoken. Articulate even. Val reached out for a handshake.

John Henry looked down at the grease on his hands.

"Just a second. I'll get right back to you." He smiled as he spoke. Val instantly saw a kind soul. She returned the smile.

John Henry cleaned his hands with the GoJo. Val always loved the way GoJo smelled, and smiled on the inside. He returned to her and extended his hand. It literally enveloped hers. She liked a person who wasn't afraid to shake a woman's hand. He looked down at her from what seemed to be three feet. She chuckled.

"If you're wondering, six feet, five and a half inches," he said with a smile. "And no, I never played basketball," he added, chuckling.

"I *was*...wondering," Val said. "But I was pretty dang close—off by only a half inch." They all laughed. "I have to thank you for the lovely dinner at Nicki's. I don't know if she already told you, but that happens to be my favorite recipe." He smiled and nodded.

He sat across from Val, and Nicki wheeled on her office chair to sit between them. She pressed her shoulder against JH's arm. His broad shoulders made him appear to tower above her. His skin was a rich brownish-red, which, along with his somewhat flat, angular nose and high cheekbones, revealed a possible indigenous heritage.

"You seem to have a bit of a problem, Val," JH offered. "Anytime you buy a big tract of land around here, especially if you're going to do any sort of development, you're going to have security issues. I can help you with that. What are your priorities? Let's see if we can start this process."

"Wow. I cannot believe how friendly everyone has been. Except the jerks. Helpful. I was saying that to Nicki the other day," Val replied.

Val explained that first she was going to need a septic system, electric, and phone lines. However, she would want to confer with a contractor first. She wanted to be sure that if something was built or installed, that it could have a dual purpose for the, hopefully, inevitable growth.

"I know you don't know me, but I have quite a bit of experience in large scale building management. Mostly from the military, but I also have managed security and facilities for some large industries in the area."

"JH, if I may call you that—" Val started. JH nodded in agreement. "I would never *need* to see a resume, although I would love to see one. Not one person I have spoken with sings anything but your praises."

"I lead a simple life. I am just as I am with you on this first meeting as I would be with a four-year-old or my preacher. It's too hard to be more than one person. It's important to me to die knowing I have done everything in my power to make the world a kinder and better place."

"Funny you say that," Val said. "I used to tell staff nurses a similar thing about not trying to be more than one person. 'Being real' seems to be a good way to create an instant comfort level in those you meet. It may not have worked well with drunk rednecks, but it seems to work generally." He nodded.

"Dad was a sharecropper when I was a boy, so I grew up using farm machinery, working the land, and watching deals being made at the county marketplace.

"My mom was part Muscogee, it was said. I was always told that mom's great-grandfather came from his Muscogee Creek tribe and took a young slave girl of African descent as a wife. I never knew my grandparents. Mom instilled in me a respect for nature and for others. When she fell in love with dad—he was black too—she said it wasn't his striking good looks, but rather his honesty and gentle way with people, especially young children." He paused and looked up. "They were good parents. And, of course, my good looks are from dad...or so said dad." They all chuckled.

"John Henry, it is a real pleasure to meet you."

"I told you so, Val," Nicki said as she looked at JH and smiled. "And I told you that you'd like Val." Nicki looked out at the laundry floor and excused herself to help one of the women reading the machine instructions in a way that signaled English might not be her native language.

"Val, I think it would be in your best interest *not* to live out there right now. At least until you can secure the area," JH said.

"Everyone has said that, even Sheriff Jenkins," Val replied. "But I'm pretty determined. What I do need though, is some professional advice. I'm glad Nicki left the room so I could run this by you. My project is controversial. If we're going to discuss it, I'll ask you to sign a non-disclosure agreement. I trust you, but I can't be too careful."

"You need not worry," JH replied. "I've worked with enough corporations to know that is pretty standard."

They discussed meeting times for the next few days and a general salary figure. John Henry wanted to consult, unpaid, as a friend, but Val insisted the reason she was here was to provide employment income to residents, whether they acted as consultants or employees. She wanted to pay those who were providing services. Val made a quick call to Sandy Ann to see if she could borrow the realtor's conference room for a few hours. Sandy Ann agreed, and said she was thrilled to be involved in any way, even if she was not privy to details. It was settled. John Henry would meet Val at the realty office the next day at ten a.m.

"Tell Lucky I'll see her tomorrow sometime," JH said. He wrote something on a napkin on Nicki's desk and left through the back door. The note, in beautiful cursive, said simply, *Paid in Full. Your smile was worth my time today. JHE*

Nicki returned, put the "gone for the day" sign on the top half of the office door, and locked it from the inside. She walked to Val and put her arm around Val's shoulder.

"Did JH leave, doll?"

"He did. And he said, 'Tell Lucky I'll see her tomorrow sometime.' He put an invoice on your desk. We're going to meet tomorrow in an official capacity for my project."

Nicki looked at the desk from across the room and appeared to be reading his handwriting. She walked to the desk and picked up the note.

"Sweet. Such a solid guy. So kind and giving."

"Seems like he thinks a lot of you. That's obvious."

"Of everyone, it seems like, but yeah, he's like a big brother...or maybe a dad." Nicki hopped up to sit on the desk. "I've never met someone with such a big heart.

"As his parents aged, JH took them into his home. He built a small living space for them. JH's wife, Sarah, cared for them while JH was in Kuwait. When he returned, they were close to death. He spent as much time as he could doing whatever they needed. Doctor's visits, cooking, cleaning. When they were dying, he acted as an aide. He even bathed them. After they passed, he had them buried on a small plot at the edge of their yard. He had to check it out, you know. I didn't even know that was legal, but it is in Georgia. Then, as a headstone, he put a beautiful wooden carving with animals and fish and weather features encircling the Earth, done by a Cherokee artist from North Carolina. I hope you can see it sometime.

"Jeez, sorry. I'm just going on and on," Nicki said. "You want some water or a soda or something?"

"I'm good. This is fascinating, actually. Before he said, I wondered if he had an indigenous heritage. So, I was interested, but really, knowing his backstory is so wonderful."

"Okay, then. I'll keep blabbing." Nicki locked eyes with Val. "I like you, you know."

"Mm-hm. Sorta guessed as much," Val said with a smile and a wink. "Well, go on." Val's open hand swept the air quickly toward herself in a circular motion from the wrist.

"Okay, okay. In Kuwait, he worked as a cook. He told me he liked serving the guys, but his captain had recognized his aptitude and natural intelligence. My interpretation. He wouldn't have said that. After he repeatedly repaired one of the ovens, his captain evidently investigated JH's files, looking for his aptitude scores. The captain took JH aside one day and apologized for his having been placed as a cook. He said he thought it was because JH was African American. The captain recommended a promotion of rank and assignment. JH was sent into mechanics as a trade specialist. Later, he worked in several other assignments. This meant better money for his family, but he learned the ins and outs of other large pieces of equipment. After his first re-enlistment, he was essentially managing facilities operations at one of the Army's regional bases." She looked at the wall across the room, as if she were a thousand miles away. "He is something else," Nicki added, shaking her head, and tapping JH's invoice on her palm.

"If *I* had done anything for you, I would have written the same thing. I like the guy." Val smiled.

"Oh, you've *done* something all right," Nicki said as she jumped off the desk. Again, that devilish smile. She leaned into Val and pressed her lips against Val's. Val's breathing changed, and she was warmed. Nicki's tongue found Val's.

"What are you doing this evening, doll?" Nicki asked as she pulled out of the kiss.

"Going home to get some sleep," Val replied, emphasizing the last three words distinctly. She was exhausted, but for the most delightful reasons. "Please, don't tempt me." Val loved the way Nicki called her *doll*. She was sure it was just a generic pet name, but the way Nicki said it...

"Okay then. I need to pay bills, do some shopping, and wash some clothes. Can you believe it? The laundromat owner has dirty clothes." Nicki smiled. "I'll stay here until I close up. If you change your mind, you know where to find me. And when."

Val kissed Nicki goodbye. Nicki caressed Val's firm bottom as she pulled Val against her pubic bone.

"Mm. I love how you feel." It took every ounce of Val's willpower to pull away and shut the door behind her.

"Sleep well, sweet lady. See you soon." Val heard Nicki's soft voice as the door shut.

***

Nicki reviewed the mental list of chores ahead of her. *These are the things that get backed up when I spend time doing something other than work or school*, she thought. *I don't have time for anything lovey dovey right now!*

"I have to have a life, though, don't I?" she exclaimed to the ceiling. She wondered if it would simply take too much energy at this point. *But it feels so nice.* "It does, but you sure don't have time for daydreaming right now, now do you?" She blew out a raspberry.

Chapter Nine

VAL WAS WAITING ON one of the padded, teak outdoor chairs on Sandy Ann's office porch when JH's panel van drove up. JH held open the door as they exchanged their greetings, and the two of them walked into the conference room after locking the front door. Sandy Ann had run to a meeting, but she told Val the room was set up for them. A carafe of coffee, a box of pastries, plates, silverware, and fixings for the eats had been arranged on one end of the conference table. *Why am I even surprised?*

"That Sandy Ann," she said. "Don't want to let her down." JH nodded in agreement.

"No. We're obligated here, don't you think? Glad I only had one cup this morning."

"Wish I could say the same, but I am a sucker for a morning snack."

They chatted as they snacked. Val talked about the campground, and JH gave her a quick history of the carwash across the street and the pool hall that used to be there.

"You know, I'm glad you said you were used to these non-disclosures," Val said.

"Oh yes, Val. Please, don't worry about that in the least. Let's see what you have." He smiled and reached for the papers. It appeared he read them thoroughly.

"Sure," JH said as he pulled out a pen from his shirt pocket and signed.

"Okay, good. Thanks. Here goes."

Val pulled out a set of plans drawn by a dear friend who worked as an architect in Athens. He was not an industrial architect, but he knew the construction and design fundamentals. Val had sought someone whose discretion was golden, and she knew this would be as protected as the bounty in Fort Knox. JH sat up straight against the back of his chair as Val revealed details of Amazing Grace.

"The keystone of the project is a non-profit casino—Amazing Grace. The theme draws from our rich religious imagery. Briefly, we use a sort of tithe, a portion of each win, that turns into a donation to one's chosen church or service organization." Val paused.

"Now that's not something we find around these parts," JH said as he nodded and smiled. "Wow."

"I'm just hoping it'll take the stigma out of 'casino.' I mean, is it bad if it's helping your church? Or the community."

"I understand what you're saying."

"About the campus. The casino building will be a sixty thousand-square-foot anchor building, occupying the center of the land tract. A smaller security and facilities building would sit on the back side of the tract. On one side, in close proximity to the anchor, would be a five-story, three hundred room hotel. Parking would surround both the anchor building and hotel. At least three acres would be set aside for a small solar farm to help defray electricity costs. The entrances from either side of the county or state-maintained roads would feature bucolic scenery, trees, and native plants. The property Sandy Ann brokered features a fifty-acre pond at the bottom of a hill near the existing main entrance. I can just see a beautifully landscaped drive snaking around the pond's edge to the anchor building, highlighted with the stunning, large, gate-shaped, lighted sign for Amazing Grace Casino."

"That's different, Val. I'll give you that, but do you think it's feasible? In Georgia, I mean?"

"Well, we know Georgia's one of those Southern, anti-gambling states. Has been. I mean look how hard Zell Miller had to work to get the lottery in here. Even with the promise of the Hope Scholarship. And now look at how many kids go to college on that."

"Yep. You're right about that."

"Destination resorts, as they call them, have gaming proponents lobbying to relax the state's existing restrictions. Georgia has historically been one of the typical, Southern, anti-gambling states. Getting legislative leaders to legalize casinos or other gaming establishments has been unsuccessful. You know the arguments. Gambling leads to organized crime and gangs. Money brought in by casinos should go for service-related industries. Well, with Amazing Grace, it will."

"Yeah, I can see that it could have a huge impact on new jobs, tax revenue, and reinvestment—not only to the community—but also to the state, the way you're describing it."

"It's not a particularly complicated idea. It isn't new, either, but it is for Georgia."

"Especially where gambling still isn't legal. Unless you consider the lottery and casinos both gambling." John Henry tapped a finger on the table. "Hm. It's interesting, for sure."

"The good news is that anti-gaming sentiment diminishes each year."

"I remember Miller's fight, but I haven't kept up with the gaming industry. You probably know that we couldn't hold a 'lottery' at church for a cake. You could sell tickets, but you couldn't say it was a 'chance.' My grandmother wouldn't buy one of those tickets, because she swore it was gambling." He shook his head. "I don't know, Val."

"Okay, so here's the brief plan. My corporation, Valiant Expeditions, would be doing business as Amazing Grace. It would be one of those destination resorts...just on a smaller scale. Amazing Grace, the casino's operational name, would become a non-profit organization satisfying multiple needs. The organization would function as a casino, but rather than the house taking the majority of the spoils, the revenue would directly serve the community and state."

"Yeah. Gotcha so far."

"Casino patrons would be eligible to join a players' club. However, the club would be set up differently than most casino membership clubs. You know, not to get perks like free hotel rooms or comped meals. Instead, when joining, one designates which religious or service organization would receive ten percent of their winnings. For example, if individuals wished to *tithe* to the Southern Baptist Convention, or the Jewish Federation of Macon and Middle Georgia, or they wished to donate to their favorite service organization, their payout slips would automatically have ten percent directed thusly. At the end of each month, a drawing would be held from the designated organizations to receive an additional donation from Amazing Grace, depending on the amount of money raised each month. Visitors from other areas or who were not players' club members would automatically have ten percent put into the house's monthly additional donation pool. You can't just win and put your money in your pocket. Some of it has to help the community."

"That might make it a little easier to swallow for gambling critics. It might at least have them turn a blind eye." JH cocked his head as if considering the information. "Maybe."

"I hope Amazing Grace can provide jobs and benefit the community through donations. I also hope to provide both sick and well daycare for employees' children, plus day programs for aging relatives of employees.

"As an outreach, we'll partner with one of the area healthcare agencies to begin a mobile kidney disease education and screening program. I've already seen how other health education might help the community."

"Val, I don't know what I think of the feasibility of this project, but I would be honored to be a part of it," he said earnestly. "Truly, it's exciting. I will tell you, though, it's going to be hard to keep this from Lucky."

"I've thought about that. It will be hard. I haven't told her anything specific. And Sandy Ann only knows the rough size of the buildings. I think she thinks it's going to be an outlet mall or a sales distribution place."

"You know, I can help you with some of this prep work. Because of the work I've done with the manufacturing places, I know a few folks who do the sort of work you're looking for with the project. You need a huge septic system. Plus, you need for your tiny house to tie into that system. I know just the firm. And the estimates you've received are probably based on residential zoning rather than commercial."

"I never even made that distinction. See. I need you."

"We can negotiate with the county to see if they would provide a tax discount or deferment, either commercial or non-profit. Sometimes, counties will provide public water service rather than approving huge private water systems with their own pumps and treatment facilities."
Val recognized this was just the person she wanted on her team.

"With your permission, I'm having business cards printed for you. I'm thinking 'Valiant Expeditions. John Henry Evans. Operations and Facilities Director,'" she read out loud from her notes.

"How about 'Facilities and Security Director' instead?"

"Brilliant. Sold. Welcome to the team." Val reached for JH's hand to seal the deal. Instead, he came around the table to stand in front of her and shook her hand. During the shake, he put his other hand atop hers.

"Thank you, Val. Your trust means the world to me."

"And to me, JH." She smiled.

As they were leaving, JH turned to Val. "Val, as my first order of business, may I please make those calls on your behalf?"

"You certainly may. Now, don't make me lazy, though," Val joked. He shook his head and beamed.

"I'll need that list you made." Val handed it to him. JH put his hand gently on her elbow as if to escort her down the stairs.

"Thank you, boss." Val smiled up at him, and they both laughed.

***

Val called and left a message for Nicki. Nicki called back in a few minutes, but Val was driving and couldn't pick up.

The squatters were sitting outside, again. Val considered what it must be like to live with the outside as your living room. That notion had its charm. Val wasn't sure she would want that in early February, even in Georgia. The usual smiles and nods were exchanged as she drove by. As soon as she arrived at Bambi, she called Nicki back. She left another message regarding phone tag.

This time when Val's phone rang, she picked up. "Success. Finally. Good evening."

"Ugh. Not so good. It's that time of the month, and I feel like shit," Nicki said. Val remembered that feeling from the past. She had a hysterectomy at age thirty. She wouldn't recommend it, but she could not say she missed anything about her period. Sometimes, she forgot women had that experience.

"I'm so sorry. You're welcome to come here, but if you have the cramps I used to have before I had a hysterectomy, all you'll want is a heating pad, eight hundred milligrams of ibuprofen, and a pillow to cover your head."

"Bingo," Nicki replied. "But don't brag about it, okay. I miss you, I have to say, but I think I'd be better off at home."

"You know, I heard once that an orgasm is one of the best ways to alleviate cramps," Val said in a sultry voice. "Not that I would know anything about that."

"I will give that remedy a try. Sorry I won't have any help." Val could hear the smile in Nicki's voice. "Later, doll."

"All alone again. I can't believe I'm all alone again," Val sang to herself in the style of the familiar Willie Nelson tune. *Oh well.*

Chapter Ten

VAL WOKE UP TO a crash, her car alarm, shouting, and a vehicle turning gravel under its wheels. She jumped out of the bed, threw on a coat, grabbed her keys, flipped the awning lights on, and ran out the front door. No thought, just action.

Trying to figure out what was going on, she pressed the lock button to shut the alarm off and heard a man's voice.

"Ma'am, I'm sorry." Val jumped, then thought she saw the silhouette of one of the squatters.

"What? What just happened? What the hell!" She held her hand on her chest.

He seemed nervous and disturbed. "I'm sorry, Ma'am. I shoulda given you a little more warning. I was sitting at the table looking up at the sky. I heard a car coming down the road in here, real slow-like...thought maybe they were looking for their campsite. It was a blue-looking pickup with no headlights on, and I didn't like the looks of that. I can't see your site from my table, so I walked up to the rise for a better view. Three men got out of the truck. One of them had what looked like a baseball bat and just took a swing at your back window. That's when I started yelling at them and running down here. They jumped back in the truck and took off, lights on." He put his flashlight onto her truck. Val walked around and saw the bashed-in glass.

"God damn it! Those fuckin' assholes. Oh, sorry," Val said as she shook her head. She told him what had happened Sunday. "I gotta go call Sheriff Jenkins. Thank you for looking out for me. I have a feeling he's going to want to ask you for whatever details you can remember."

He nodded. "I'll be right here until you return, okay?"

She ran up the hill in the center of the campground to make sure the call would go through. After the call, she ran back down to her site. Her eyesight had re-adjusted to the dark after using her phone. She sought out the squatter who had approached her, who she now recognized as the squatter who seemed to be the group's leader.

"Don't know when I've been so freaked out." Val held out her shaking hands. "You remember anything else? I was dead asleep."

"Pretty sure it was a dark blue truck. Saw that when they finally turned the lights on to get outta here, but when they turned the truck lights on…" He paused, grinned, and squinted his eyes playfully. "The light came on at the license plate. And guess what? I got the number…dumb fucks." His expression returned to a more serious one.

"Oh, wow! I appreciate what you did. I mean, you don't even know me. But that scared the shit out of me."

"Ma'am, I don't like any folks bothering others. You haven't ignored us like so many campers do. There are four of us over there. We've all struggled fitting in, but regardless, it's just the right thing to do…to help out others who need it," the man said. "If you ever need anything, please ask."

"Thank you again," Val replied. "I'm Val Scott." Val extended her hand. "Nice to meet you after so many weeks."

"Frank Thompson," he replied. "Nice to meet you, Val." Frank shook the extended hand. "I'll be awake if you need anything." He headed back on a straight line to site fifteen, without using his light, and obviously without needing it.

Jenkins had called one of the guys who happened to be on patrol not far from Hamburg. The State Patrol car rolled in with blue lights flashing, but thankfully, no siren. The trooper got out and walked toward Val. She stood with her arms crossed in front of her to hold her coat closed.

"Hi, ma'am. You're Ms. Scott? Jenkins told me what happened. Describe it from your perspective?" he asked as he shone a beam onto her broken window.

"I heard yelling, my car alarm, and a loud crash. Woke me up from a dead sleep." Val shook her head. "When I ran outside, one of the campers from fifteen, Frank Thompson, was standing outside. I had heard some sort of vehicle driving fast, kicking up gravel, but I never saw it. Frank said he saw a 'blueish' truck driving by their site." Val pointed at site fifteen. "When the truck stopped here, Frank said he headed here as quickly as he could. He saw three men get out, one of them with what looked like a bat. When he saw the one with the bat swing at my truck window, he started yelling. He said the men jumped into the truck and drove away. That certainly makes sense based on what woke me up. He could only see rear lights and the plate light by the time he got here." Val handed the plate number Frank had given her. "Frank said come see him if you need to."

"Don't worry. I have to have his statement for my report," Trooper Jones said. Val made a mental note of the name on his name tag. *Michael Jones.* "But I'll tell you, Ms. Scott. I think I recognize that plate. And it does belong to a blue pickup if I'm not mistaken. We'll take care of this." His flashlight beam focused again onto Val's shattered truck window. They looked up at headlights of two golf carts headed their way. Lights were on at the park staff residence, so Val assumed they were curious about the excitement.

Two disheveled park rangers in separate carts rolled up.

"What's going on?" one of them asked.

The trooper explained he had received a call from the Sheriff's office reporting a suspicious truck and perhaps some vandalism.

"Luckily, one of the campers was up and saw the whole thing. Nobody's hurt, just a broken truck window. We have this under control, guys. Go back to bed. I'll send a copy of the report." They turned around and headed home.

"Thanks, Officer Jones," Val said. "I think I'll go back to bed myself. You know how to find me."

"Sure. You may hear me out here for a bit," Trooper Jones reported. "I have to take some pictures, but I'll be as quiet as I can be when I leave." He reached into his car and turned off the blue lights. His headlights seemed to give enough light to see his way around the truck and onto the campground road for any trace of the fast getaway.

Val tried to sleep, but her mind was spinning. Enough adrenaline had flooded her to keep her awake for a week. *No one to call at this time of night. Three a.m. Ugh.* She thought of Nicki...her smile, and the past two times they had made love. It was not lost on Val that whenever she thought of Nicki now, she longed for her touch. She was, if nothing else, in lust.

It wasn't just lust, though, Val thought. During the past two weeks, she had spent quite a few hours at the laundromat. She would read, use the internet, or ride her bike up for lunch. She even helped out on the floor some when Nicki was studying.

She loved watching Nicki rush out to help one of the laundry customers struggling in even the most mundane of ways. Nicki was incredible with kids. When a child was crying, she would run out of the office with a finger puppet on each index finger and give a little performance. Within minutes the kids were laughing or at least enthralled by the show. Val had heard Nicki give little pep talks to young mothers and other women who seemed to be struggling. Val knew Nicki understood their circumstances. Val had even seen her give a roll of quarters to a woman and push her dollar bills back and tell the woman to "keep it."

But she had also seen Nicki run out to the car of a guy smoking in the driver's seat who was yelling insults at a woman carrying three baskets of clothes at once. She put her face right to the window and let the guy have it. She was amazing. Val wondered how a thirty-two-year-old woman working on an MBA and holding a bachelor's in social work would be satisfied to run a laundry at the age she should be in the prime of her career. Val thought again of the stability that work at the laundromat had given Nicki when she needed it most. Val acknowledged an infinite respect for Nicki.

It was not long before the infinite respect thoughts were melted away by thoughts of Nicki's kisses. She wished she could feel Nicki again. Nicki's mouth on her breast, tongue circling her nipple. As her hand moved from her breast to between her legs, Val thought of Nicki doing the same.

***

An annoying chime from the phone sounded. After cursing her alarm, she realized it was a call coming in.

"Hello?" Her voice was gravelly.

"I woke you up. Sorry," Nicki said. "What the F happened last night?"

No privacy anywhere. Not that she minded Nicki knowing what had happened. "Yeah. Not a great night, I'm afraid, but I'm okay. I have to figure out where to get the window fixed, I guess. Hey, how are *you* feeling?"

"I'm fine now. That remedy worked...if you were wondering." Nicki was smiling. Val could tell that much from her tone.

"It's good to hear your smile. I thought of that smile this morning. It helped me relax and go back to sleep after that rude interruption to my night," Val said. "That, and the same remedy I suggested for you."

"Hmm. That'll be something I will *not* think about today as I'm studying," Nicki said.

"Studying, huh? That's your excuse?"

"No excuse. I have an Ethics in Management essay to compose for my online class. The class is discussing ethics in human resources.

Tonight, the instructor will give us a scenario, and we have to devise a solution. I'd like to ace it, but any distraction might trip me up."

Val doubted that, but she understood Nicki's point.

"Never let it be said that I thwarted anyone's career path. Even if you might thwart *my* plans," Val taunted. "I'm hoping to hear from the tiny house folks today. The house may be here today or tomorrow. After it's set up, and a few things are moved in, *then* I'll have you visit."

"I hope you'll let me help you with that, doll," Nicki replied. "JH and I would be happy to help you move in. We've already discussed it."

"Can we see one another tomorrow, regardless?" Val cringed as she asked, hoping she wasn't invading Nicki's space, or worse, seeming needy.

"Count on that, my dear." Then silence. At first Val thought they were cut off. Nicki sighed. "I miss you; I'll be honest." Another pause. "I noticed that I could smell you on my sheets. I think I came because of that. I can't even believe I'm telling you that, but you're in my head. And other places, too," Nicki said cautiously. "I'm...crazy for you...Look. I gotta go." Nicki hung up abruptly.

Why did she hang up so quickly? Is Nicki pulling away? Scared? No. Please, no. Can she be any more scared than I am? She would give Nicki space today, as requested. Luckily, Val had many distractions. Her truck window, for one. And she needed to get phones for her and JH. Business phones with different numbers from personal cells. *Wow. This is really happening.*

***

Val called JH on his personal cell. He answered. He was at the laundry since Nicki was home studying. She decided to swing by to drop off the phone.

As she handed JH the phone, she told him this would be the number on his business card. She was on her way to their nearest department store to get some pre-cut business card sheets since JH had meetings coming up imminently. She would set them up on her computer and find him tomorrow to deliver the cards. In the meantime, the phones should be good to go.

It was clear by his expression that JH was impressed by Val's "get 'er done" work ethic. He nodded and opened the box, pulled out the phone and turned it on.

"I'll read this," he said as he shook the phone's quick reference guide. "It's a bit different than mine, but I'll figure it out. By the way, I'm sorry about last night," he said. "I'm pretty sure they arrested Ben Linton. He's a local and a regular in the police blotter."

Val explained what Trooper Jones had said. It seemed pretty open-and-shut. "I need to take the truck somewhere to have the window replaced, though."

JH instructed her to call her insurance company. They would probably send someone to a place of her choosing, even the parking lot here, to put in the new window. It would be covered without a doubt, even if the insurance company decided to sue the vandal for damages.

"See you soon, JH," Val said as she turned to leave. JH nodded and smiled broadly, pretending to take a selfie. *Adorable.*

Chapter Eleven

VAL FOUND IT DIFFICULT to contain her excitement this morning; the tiny house transport company had called. Heading out of Chattanooga, they expected to be in Marshall by one o'clock at the latest, depending on traffic through Atlanta, weigh stations, and highway construction. She agreed to be at the property a little earlier, just in case. She called JH at nine and told him. He said he'd be able to meet her there. As luck would have it, the septic folks were scheduled to come tomorrow to dig. To circumvent any placement problems, he asked her to bring both the plat and the facilities office building plan.

Val had started batches of chocolate chip and oatmeal raisin cookies for Frank Thompson and his band of squatters. *Stop it, Scott. They're not squatters. They're campers. Remember what your mission is.* She regretted not trusting her first instinct to bake them cookies, but she certainly wasn't going to delay seeing that through. Bambi's convection microwave was small, but it worked. She would have to bake the cookies in four batches of six. She could not afford to spend all day baking, so she decided two dozen would have to work.

On her way out, she drove back around the circle, and pulled into the campers' driveway. They were, not surprisingly, seated around the picnic table. Frank stood up and came to the truck.

"Hi, Frank," Val said. She walked toward him and shook his hand with her right hand. She handed him the plate of cookies with the other. "I hope y'all will enjoy these. I so appreciate what you did for me the other morning."

"Ma'am. We thank you," Frank said. The other guys were nodding their heads in agreement. "We may look rag-tag, but we're good men who've seen better days. That's Pops over there in the blue shirt. Noodle's standing right behind him. Then George there at the tent." Pops and George waved when Frank introduced them, but Noodle looked down and crouched behind Pops.

"Hi guys. Being kind and looking out for others is all we can hope for in people, isn't it?" Val replied. "I've got an appointment, so I've gotta run. I'll be leaving the campground at the end of the week. My new home is supposed to arrive today. It's one of those tiny houses."

"I've seen those on the road before, being pulled. They look so small, but I guess they ain't no smaller than our tents are!" He laughed, and she followed his lead. "We appreciate this ma'am. We do."

"I'll see you soon, Frank," Val said as she opened the door of her truck. She drove back around the circle and out of the park. She wondered when she'd get the nerve to ask for their stories.

***

Val had been sitting at the property for thirty minutes when JH pulled up in his panel van. Val opened her tailgate so JH could spread out the drawings. He looked around at the current tree line on the property, eyeing the lay of the land. He looked up at the sun to verify their positions. He asked Val if she had a floor plan of the tiny house. She pulled up an image on her new work cellphone, grateful for a good signal. He looked at it carefully, looked back at the tree line, and studied the plan a minute.

"Let's move our trucks there," he suggested, pointing. "But you can wait until the movers arrive. We might need your table again when they get here," he said, nodding at the tailgate. JH moved his truck what seemed to be a mile away.

He cut down a few small scrub trees with a knife he had strapped on his left thigh. She hadn't noticed JH was a "leftie" when he signed the papers. She supposed attacks and advances had distracted her lately. She smiled to herself. *Advances.*

JH created a diagram outline for placement of the house, giving the tiny house porch the best view, but making it accessible from a parking spot which did not currently exist. She mentally pinched herself to make sure she wasn't in heaven. JH certainly seemed to know what he was doing.

They first heard, then saw, the truck pulling onto the driveway. Once he saw the size of the tow vehicle, JH asked her to move her truck quickly next to his, but to bring the plans back with her. She moved just as the truck backed the house into position. JH explained to the driver where this and where that would be. He exuded confidence, and they followed his lead.

As they prepared to leave, JH handed each man a fifty and one of the cards Val had prepared for him. He shook each man's hand and thanked them for coming. They handed JH the keys, nodded at Val, and told her to enjoy her new home. They drove off with big smiles.

"The cost of doing business. I guess I should have warned you." JH smiled.

"I trust you implicitly, Mr. Evans," Val said, smiling. She squealed, uncharacteristically. "Let's go in!"

As small as it might be, it looked spacious enough sitting amidst the huge expanse of open property. As they walked up onto the porch, she could picture sipping coffee in a rocker.

"Shall I carry you over the threshold, ma'am?" JH smiled at her, bent at the waist, as if to serve her. He then handed her the keys. She laughed out loud, threw the door open and walked in. JH ducked, until he reached the vaulted opening between the double lofts.

"This is nice, Val. I love the smell of cedar."

"Just in case, please." Val handed one of the key sets back to JH. He nodded.

Val shook her head, dumbstruck. They investigated the appliances, the small downstairs bedroom, the bathroom, and examined all of the nooks and crannies. She climbed the stairs to the loft, and looked across at the other loft, which she planned to use for storage. The queen bed would fit up here fine.

"JH?" She made sure he was still inside. "I wouldn't advise your coming up here." He laughed from below.

"It is interesting. Fascinating, but I couldn't live here," he said. She agreed that would be rough, though she told him she'd seen a tall guy on HGTV living in a tiny house with his wife and their child.

"No way." JH shook his head. "I have to have space above my head. It's a thing."

Both lofts in the cottage-style house seemed larger because of the two dormers on both ends. The twenty-six foot long home had a lower level of less than two hundred square feet, but the lofts added roughly one hundred fifty square feet. It was larger than Bambi, and she now had a gourmet kitchen. She was excited to have a real oven again, even if it wasn't full size.

"When are they going to bring me some power, oh wise one?" Val joked.

JH explained the process of bringing a power pole and running lines. Since she was able to have fiber optics, he wasn't sure if that was going to help or hurt her prospects. Since power was coming out as a commercial venture, power company representatives typically fell on top of one another to please a client, he explained. He assumed within a week, she'd be up and running. He had a guy coming to put the pole in tomorrow. Septic started tomorrow also. Home in place. The pod storage folks were waiting on her call, and they would come with her furnishings.

"By the way, Ben Linton pled out, I hear. He agreed to some jail time and mandatory rehab with follow-up. Heard it when I was at the courthouse."

"Good news."

"You know, Val, I took the liberty of speaking with a county commissioner yesterday, and unofficially, he advised us to ask for some time at the next meeting to discuss the project."

"Whew. I know we need to get going on this, but I have to find someone to discuss short- and long-term prospects with our representatives," she replied. "Until we have a go-ahead that non-profit gaming has a pretty good chance of passage, I can't risk revealing anything. And without revealing our buildings' purpose, we're at a standstill."

"You may think I'm dreaming, Val, but I'll tell you who would be effective in that type of front-man position. You know her already." JH looked her straight in the eyes.

Val thought a moment. *Sandy Ann isn't going to want this job, is she? She could talk a miser out of a pot of gold, though.*

"Go on," Val said.

"Nicki Williams." He didn't flinch. He kept his focus on her countenance, as if trying to read her response. "She has a college degree. She's smart as a whip. She'll soon have that MBA. She's been planning for her final project. She wants to do something with non-profits. Something fresh."

"Damn. I hadn't even thought of that. She *is* smart. I've seen how she interacts with her customers and their children. I haven't even shared the details with her." Val loved the idea, but it filled her with dread for some reason. She would have to explore that feeling some more.

"Let me think on it. Please don't say anything to her."

"I've only told her she should talk with you about the project. I told her you probably had some interesting experiences and ideas having been in hospital management," he said. "Val, I web-searched your name. After I saw the initiatives you championed, I told Nicki to check that out. I thought she would see how you might be a good resource."

Val was touched. And horrified in some ways. What else might be on the internet that she had forgotten? She chuckled to herself.

"She's a good lady, Val. Breaks such as this come once in a lifetime for someone like Nicki." Val certainly knew that could be true. She remained silent as she thought through JH's insights.

"From what she tells me, y'all have quite a history. You sure know her."

"That I do. After I retired from the Army, I kept close contact with the VA. My healthcare is based there, and I was troubled by the number of soldiers who came home with PTSD. From talking with them in group, I thought I might have an ability to help calm and re-focus these guys and later, gals. Even during my full-time criminology classes, I continued the support groups. That's when I met Nicki. I had just lost my wife to cancer—"

"Nicki told me about your wife. I was so sorry to hear that. Sarah, right?"

"That's right." He smiled as he ran his fingertips over the ring finger of his left hand, presumably where his wedding band had been. "I could see Nicki's helplessness and hopelessness, similar to mine at one point. Sometimes we'd meet for coffee, and I'd talk her out of something desperate. Helping Nicki through this time period really helped me process my own grief." John Henry leaned against the porch rail and blew out a sigh.

"Nicki became more involved in the laundromat as her aunt became too ill to manage it. She'd ask me to help with washing machines or coin changers and vending machines. She wanted to be able to do it herself, so I started teaching her some basic repairs. Soon, she was making a little money, and she wanted to pay me. Often, I wouldn't charge her, or I'd charge her some small amount.

"I loved watching her confidence grow. She was becoming emotionally healthier, but recently, in the past few weeks really, I've seen something else. A spark." He smiled. "Nicki mentioned she'd met a lady at the laundromat who had just come to town, and how she helped the lady out. You."

"Yeah. Me." Val smiled.

"What I've seen is Nicki moving up Maslow's Hierarchy of Needs. First, she needed basics, you know, which she now has. Now I see those needs of belonging and closeness being met. At least it seems that way to me. She can move on up now. I think we'll see her reach her potential here soon." He looked at Val and slapped his leg.

"Wow. I haven't thought about Maslow for years. You're right. Basics first, food and shelter. All the stages of a pyramid before you can reach the top—self-actualization."

"Well, let's get out of here. Do you want me to lock up?" JH asked.

"No, not yet. I'm going to sit out here a while longer. You've given me a lot to think about. I'll head out before dark, though."

"Please don't stay too much longer, Val," he requested. "Let folks see me out here a few times. Word will get around."

"That's one thing I can count on for sure!" she replied as she patted his back. "I have to say, I feel a lot better with Ben Linton behind bars. Hopefully no one posts bail for him."

"Not likely, if history is any guide. See you tomorrow." He turned around, walked to the van, and smiled back at her.

Before Val left, she phoned Nicki. Nicki picked up on the second ring. "Good evening. Whatcha' wearin'?"

Val heard that devilish smile.

"Ha. Ha. I'm sitting on the front porch of my new home! Can you come see it tomorrow, maybe?"

"Tomorrow would be great. I think. I have plans tonight," Nicki replied. "I mean, I would love to come tonight. I just can't. I'll tell you tomorrow. It's a work thing."

"Hmm." A few beats passed.

"You sound jealous!" Nicki laughed. "Are you?"

"Just a tad, but if it's something I would be jealous about, I might not want to know," Val joked. "No, Lucky. Not jealous. Excited. I'll tell myself that anyway. Why should I feel jealous? We've only known one another just over a month!"

"Oh, don't even think like that. If you're not enjoying it though..."

"You're funny. You know I'm enjoying it, it's just—"

"Oh, shush. I'm teasing you; but just so you know, it is a work thing. Look, I'll be over first thing in the morning after opening up. Okay?"

"Well, then. That's that. No fun tonight. Guess I'll just tuck my tail between my legs and scamper on home to Bambi." Val chuckled.

"C'mon now." Nicki blew out a raspberry. "Behave." Val recognized Nicki's teasing.

"I'll see you tomorrow. I kinda like seeing you."

"That's more like it...tomorrow...and I'm looking forward to it."

As she drove by the squatters, they waved her down, all four of them running up to her truck. *Scott! Not squatters. Try Frank's place.*

"Hey, Val!" they shouted, smiling. *Whoa.* "You got the window fixed!"

"Yeah. It was easier than I thought."

"We sure did enjoy those cookies." Frank shook his head with delight as he spoke. The other guys chimed in with "Thank you."

Val beamed. *A little nice goes a long way.*

"Well, that asshole...oops, sorry. That Linton fellow will hopefully be away for a while." They all smiled and exchanged good-byes, and she made her way around to Bambi.

As she drove up, she noticed the two camp chairs under the awning. *Perfect.* She picked them up and put them in the back of her truck, wrapping them in a tarp with a bungee to keep them from getting wet or blowing out in the morning when she would drive back to her new house.

A glass of wine, grilled cheese sandwich, and an apple seemed a comforting supper. *Why are simple meals so delightful,* she wondered as she pulled apart a piece of sandwich, catching the cheese string before it dropped. Then a crunch of apple followed by a sip of wine. *God that's good.* After placing the plate and glass in the sink, she snuggled into her bed. The flannel was warm, and the heavy cotton blanket was soft against her arms. She pulled her knees up and retrieved the book from the edge of her bed, knowing sleep wasn't far behind.

Chapter Twelve

VAL WANTED TO ARRIVE early at her tiny house to prepare for Nicki's arrival. She gathered all the items she could think of to ensure a romantic evening. After assembling the items and loading them into the truck, she thought, *I'll be glad not to be living in two places at the same time!*

She was glad Nicki hadn't arrived yet. She placed the chairs neatly on the porch. The other items she left in the truck. *A surprise, I hope. Seven-thirty. Nicki should be here any minute.* Val sat down in one of the chairs, hoping she would look cool and relaxed as Nicki pulled up. Val felt nothing of the sort. The mere thought of Nicki woke up what seemed like a jar of butterflies. That, and the excitement of showing off the tiny house.

As the pickup pulled in, Val saw Nicki's brilliant, ear-to-ear smile. Val was too excited to remain seated. She stood and leaned an arm on the porch column, returning the smile.

"Wow, Val. This is so cool. It's beautiful. Wow." Nicki's awe was evident as she exited the truck and walked onto the tiny house's porch.

"I love it, Nicki. It doesn't even have my stuff in it yet, but I still love it," Val replied. Val showed Nicki all of the amenities she had explored with JH. Nicki scrambled up the stairs to one loft.

"Oh wow! This is so cool!" she repeated. "I've always wanted to see one of these. You know, when Mike and I lived in that cabin, I thought that was what a tiny house would be, but this is a teeny mansion compared to that. I mean, the kitchen alone!" Nicki looked down from the loft at Val.

"God, I didn't even say hello. What a dolt!"

"It's not too late, you know." Val smiled. Nicki ran down the stairs and enveloped Val in a bear hug.

"Oh, Val," Nicki said softly, "I think this is wonderful. Your place. And you." She kissed Val gently. "Thank you for sharing this with me." Her tone had changed from that of wonder to one of sensibility.

"Hey, can we bring those chairs inside? Normally, you know I'd be outside, but right now, I just want to look around and smell the cedar." Nicki ran back up into the loft.

Val brought the chairs into the great room as Nicki descended the stairs.

"Oh look!" Nicki said as she noticed the storage spaces under each stair, putting her hand in each one, outlining them with two fingers.

"Just so I can get this out, right now—," Nicki began. *Oh no, this doesn't sound good.* "I've hired a young girl to help me out at the laundromat. She's going to be living in the office."

"Why didn't you just say so on the phone?" Val asked.

"I couldn't. She was sitting at the desk reading one of the machine manuals. I was afraid you might judge me in some way. Or maybe be angry. I don't know. I know it's my business."

"Oh, Nicki. It takes a lot to irritate me or cause me to judge. Even when I do judge, I have to think long and hard about my reasons for doing it. And please, nothing I have seen so far leads me to believe you don't think about your business decisions!" Val took Nicki's hand and kissed her palm.

"She just finished high school in the spring, and still hasn't found work. She's pregnant, too. She needs the job. I was in the pizza place the other day, and Peggy told me her niece needed a job and a place to stay, because her daddy had kicked her out of the house. Turns out she's sharp as a tack. She sat with me all of one day, opening to close. The next day, when she wasn't throwing up, she did all of the things I do, except the books."

"Ben Linton's daughter?" Val slowly shaking her head. Nicki confirmed with a grimace. Nicki was so adorable Val could only smile at her.

"Ashley. That's her name. She and her secret sweetheart evidently went too far one night. He reluctantly dumped her the minute she told him she was pregnant. Ashley thought he might come around, but he was scared of her daddy. When Ben found out the father was African American, he blew his top. That was probably the day they accosted you."

"The guy certainly has a right to be scared, but it's not cool to just drop her. He's not willing to give any support?" *God, these small-town antics. Am I going to be able to take this?*

"Hasn't looked like it so far. I guess we'll find out, though. Not surprisingly, I identify with the girl's situation. When I recognized Ashley's potential, I made the offer to her. Room and board at the laundry—not glamorous—but safe, in exchange for me having time off."

"Sounds reasonable to me," Val replied.

"I start my final project for school in a few weeks. It'll take most of my time. I've struggled with how I could keep the laundromat running, especially if I have to go to another city for my project. My rough idea has been approved by my professor. I want to find a struggling non-profit and develop a business plan aimed at setting an improved course for the organization."

"That sounds great." *My old buddy's saying is so appropriate. See how things turn out to the glory of those who serve the Lord.* Lisa had been a believer, but she used the saying whether or not she felt the spirit at that moment. She would have loved Val's casino concept. And she would have loved seeing the way things appeared to be falling into place. Val briefly looked up as if paying homage to Lisa, who had died of breast cancer years earlier.

The next two days were to be a trial run for Ashley, to see if she was up to the task, but Nicki was, after opening that day, planning to let Ashley manage the two days alone. Ashley was driving one of Peggy's kids' cars that needed new tires, but she'd only drive if she had to go anywhere.

"And Ashley will call me or Peggy if she has questions or needs anything at all, but I don't think she'll call," Nicki said confidently. "She's so *smart.*"

Val stood up from her chair, walked the step to Nicki's chair, and kneeled in between Nicki's knees. Val put her arms around Nicki, and Nicki kissed Val's head. Val looked up at her.

"Nicki Williams. You are an amazing woman. Kind. Insightful. You are showing the skills of a great leader." Val was not prepared for Nicki's blush. "I need to talk with you, too."

"Okay. You're scaring me a little being so serious. What's up?"

"Nothing bad, I promise. I think I have a final project for your master's program. I need a business plan. It's a non-profit, but it isn't even off the ground yet. You could say that is struggling, couldn't you?"

"Yeah," Nicki said, dragging the word out slowly. "I'm intrigued. Go on."

"The only thing, and don't be offended by it, is that you will have to sign a non-disclosure agreement, with some stipulations. I get it if you think it would be weird to work together. Though you would be the perfect person; you can thank JH for his idea to recommend you."

"I've studied non-disclosure. Might be hard to navigate a project if I can't share the details with my professor."

"It'll be easier once papers are filed with tax agencies and the Secretary of State. Your professor will likely be familiar with the need to keep things on the QT, especially when starting up.

"There's a lot of work ahead, I'll admit. You're in a much better place to be credible speaking with potential stakeholders than I am as a retired nurse who's only recently relocated here."

"C'mon. You've built this up; you're clearly excited. Let's do it." Nicki extended her arm and waved her index finger in a "hand it over" gesture.

"Good decision." Val smiled as she pulled the document out of her briefcase. "Just sign here and initial this." As Nicki read and signed, Val spread the plans on the table. She placed the signed agreement back into the briefcase. "As I lay out my plan, you think about what you might need to scale down for your project." Val grabbed a legal pad and pen from her briefcase to capture Nicki's questions.

"Here's where it gets fun...at least for me. You can see the taped off areas out there along the drive. The largest of those will be a non-profit casino—"

"No kidding? You think that's going to fly?" Nicki grimaced in disbelief.

"Look. Keep an open mind about the concept. Amazing Grace casino is the keystone of the non-profit, Valiant Expeditions. Instead of the house keeping the profits, those funds go back into the community and state." She laid out the high points of the casino's theme. "JH and I have had numerous discussions. We both think there's a benefit to the community. And even the community building can house multiple sizes of groups. Like the grief support and domestic violence groups. There'll even be a concert venue, and eventually a hotel." Val tried to discern Nicki's facial expressions as she jotted onto the pad. "So? What do you think so far?" She had known Nicki long enough to know she could appreciate the concept.

"You know, we need a timeline for each part of the project. I can make a spreadsheet, but I'd like to use project management software to capture these," she said as she dotted the pen onto the pad. "What's our completion target for each task or each phase? Who are stakeholders for each phase? Who will be responsible for each task? How many employees are we thinking? Do we need grants?" Nicki's ability to see the unanswerable questions of the bigger picture solidified Val's belief in Nicki's importance as a team member.

It was three in the afternoon, and they had not stopped to eat.

"Val, I'm starving," Nicki said. "Should I run and go get us something to eat?"

"I've taken care of that. I hope I brought enough food, though." Val set up the camp table, covered it with a folded tablecloth, and placed the napkins at their places. In the kitchen she began slicing cheeses. She realized she had not brought plates, so she used the cutting board, and neatly arranged an hors d'oeuvres tray for finger food. After placing it on the center of the table, Val returned to the kitchen and pulled the glasses and champagne bottle out of the cooler. As she was wiping the bottle with one of the towels, Nicki came in behind her and slid her arms around Val's waist. She nuzzled into Val's neck and lightly nibbled.

"If you're hungry—" Val started.

"Oh, I'm hungry, all right. But..." Nicki trailed off. She remained with her face against Val's neck. Val turned around, still holding the champagne bottle. They kissed. Just as Val thought she should put the champagne back in the cooler, Nicki pulled back gently, and grabbed the glasses.

"Let's toast!" She pecked Val on the cheek and led her back to the table. Nicki placed the glasses on the table, took the bottle from Val, and wrestled with the cork until it popped, flying up and landing in one of the lofts. They both laughed. Val grabbed a napkin to control the liquid bubbling onto the floor.

"Crap!" Nicki jumped to grab one of the towels and mopped up the spillage. "Sorry."

"Isn't that what happens when you break the bottle on a ship?" Val replied, smiling at Nicki and shaking her head. Nicki poured carefully so as to avoid additional mopping.

"To your new adventure!" she said as she raised her glass toward Val's.

"To new adventures for all of us! And to Amazing Grace!" Val offered.

"Hear, hear!" Nicki followed with another clink.

After a sip or two, Nicki pulled her legs under her in the camp chair and started noshing with aplomb. She spoke with her mouth still full, and cracker crumbs blew out. She covered her mouth and laughed, which Val noticed was not helping the situation. Both of them laughed even more.

"When you're able to talk...How did your essay go the other night?"

"It went okay, I think." Nicki paused. "Truthfully, I think it went great." She smiled at Val proudly.

"Really, Nicki. What do you think...I mean, about the project?"

"I can see I need to do some research, but I do remember the Zell Miller, Hope Scholarship for school desks then tuition era. That seemed to be a tough sell sometimes. I know a lot of folks were worried it would negatively impact the poor. Don't know how that's played out, but I should add that to my research."

"I've done a little research on the gaming industry in Georgia. Enough to put my eggs in a basket."

"That's a lot more than I know. I should probably find out who the prior lobbyists have been...maybe talk with them directly. New territory for me, for sure. You know, the most political thing I've ever done, other than vote, is to write letters to legislators or congressmen, mainly about bills serving veterans or helping to prevent domestic violence."

"I visited the state legislature once with a professional nurses' organization. Immediately prior to meeting with them, we had an in-service on how to approach them, the types of things they wanted to hear, and how to elicit support. I've spoken with muckety-mucks in the hospital setting, but it's definitely not my cup of tea. You don't seem to have trouble speaking to anyone."

"Ha. I guess one could call me outgoing." She smiled at Val. "But I've never spoken with muckety-mucks," she teased.

"You joke, but I'm sure you realize that movers and shakers often use informal settings to advance ideas and gather intel."

"Well, look at us. Two professionals having a professional discussion....and not even interrupting it with hanky panky."

"Nicki. Speaking of that...I want to ask you something; and I want you to be honest, please."

"What?...*What?*" Nicki looked hesitant, nervous.

"The other night on the phone...you sounded so intense. Then you just ended the conversation abruptly. I mean you said goodbye, but...I don't know. It didn't sound like you had a customer or something. What was that all about?"

"Oh yeah. I know. That wasn't fair, but it was the best I could manage at the time," Nicki started. "I—I—" She paused again, her head turned, but facing the floor.

"Look at me, Nicki. *Talk* to me." Val was asking, but firmly. When Nicki raised her face, Val saw she was teary-eyed. She knew Nicki would not want Val to see her cry again.

"Do you need to wait to discuss whatever this is? I don't want to wait, but I will."

"Val, I said things to you. I meant those things. I am crazy about you. And it scares the shit out of me. Everyone I've ever loved—"

"You've had horrible loss, Nicki. I know that," Val interrupted. "But look at what you have. You have JH. And Ashley. You're giving back to Ashley. Helping her grow. Look at what you're becoming. I've never met anyone so strong, working so hard to achieve a dream. A dream to make others' lives better by heading some non-profit. No one can stop that dream, girl." Val knelt in front of Nicki's chair and put a hand on Nicki's knee.

"I was terrified when I told you I was crazy about you. I know that. I hope you see, though, that I didn't let it rule me. It didn't get the better of me in the long run. Thank you for trusting me enough to..." Another pause. "To stick around and make me talk."

"That's what we should do, right? Talk? Open communication is a huge factor in successful relationships." She looked away for a beat. "It's not always easy...for me, too. But I don't like heavy conversations hanging over my head either." Another beat passed. "I'm quite fond of you, you know."

Nicki pulled at Val's shoulders as if to encourage her to sit on her lap.

"That ain't gonna work, girl." Val laughed at the thought. "And...I don't want any more champagne on the floor."

"You are a doll. I've never met any—" Val stopped Nicki by kissing her.

"I'm going to clean up quickly and throw these things in the truck. Come back with me to Hamburg. Let me drive," Val said quietly.

"But my truck—"

"I promise I'll bring you back whenever you're ready. Unless you want to sleep in the truck or on this hard floor tonight."

Nicki shook her head. She knew she shouldn't drive. The champagne had certainly worked its magic.

"You're okay to drive?" Nicki asked.

"I will be."

When Val had loaded up her truck, she led Nicki out, locked the door, and stood by the porch looking up at the partly cloudy sky. It was dark. A rising, late gibbous moon was casting enough light, though, for the two of them to walk without a flashlight. Nicki backed into Val as if to indicate she was chilly. Val put her arms around Nicki, and they stood together for several minutes, looking up.

"Let's go," Val whispered into Nicki's ear.

When they arrived back at Hamburg, Frank's place was dark. Val wondered if he was sitting watch tonight. She wondered if the other campers pitched in and did the same. What would they be watching for? Did they have to take turns for a spot on a mattress inside the tent? She drove slowly, trying to be as quiet as she could.

When Val pulled into her drive, she thought she heard the cry of a loon. *Could that be possible?* Nicki had perked up, moving from the truck's heater to the cool air outside. She walked to Bambi.

"Hey, do you want to walk to the dock with me?" Val whispered loudly enough for Nicki to hear. "I think I heard a loon, but I'm not sure it's the right time of year. I don't think it was a screech owl, though."

"Why not? Let's go." Nicki sounded game. They placed most of their stuff back in the truck bed. The walk was short, but Val had brought the chairs just in case they wanted to sit. As they walked onto the dock, Val saw a figure sitting in the dark.

"Hey, Val," Frank's voice wafted quietly toward them as they approached.

"Frank," Val whispered. "What are you *doing* out here?"

"I was listening to the loons," Frank replied in a whisper.

"I wondered! I thought I heard them, but thought it wasn't quite the right time of year," Val explained, again in a whisper.

Frank replied that it would be uncommon for loons to be mating or nesting in this part of Georgia in the winter.

"Uncommon, but they're here sometimes. I wonder how all this climate change stuff might be messing these birds up," he said, shaking his head. "I worry where we are headed."

"Yeah. Me too...oh my goodness, Frank. Excuse my rudeness. This is my good friend, Nicki Williams. Nicki, this is my new good friend, Frank Thompson. He's the guy who shooed off the infamous Ben Linton."

"Good to meet you, Frank. And thank you," Nicki replied.

"The pleasure is mine, Ms. Williams. You own the laundry, don't you?" Frank asked.

"Guilty as charged. Please, call me Nicki. It was my great aunt's place. She took me in after my parents died, and again after I lost my husband in Iraq. I've been in that laundromat pretty much my whole life."

"Nicki, I'm sorry for your loss. I was in Kuwait, but Noodle there—," he gestured to his camp, "was stationed in Iraq and Afghanistan. He suffered a brain injury, but he's a good fellow. I, for one, appreciate your husband's service. And again, I'm sorry for your loss."

"Thank you for that, Frank," Nicki replied. "You ever go to the Milledgeville VA? My friend—" At that moment a loon called eerily. Then another.

"Oh my god, y'all. I've never heard one in real life! It's beautiful!" Nicki exclaimed softly. "Mr. Frank. Frank. It was a pleasure to meet you, and I hope I'll *see* you when it's light sometime, but if y'all will excuse me, I think hearing that loon has excited the pee out of me. I *gotta* go." They all laughed.

"Hope we didn't disturb your peace, Frank," Val said. "I'll see you soon. By the way, I'm moving out in a few days. My house arrived, so I'll be moving my camper to my new property." Frank nodded his head.

"I'm going to join her inside," Val said as she turned to Nicki.

"She puts it out there, doesn't she?" Frank said with a soft chuckle.

"She does indeed." Val turned back toward Frank.

"Seems like a nice lady. You seem to be quite fond of her. Thanks for introducing me."

"Of course. Thanks, Frank. She is, and I am." Val beamed, not knowing if Frank could see her face or not.

"Have a nice rest of your evening," Frank said warmly. She gave him a wave as she stepped inside Bambi.

"You too."

Chapter Thirteen

NICKI EXCUSED HERSELF TO Bambi's tiny restroom. Val sighed at the thought of Nicki, and where the rest of the night would lead. Nicki came out smiling. And naked. She was holding her folded clothes, which she put on one side of the dinette. She slid into the far side of the double bed. *Devilish smile.* Val turned off the interior lights.

"Hey, no fair," Nicki said when the lights went out.

"The fair left in October," Val replied. Nicki hmphed. Val loved that retort. The nursing staff used to needle her for her 'stock answers.' She was nothing if not consistent.

She stepped into the bathroom and felt for what she needed in the dark until her eyes adjusted. She freshened up. When she came out of the bathroom and put her clothes on the dinette seat, her feet were cold. She reached into the drawer and pulled out socks. Nicki's eyes had obviously adjusted enough to see what Val was doing.

"Oh no you don't!" Nicki said.

"But—" Val started.

"Come here, bare feet and bare everything else, I hope." Nicki was smiling and Val could hear it.

As she slid in against Nicki, Val melted inside. Her groin was warm. She slid her right arm under Nicki's neck, and with her left hand on Nicki's bottom, Val edged herself closer. Nicki's mouth was incredible. Warm. Soft. Wet. Nicki's tongue found hers. Val was already pulsing with that now familiar ache.

"I missed you. I missed this with you. With *you*." Nicki softly spoke into Val's mouth.

***

Val did not stir when Nicki crawled across her the next morning. Nicki straddled Val to jostle her awake. Val looked like she was sleeping soundly. Nicki frowned and hmphed. She was hungry and needed coffee. After a bathroom visit, she looked around in drawers and cabinets until she found coffee, filters, and a spoon.

Nicki pushed on the bed with her arms, shaking it, hoping to wake Val. It took a couple of good shakes, and Val turned to the edge of the bed. Her elbow across her eyes kept out most of the morning light.

"What time is it?" Val asked.

"Nine o'clock, sleeping beauty."

"Shit. I haven't slept that late in—" Val stopped and looked around.

"Oh, hush," Nicki replied. "You needed it obviously. Coffee?"

"Ugh. Of course, but must I get up?"

"I don't know. Must you?" Nicki teased. She crawled up onto the bed and pushed Val onto her back and straddled her. She had on one of Val's large, pinstriped men's shirts that she used for a robe or whatever. She didn't have on panties.

"Hey, now. Don't get me riled up this morning."

"I've already tried once, and you didn't wake up. You're no fun." Nicki smiled as she leaned in with her lips just above Val's. Val pulled Nicki's bottom down with hands on both cheeks.

"Mm," Val moaned. She kissed hard and bit Nicki's bottom lip softly.

***

Two hours went by sweetly. Val rolled out of bed. "My coffee's cold, Lucky, but you, my dear, are not," Val teased. "C'mon now, you're not usually one to blush."

"No. You're corny and all, but it's sweet when you call me Lucky. You don't do it all the time," Nicki remarked. Val thought a moment. *No. I don't. Hmm. Wonder why?*

"Here's a coincidence for you. I like it when you call me Doll. It's *hot*. Well, in fact, it makes me *warm*. In a certain place. I guess it's a good thing you don't do it all the time."

"I need to go home, *doll*." Nicki whispered as she sidled up to Val's side.

"Sure. Let me throw on some clothes. And I suppose *you'll* need to put on some pants," Val said, checking out Nicki's legs and ass. "Mmm. Quit tempting me."

***

Val was getting used to driving around here. Everything was ten miles away unless you were in town. Ten or more. Distance seemed so

83

relative, especially when she compared driving and cycling. She knew tomorrow she'd be moving Bambi to the property, and it seemed like a ride could be worked in today, so she headed back to Hamburg. On the way in, she waved to the group at Frank's place as usual. She was pumping her tires and doing the pre-ride check when she saw Frank walking her way with one of the other guys. They were carrying a cooler, one man on each side.

"Hi, Val. Hope it's okay—we've got something for you."

"Oh, Frank. Y'all are too nice. Whatcha got in there?" Val was expecting beer.

"A whole mess of bass, cleaned, and cut into nice size filets. We put 'em on ice 'cause we figured you wouldn't have a big enough refrigerator in that." Frank tilted his head toward Bambi. "And Val, this is Noodle. I was telling you and your friend about him."

"Hi, Noodle. Nice to meet you." Val smiled as she extended her hand to him.

"It's okay, buddy. You can shake her hand. She's all right." Frank put his hand on Noodle's back. Noodle extended his hand tentatively. He shook Val's hand and pulled it away just as quickly.

"Thank you for your service, Noodle. And thank both of you for the fish. I'm going to be making dinner for a couple of friends tomorrow. Now I have the perfect main course!"

"You're welcome, ma'am," Noodle said. Frank indicated with his head that they were going to carry the cooler and place it under the tree next to the camper.

"Let's keep this in a shady spot," Frank explained to Noodle. "Val, you may need to add another bag of ice tonight. I would if I were you."

"Y'all are the sweetest. Thanks again, guys," Val said as they headed across the campground to their site. *Man, that's nice of them. I should be helping them!* She patted the top of the cooler. *Who would have thought? Just amazing.* "Amazing Grace indeed!" she said aloud as she looked up and pointed to the sky. She walked the bike out to the road and started the ride. She'd have a good two hours, so she decided the big loop would work today.

***

When Val returned, Nicki was sitting in one of the camp chairs under the awning looking oh so hot in her sunglasses. *Damn!* It was a nice day, not too chilly. Val couldn't tell if Nicki was asleep or resting.

Her face didn't give anything away. No smile, so maybe she was asleep. As she drew closer, she quietly studied Nicki's face. Her full, pink lips were apart, shiny from sunscreen gloss, Val guessed. Nicki's neck, cheeks, and forehead glistened from light perspiration. The slow rhythmic rise and fall of her chest indicated Nicki probably *was* asleep. Val couldn't blame her.

Val looked around to see if any campers might be watching. The coast looked clear, so she leaned in, softly placed a hand on Nicki's cheek, and kissed her. Nicki moaned softly, stretched her arm and grabbed Val's bottom, pulling her close. She leaned into Nicki's lips and breathed a quiet sigh.

"Watch out," she whispered into Nicki's mouth. "You look *hot* in those shades." Nicki's hand slid slowly along the lycra of Val's shorts.

"You feel pretty hot right now. Slippery. Mm." A couple of beats passed. "Damn. A car's coming."

"Damn's right," Val agreed as she pulled away and looked at the vehicle driving through. "Hi," Val said quietly as she returned her gaze to Nicki.

"Hi yourself. That was a nice way to end a nap." Nicki moved her arm to her forehead to block the sun.

"I enjoyed it." She brushed her hand across Nicki's forearm.

"Did your buddies bring you those fish?" Nicki straightened up in the chair.

"They did. Frank and Noodle brought 'em. Sweet, wasn't it? I'm going to make that for you and JH tomorrow out at the property...using the outdoor grill."

"You know it's going to rain tomorrow, crazy girl," Nicki informed Val, smiling. "After we get ol' Bambi situated, let's all come to my place. We'll cook there."

"That'll work."

"Our buddy JH is probably going to want to cook, though. He loves to cook for others. He will *never* let me cook for him. And I'm not a bad cook," Nicki explained.

"I won't argue with him. I love being cooked for. Who doesn't? Other than *him*!" Nicki laughed.

"Have you been tempted to go by the laundry to check on Ashley, or call?" Val asked. "I know it must be hard to have someone else in charge."

"It's all good, I think. I drove by earlier on the way to the grocery. The building wasn't on fire. Ashley's car was there. JH was not. That means I'm free for the rest of the day. What's left of it, anyway."

Val thought through what she needed to start today in order to have things ready tomorrow. Val mentally ran through her list of tasks that had to be done today to have Bambi prepped and ready for the move to the new property as well as setting her back up.

"Well, don't seem so excited." Nicki snarked.

"Come on now," Val replied. "Remember. I'm much older than you are. My mental powers are slower than yours." Val felt lucky her stroke hadn't left any residual damage, but there were times when she wondered if her thoughts flowed slower than others her age. She joked in a self-deprecating manner from time to time. *Not really one of my best qualities,* Val thought.

"Oh *brother*," Nicki said as she rolled her eyes, watching as Val walked inside the camper. Nicki followed her in, shut the door, and stepped close to Val as she reached into her cooler to grab a cold water. Nicki slapped Val's bottom. Maybe a little too hard, based on Val's response.

Val pushed Nicki onto the bed and held her down.

"Whoa, now. Easy. Sorry if that was too hard," Nicki said apologetically. Val did not let up with the pressure on Nicki's wrists or legs. She did not smile, and she didn't reveal her thoughts.

"Val. Are you teasing me? God, I hope so. I'll give in here if you are and enjoy this. Give me a sign." Val saw the concern in Nicki's face.

As she loosened her grip, Val trailed soft kisses from Nicki's neck, up to the side of her face, and landed tenderly upon Nicki's lips. "Yeah, I'm kidding. Sorry," she whispered. "I see that was a little harsh. Maybe a little overboard."

"Whew. Thank you," Nicki replied, smiling back at Val. "You feel nice in lycra. Especially tight lycra." Val loosened her grip completely and rested her hands in Nicki's.

"Hey, can I talk you out of that lycra?" Nicki asked. "Come to my house for your shower, though. The tub is big enough for two. We can start in the shower and finish up in the tub."

"Tempting," Val admitted with a grin.

"And, you can put that fish in my refrigerator when you come."

"Tempting...*and* a good idea," Val said softly as she leaned again to kiss Nicki. "Should I bring an overnight bag?"

"If you want," Nicki said. "And Val. I don't think of your age, whatever it is. I want you to know that." Nicki breathed softly onto Val's cheek, and with her own lips and face, she turned Val's face so their lips would be closer. "You are the hottest person I have ever known. I'm serious."

"I find *you* mesmerizing. Your energy is endless. It makes me *feel* younger. That's you, Nicki. You bring that out in me." She rolled on to her back, bringing Nicki on top of her.

"If you leave here, I'll follow you, but if you stay any longer, we're staying *here* tonight," Val added.

"I want to be at my house. With you. Tonight. *Please!*" Nicki stated firmly. "Come to my place. Come. *At* my place."

"I'll come. No doubt." Val whispered into Nicki's mouth again as their lips touched.

Nicki's devilish smile appeared as she slid off Val, applying pressure to Val's sensitive parts. Nicki did not take her eyes off Val as she backed out the door.

Val groaned as she sat up. *She is killing me. Killing me softly.* Val hummed the song in her head. She gathered a few things together and removed the remaining items from the back of the truck, putting them under the awning for protection from the coming rain. She noticed the cooler was gone. *Nicki.* She had taken it for Val.

Val's concern over their age difference seemed to sit constantly in the back of her mind. It tapped its finger on her shoulder in quiet moments, vexing her. Val may be older than Nicki, but she could name plenty of couples with age differences. *They* didn't seem to be having any problems relating as lovers or friends. This relationship was still new, though. Val pondered Nicki's childhood. She was raised by grandparents and a great aunt. She was typically with people much older than her actual parents would have been. Val wondered if Nicki's perspective was influenced by this. "Leave me alone! Let me enjoy myself," she snapped at herself. "Maybe she doesn't think about our age difference." *Does it matter, though? Might it matter in the future?* "The future! Val, girl. You're thinking future? Whose perspective may be changing?"

Chapter Fourteen

DISTRACTED, VAL VEERED OFF the road on the way to Nicki's, almost hitting a mailbox. *That was lucky. Ha. Yes, it was. The nickname, Lucky. How appropriate for Nicki to be involved in a casino project!* Val decided to consider that a good omen.

She arrived at Nicki's no worse for wear. She still had on her riding clothes because she wanted a shower before any tomfoolery. Nicki was busy putting away the fish. She spotted Val, held up her hands, and made a face that screamed "yucky."

"Wash your hands in lemon juice. Do you have any Doctor Bronner's? That helps," Val advised.

"I do, but I don't want any soap residue left." Nicki narrowed her eyes and sported an evil grin. "That peppermint might be uncomfortable for you," Nicki teased. Val rolled her eyes.

"Oh my. You're a *mess!*" She chuckled. "Let me take a quick shower to get this road grime off me. Do you have any Jack here?"

"I sure do. Great idea. I'll get that ready for you," Nicki replied.

The shower felt great. The water pressure sure beat Hamburg's comfort station. And Hamburg's beat Bambi's. When Val visited before, she'd fantasized about Nicki in that two-person tub. *Ooh la la.*

Outside of the shower, Val heard Nicki rattle ice in a glass. Val quickly dried off, eager to taste both the Jack and Nicki's luscious lips. Val opened the shower curtain to step out of the tub.

"Where are *you* going?" she heard Nicki say from the other room. Val saw the glasses of Jack on the rocks sitting on Nicki's bedside table.

"I'm coming out."

"We'll see," Nicki answered. Val could tell Nicki was speaking through her devilish smile. Val had brought one of her big, boy's shirts, and she slipped into it. She had a feeling it wouldn't be on long. She stepped into the bedroom and picked up a glass. She brought the glass up to her lips, allowing the warmth of the whiskey to coat her tongue before swallowing. *That's good stuff,* she thought. Before Val could turn around, Nicki came up behind her and pressed into her. Nicki giggled.

"What are you doing?" Val shivered at the warm breath on her neck.

"Have another sip," Nicki urged.

Nicki picked up her glass, still behind Val, and did the same.

"Mm. Don't turn around," Nicki placed her glass back on the table. "Here, I'll take yours," she whispered as she removed Val's glass and returned it to the table. "Good." Her hands trailed down Val's sides and settled lightly at her waist.

"Remember, don't turn around. Just walk to the tub. I'm right behind you." Nicki lightly pushed Val from behind.

"Okay, okay. I'm walking."

As they walked to the edge of the tub, Nicki eased her hands along Val's side and onto her shoulders. "Okay," she whispered from behind into Val's ear. "No peeking." She carefully slipped Val's shirt off from her shoulders, leaning back to allow it to fall to the floor. Val shivered even as the warmth spread between her legs.

"Step in and sit. Close your eyes, please."

"Oh god. Anything you say." Val swallowed a moan as she pushed back to feel some part of Nicki, who turned on the shower to a trickle of warm water.

"I just dried off, but I'm so wet.," Val forced out with a sigh.

"That's okay. We'll both be wet, but don't peek." Nicki stepped into the tub and straddled Val's legs.

"Nicki, I—" Val struggled to finish the sentence against a sigh.

"S'okay. You can open them now." When Val opened her eyes, she saw Nicki was wearing the same mid-thigh, shirred black dress she wore the first time Val visited.

"Nicki!" Val's exclamation sounded more like a moan. Nicki leaned forward and pressed her lips on Val's.

Oh my god. Val was close to orgasm just from looking at Nicki. Nicki smiled at Val, hiked the dress, and slid up Val's legs, avoiding putting weight on them. Nicki was wearing nothing underneath the dress. The sensuality left Val weak. The dress, the water. Nicki.

"Nicki." Val moaned with pleasure. Nicki guided Val down to the end of the tub without hardware. Water splashed onto Nicki's back and across both of them as Nicki slid against Val's body, dress and all. Val pulled at Nicki, but she resisted and slid down, resting her lips on Val's breast.

"Oh, yes." Val's voice dropped an octave as she spoke, and she clenched the fabric of the dress in her fists. "I want to feel you." Val sighed as she arched her back against Nicki's body.

Nicki dropped her face between Val's legs. She lightly sucked Val's wet softness, as if using her tongue to discover what would make Val rock her hips. When she did, Nicki seemed to focus on it.

"Oh yes. Please." Val's voice was strained, almost feral. Val stroked Nicki's head, water splashing, letting her movements and moans guide Nicki's course.

"I want your mouth," Val's whisper demanded.

"Almost there."

When Val climaxed, Nicki slid up to hold her. She rested her lips against Val's as she softly bucked and moaned. Val was spent physically. She briefly drifted into a state of lucid dreaming for a minute or two.

Nicki moved, and the water splashed onto Val's face, bringing her back to the present.

"Sorry, doll. I had to turn," Nicki explained. "You are absolutely gorgeous. I can't seem to get enough."

"Lust is wonderful," Val replied softly. She pulled Nicki into another kiss. Val couldn't believe Nicki was still wearing her dress. She shook her head in awe of Nicki's allure.

"God!" Val said, moving her mouth across Nicki's breast and down the dress to her waist and finally, between her legs. Nicki leaned forward enough to pull the dress off. Val pushed her hands away.

"No. Please. Leave it on...at least for now," Val whispered. She slid the front of Nicki's dress up to just above her hips.

"Nicki. Nicki. Nicki."

Val pushed one of Nicki's legs up as she leaned against the curved back of the tub. Val lightly nibbled and slid her tongue into the slit. Nicki's body writhed in response to the erotic sensation, her breathing barely audible. She was quieter in general during lovemaking than Val. Val wondered what might make Nicki moan. As she explored, Nicki held the edge on the back of the tub. Val was aroused even more now by the position of Nicki's dress and water still streaming on them. She slid up to kiss Nicki. The smells of both of them mingled on their faces.

Val was beside herself with the aching pulse of arousal. She was worried she would come again, even before she could satisfy Nicki. After one more kiss, Val returned between Nicki's legs. After soft kisses, she slipped her tongue deep inside. Nicki arched up and gently pushed Val's face against her. Val moved rhythmically. Nicki called out in soft moans. She bucked and shuddered with Val's movements.

"Just. Like. That," Nicki whispered as she kept a guiding hand on Val's head. Nicki bucked again and shuddered. She moaned a guttural

"Oh." She pulled at Val's shoulders, guiding her onto her partially clothed body. Val came again when she felt Nicki's lips and tongue. Spent, exhausted, Val rested her head on Nicki's shoulder, and Nicki draped her arm across Val's waist. They held one another for what seemed like hours, water flowing.

After a few minutes, Nicki reached up and turned off the water. With her body against Val, she pulled a towel down for both of them. Nicki put the towel around Val's shoulder. "Come to bed with me, Val. Sleep with me, please," Nicki said softly.

***

Light was streaming through the window when Val woke up. For the last few years of being single, she had missed lovemaking, but making love with Nicki was something beyond her experiences. The scents of their bodies warmed her again. She closed her eyes just to savor the feeling. She heard Nicki in the kitchen.

"Nicki," Val called. Nicki stepped just outside the bedroom and looked in, smiling.

"Come have coffee. I'm making some cheese toast. Want some?" Val nodded her response.

Val slid into a pair of jeans and the long sleeve T-shirt she'd brought. She'd get properly dressed after coffee. As she sat bending to put on some socks, she noticed her pubic area was sore. *Too much action*? She smiled.

The warm coffee slid down Val's throat. "Mm. That's good, Nicki."

When Nicki brought the toast to the table, she sat across from Val. She stretched her arm and took Val's hand in hers for a minute or two. They didn't speak. After breakfast, Val returned to Nicki's bedroom and finished dressing.

"Come. Shower," Nicki said as she leaned against the door frame. Val looked at Nicki to determine if she meant it as a double entendre.

"I'm going to wait until later," Val said as she looked in the mirror and combed her hair back with her fingers. Nicki frowned.

"I'd like to look at you. Or more." She walked to Val and kissed her. "I enjoyed last night. I—" Nicki stopped and turned to walk out.

"Me, too. You what?" Val asked. Nicki shook her head and diverted her eyes to the floor.

"Sorry, Val. Nothing I say would sound appropriate right now. When I have the words worked out, I'll let you know." She smiled and shook her head again. "I'll say it when I can say it right." Nicki gently placed her hand on the side of Val's face.

Val took Nicki's hand and kissed her palm. Nicki pulled Val closer with that hand. They kissed again. Nicki's lips were intoxicating. Again. What a spell she had placed on Val!

"Nicki, I need to go. I told the ranger I'd be out by one today."

"I'll come help you," Nicki said, and turned to scan the room for some shoes.

"Nah. I have a system. It's better if I do it myself. I get into a groove, you know. And then, I get irritated if I'm interrupted. Trust me. Thanks, though. I'll call if I need any help."

"Okay. Fair enough. I'll see you tonight, then? Here, but what time?"

"Let's say six-thirty for dinner. Hopefully that'll suit JH. Otherwise, we'll use the fallback plan of grilling the fish for him. And that'll never happen." Nicki chuckled.

"But come anytime. I enjoy you being here." Nicki pulled Val back for another kiss.

"I like the way it feels when I'm here. I like the way I feel when you're *there*," Val whispered into Nicki's mouth. *What is she doing to me? I'm afraid I'm really falling for her. Like seriously.*

***

"Shit," Nicki exclaimed as Val drove away. She kicked herself mentally for not saying what she felt. She knew it was early in the relationship, but she had been taken off guard by her feelings for Val. She wasn't one of the usual flings she had had over the past two years. Val seemed to understand her in a way others hadn't. And the sex was tender, sweet...and *hot*. It may have been hot with a few of the gals, but definitely not complicated. She shouted, "I don't have time for complications. I just don't have time." Tears filled her eyes, and she acknowledged to herself that she would be genuinely hurt if Val ended things. She hoped she could push it out of her mind long enough to finish a paper for her class.

***

Val's move was uneventful. Frank came and said goodbye. He wasn't sure how much longer they would be able to stay. The ranger was letting each one of them register separately for a fourteen-day stay. They were on their fourth stay; Val was on her third. If the park stayed this empty, hopefully the ranger would let them cycle through at least one more time.

She asked Frank if it was okay if she told John Henry about them. Having been in Kuwait, he would understand their situation. He might have some pull at the VA if they needed anything. She relayed JH's involvement in the grief and PTSD groups. Frank thanked her. He said yes for now, but hoped it would be okay if he changed his mind later. Val assured him it would. She handed Frank one of JH's new cards.

"Call him if you ever need anything. I don't have a card yet, but you know how to find me." She chuckled and Frank laughed.

"Sure do! We'll just drive around until we find your truck, but only in the daylight."

He's a funny guy, that Frank. She hadn't expected that.

***

Before she left Bambi at the property, she turned on the outdoor light. It would make it easier to come into the property and have some bearings if the light was on. She knew it would pull from the battery, but LEDs had a low power drain. Having had full hook-ups at Hamburg, Bambi was fully charged, and her freshwater tank was full. Val couldn't live it up, but she could eke it out with the bare necessities. She was confident she could get by with a little help from her friends. She began singing in her head again.

***

JH was already at Nicki's when Val arrived at five-fifteen. The cooking smells were delightful. Nicki greeted her at the door with a warm hug and a kiss. Val stepped into the kitchen and said hello to John Henry.

"Sure does smell good in here!" John Henry smiled at her and nodded in agreement. He was in his zone, chopping—maybe cabbage for slaw.

"Come sit." Nicki patted the place beside her on the couch. "Something to drink? Chardonnay or Jack or water?" Val settled on the chard as long as it wasn't Australian or Chilean. Nicki assured her it was good ol' U S of A, Californian. She brought Val a glass and returned to her seat.

"I need to say something to you, Val," Nicki said seriously. Val drew her head back, tilted it to the side, and narrowed her eyes.

"This sounds ominous." *Shit, shit, shit. What?*

"It's going to sound hokey, but I need to say it." Val had heard that before. Maybe this was Nicki's thing, these true confessions. "You are the best thing to happen to me since JH."

"Wow. JH is a mighty high bar. I know that's saying something!" Val said. "You're sweet."

"I'm crazy for you. I'm crazy for you," Nicki continued. Val heard Madonna in her head. *What is it with the songs, lately?*

"It's early days for us. We haven't had any real disagreements," Val said. "Lust is a powerful motivator. Remember, it's lust that triggers procreation. It has to be powerful."

"Thanks for that matter-of-fact, scientific analysis of our relationship," Nicki scoffed. Val squeezed Nicki's hand.

"It's okay. Don't think I'm *not* crazy for *you*. But we have to be sensible here. Let's not read too much into it just yet. And let's not discount where it could lead—negative or positive. Let's be open to infinite possibilities. I'm serious, Nicki. We never know. We never do. Life is too short to try to corral it."

"I'm not sure I like you anymore," Nicki said. She smiled. "But I'm afraid I—" She stopped mid-thought, frowned, and looked at the floor.

"You beautiful, wonderful, irresistible woman!" Val laughed as she spoke. "Please remember it's possible I could have been your mother. We found one another at different points of our lives. You would normally be in the prime of your professional career. I'm nearing retirement." Val had no counseling degree, but discussions with staff through the years helped give her wisdom in all types of situations. "I can't think of anything I cherish more than what we've found, Nicki."

Nicki seemed more somber. Even though she smiled, she turned partially away. Val worried that the mother thing was *not* the right thing to say, even if it were true.

"Nicki. Please." Val pulled Nicki to her. "Look at me. I'm still the same person I was last night and this morning. Don't build a wall I can't climb."

"Hey, Nicki," JH called out from the kitchen. "I have a question."

"Hold that thought." Nicki held up her finger to pause the conversation and left the room.

***

John Henry talked a lot about cooking and construction at dinner. Val caught him glancing at Nicki several times as if to see what she was feeling. She could tell he knew something wasn't right. Nicki had something on her mind. Val guessed Nicki would have to talk with someone sometime soon. Val sensed the tension, and she kept the discussions to Amazing Grace, Frank and his friends, and supplemented JH's food discussions.

After dinner, Val begged John Henry and Nicki to take any leftovers. She explained that they wouldn't keep long enough without full refrigeration, which she didn't have. They happily agreed. JH had already frozen half of the fish, and he would leave a third of those with Nicki. Since he had a large, deep freezer, he would keep a third of them for Val, whenever she wanted them.

On her way out, Val gave John Henry a big hug, and when he leaned in for the hug, she gave him a peck on the cheek. His eyes looked up to the sky, and he smiled after the kiss, not feigning the mix of embarrassment and delight. She hugged Nicki, though she was stiff. Stiffer than she was last night, anyway. She kissed Val's cheek, and surprised Val by walking her to her truck.

"I'm sorry, Val. I just need to process this whole thing. I owe you a talk, I know. It's a hard time. I feel so overwhelmed. I'm trying not to be too crabby."

"Sure. Of course. I know you'll be busy tomorrow, evaluating your protégé, but know that I look forward to hearing from you, or to seeing you...whenever you're ready. Just so you know, I've been thinking of you a lot lately. I even ran off the road on the way to see you last night." Nicki laughed and looked at the ground. Val kissed Nicki on the cheek first, and then softly on the lips. Nicki stood next to the truck and waited for Val to drive off.

Val hated to leave. She could see what seemed like turmoil in Nicki's eyes, and she could definitely feel the tension, but she wanted to honor Nicki's request for time.

Chapter Fifteen

NICKI WAS ONLY AWAY from the laundromat for two days, but she thought of this as a gift from God. She now truly understood the feeling of a weekend that was too short. It was eight o'clock, and all the lights were on inside. She pulled around back, but remembered to walk around to the front. She wanted Ashley to feel she had her own space. Nicki wanted to be a guest, but a guest who had desk privileges. She smiled to herself.

As she walked in the front door, Ashley put a trash can, newly bagged, down on the floor, and just smiled.

"I'm so glad you're here! I had the best weekend," Ashley reported. "We took in three hundred dollars. Some campers from Hamburg came in with a whole passel of laundry in garbage bags. The place was hopping all weekend."

"How are *you* doing?" Nicki suspected Ashley didn't feel any morning sickness today. "Not queasy?"

"Oh, I've already hurled twice, but I've finally gotten used to the feeling. My midwife recommended an antacid she said would be safe. I can't take it with my vitamins, but she said it was okay to take my vitamins at lunch if that helped."

"Good idea," Nicki agreed. "I have to fess up—"

"I know, Nicki. I saw your truck come by here. JH's, too! I swear." She laughed loudly.

"No. Ashley. I was *just* going to the store. I *had* to drive by. Even when the laundromat is closed up, if I drive by, I look. It's a habit. I promise. But I did call JH to see if you had called him." Nicki smiled as she lowered her head, feigning shame.

"Y'all are something else. I think I did okay." Ashley was still chuckling. "But Nicki, can I show you something in the office? I have an idea...a question, really."

"Of course." Nicki followed Ashley into the office. Ashley pushed the top door closed partially, with just enough of a crack to be able to see the floor. She reached behind the desk and brought out a half piece of poster board.

"Now, please. Before I show this to you, I'm asking you to keep an open mind." Nicki nodded. Ashley turned the sign around:

Drop off service
Wash, Dry and Fold.
Drop off in the morning. Pick up in the evening.
See Attendant.

"I got the idea when those men from the park came in. They didn't seem to mind doing laundry, but I thought it would be nice if we brought in a little more money? I mean, I already have to be here. I might as well do someone's laundry for them. In the summer especially, when folks are at Hamburg. They may not want to do their own laundry. Only one machine at the park, and it's not the best." Ashley seemed so enthusiastic.

"Ashley, I've thought of a drop off service a thousand times, but I always found something else to do, especially once I started this school program. I'd love to see that here. And let me say, I never knew you had that artistic ability! Script and block type and all."

"Nicki, I'm not going to lie to you. I talked with Aunt Peggy first. Since she has the Joint, I thought she might be a good person for ideas. And her son, my cousin, is the artist. Not me," Ashley confessed. Nicki was looking at her, still thinking through any negatives to the drop off service idea.

"Please don't be mad. I told her not to say anything to anyone. I wanted to talk to you first." Ashley had a nervous look on her face. Nicki shook her head, smiling.

"Oh my, no, Ashley! The gears in my mind are just spinning. Thinking as a person with an MBA, you know. Just considering everything about your idea. And the process of speaking with another businessperson and asking for their confidentiality? Preparing the sales piece for the idea? Ashley, we've got to get you in school, baby girl." Nicki held up Ashley's sign. "I say we post it today, if you're ready."

"Do you want to keep separate books for this, Nicki? That would make sense, right?" Ashley sheepishly advised. She held up a ledger book, cringed, and smiled a wide-open, fake smile.

"I hope I didn't overstep."

"Right on the money, girl! Literally! You're too much." They both laughed, and Nicki gave Ashley an attagirl, one-armed shoulder hug.

Ashley beamed. Nicki placed the sign on the inside of the front door that morning, just above the hours.

Nicki ran a few errands and came back to the laundry.

"Ashley. I've thought long and hard about this. I've been thinking about it anyway. I'm gonna start paying you for your time, so you'll have some spending money. Not just working for the place to live. And you should keep any of the money you bring in from the wash and fold. That's strictly labor, really. Keep track of it, Ashley. Your time, too. Your hours, I mean, but keep it separately, maybe on the back pages of the books. The regular books."

"Okay, sure, but Nicki, do you have any objection to my doing the books on a computer? I can use my laptop. It's a nice one. I can protect the laundromat's files if you're worried, and back them up to the cloud so we never lose anything."

Ashley's suggestions seemed sound. If Ashley was to consider taking control of the business at some point, Nicki wanted her to feel invested. Everything indicated she already was, but if she didn't want the laundromat, she at least needed to feel comfortable putting the experience on a resume.

Nicki hoped motherhood wouldn't derail the plan. Nicki would be finished with her project at that point, so she could cover the first few weeks of Ashley's maternity leave. Nicki didn't know if Ashley would feel comfortable caring for the baby in the office during the day, but the office was large enough for a crib and changing table. *That's going to be my gift to her!* Nicki thought. She realized Ashley was waiting for her response.

"That sounds like a great idea, Ms. Linton, but we probably ought to purchase a business laptop or desktop. Whatever you recommend. Check out what you think will work best...computer and software. Prepare a proposal for me. Nothing formal. Something I can review. I'll get back to you shortly thereafter," Nicki said in a deep voice.

Ashley smiled at Nicki. Tears ran down her face. She got up and hugged Nicki tightly.

"Nicki, I can't believe this is happening to me. I don't know what I would have done if you hadn't come along when you did."

"Don't you worry, baby girl. Your Aunt Peggy and I will make sure you always have whatever you need...as long as we're around." She patted Ashley's back and handed her a tissue as she pulled away.

"Thank you. I'm sorry." Ashley sniffled. Nicki hugged her again.

"Ashley, I'll never forget what it was like to need help. So many people here made it possible for me to survive. I'm glad I can do this." Nicki wiped the tears from her own eyes.

***

Val's phone rang. It was Nicki.

"Hi, doll. How's the laundry business?" Val asked.

"Ha, ha, ha." Nicki relayed the course of the morning's events. She sounded excited to see Ashley take such an interest and seem so motivated...and happy.

Val didn't know what income a laundromat generated, but she never thought it would sustain some*one*, much less two people.

"Are you sure you can afford all of that, Nicki?" Val asked. "Not that it's any of my business, mind you."

"It's okay. I don't mind. I own my house, a good bit of land, and the laundromat outright. My aunt left them all to me debt-free. She owned them. I only have to pay the taxes and upkeep. And of course, I have to buy or lease equipment when I need it. Other than a couple of machines, which will pay for themselves over time, I don't really have any other debt.

"When Mike died, I received a death benefit from a special life insurance policy. It was really quite generous. Don't know how much he had to pay for a policy that covered wartime, but he had told me it wasn't much. Some kind of special thing for the military, I guess. I was able to pay off Mike's pickup truck and any other little credit card bills I had, and still put some in savings. I always thought maybe I should move that into a retirement fund. I did receive a military survivor check for a few months. Mostly I put that directly into savings.

"I assure you, I'm doing just fine for little ol' Marshall, Georgia."

That's a relief. Boy, what you don't know of people's lives.

"I hope you know those are things I love about you—your generosity and your business sense. I do hope you remain cautious, though."

"Oh, pshaw, Val. I'm no dummy. But really, thank you for saying that."

After other gossipy chit-chat, Nicki added something she had forgotten regarding her vast wealth as she called it. She sold three acres a few years ago. She had wanted a cushion when she started her MBA program. Nicki now owned only twenty acres of her aunt's property in

Washington County, not far out of town. Further discussion revealed Nicki's property abutted Val's Washington County property.

Another coincidence? How can you not believe in them? Fate? Synchronicity? I don't know, but that is curious.

***

The discussion about land led Val to think of the Hamburg guys. She missed knowing they were close by. *Maybe I'll swing by and visit.* She wondered if she should bring them something, but couldn't think of anything. As she drove into Hamburg, she drove around the circle until she found their new site. Noodle stood up as she pulled in.

"Frank. Frank. Frank." He was shouting loudly. Frank walked around from behind the tent setup.

"Val!" He smiled as he used a towel to dry his right hand, then his face. His wet hair and tank undershirt let her know he was shaving and cleaning up. She shook his hand.

"Noodle, you remember Ms. Val, don't you?" Frank said to Noodle. "Pull up a picnic bench, Ms. Val. Take a load off."

"I see you decided to have a change of scenery." Val winked at him. "I wanted you to know my friend, John Henry, asked if it would be okay if he visited. I told him you had said that was okay for now. Has he come by?" she asked.

Frank indicated he came by one day, but Noodle had sort of freaked out.

"He was having a bad day." As soon as Noodle was out of earshot, Frank continued.

"Val, it pains me to say this. Noodle is on a waiting list for a group home in Augusta. They have the best services for guys like him. He's a good guy. Sometimes I cry thinking what he goes through. And what he went through before we all hooked up. People laugh at him. Needle him. It's just horrible. We look out for him, though. Pops tried up until he couldn't. Now George and I are all he has. We didn't even know him before. So many of us find one another on the streets or in waiting rooms. Those who don't...if they haven't been lucky enough to live around handy, reputable, inexpensive services...well, they're probably not with us anymore."

"JH said the same thing. How the depression and suicide rates were higher among vets."

She also shared with him what Nicki had not shared on the night she met Frank. That Nicki thought her husband may have deliberately gone on that fatal mine mission because of his depression, although his depression was not just war related. She told Frank how Nicki and Mike's daughter had died from measles. Frank lowered his head, shaking it back and forth.

"That's too much for one girl to bear," he said softly. "I hate to hear that. I'll pray for her. If God listens to us...if there is a God...he...or she...will hear me every night as I pray while sitting watch, asking for mercy on Noodle and Pops. George and I can make it, but I don't know...Noodle and Pops. I just don't know. I'll put Miss Nicki on that list, too."

"She'd appreciate that, but she's a tough one, Frank. I think she's well past her darkest times."

As Frank pulled a collared shirt on, he told Val how he and George had been on alternate watch shifts in the Army.

"We still do that. Old habits and all. Normally, George would be out here right now while I slept, but he had a bad night. Not much sleep with Noodle and Pops on his hands. I'm giving him a rest. This keeps us sane, Val. The outdoors. Looking out at clouds or the stars. Hearing the wind in the pines. Owls. Coyote. Peace."

"And loons!" Val added. He nodded in agreement, smiling.

"That night when those boys busted out your window, George came flying out of that tent. He thought he was back in-country. Freaked him right out. That was all the commotion at our place when I ran to see what was happening. I think for a minute the boys thought we were under attack."

"I met the husband of one of my work colleagues once who had been in Afghanistan with his National Guard unit. She said she hates New Year's Eve and July Fourth because he has such a hard time with fireworks now. She said she and the kids have to sleep in a different room. I hate that our guys and gals go through those tortures."

Val stood to leave.

"Val, ask your friend to drop back by and ask him to bring a fishing pole. George, him and me can have a visit. A talk. It might do us some good. Tell him I can pay him some. We all get money, you know."

"I'm pretty sure he won't accept money. He does it because he cares. He doesn't want anyone to have to go through that alone. He's one special man, Frank. You'll see. And boy, did he enjoy that fish! We all did!" She smiled as she told Frank how JH was a cook in the service, and how he took some culinary classes after leaving the service to complement the training. Frank seemed pleased that someone had cooked a meal for the girls. They exchanged goodbyes.

"That's real nice of you, Val, to come visit us. Real nice," he said as she opened her door.

Chapter Sixteen

JOHN HENRY WAS NOW working at the Amazing Grace property a few hours a day. He'd sit in the front seat of his van or under Bambi's awning making notes. He'd walk around measuring, tapping in stakes, and running orange or pink tape. Val was never sure of the meaning of new, brightly outlined plots of land when they appeared, but she trusted JH.

It was time to get to work on some of the nuts and bolts of setting up the business. She had to secure the corporation name and file paperwork with the Secretary of State. For this she needed corporate officers. She hoped to be able to use two key individuals as officers. In the meantime, her closest friends had agreed to hold those titles if needed.

Val figured she'd have to start without Nicki's help since Nicki was busy with her class. When she arrived home that afternoon, JH was putting a roll of tape and some tools in the back of his van.

"Hi, Val. You just missed Nicki by five minutes. Surprised you didn't pass her. She left you that." He pointed to a large manila envelope—two inches thick by her guess.

"Reading material, I wonder?" Val groaned.

"I wouldn't have any idea, Val. Look, I have to get to the VA, so I can't stay and chat, but it was a pleasure to see you, as always." He got into the van, stopped and looked at her pensively. After a second, he rolled the window down.

"I have to say something, Val." He paused again. "It isn't my business, you know, but I feel I need to say it anyway. Please don't take it without the friendship and caring from which I say it."

"Of course," Val replied, nodding.

"I think Nicki is falling in love with you. Or maybe she already has," he said. "I don't know that she's ready for a serious relationship, or if she even realizes that herself. I can see that her being involved in this project might complicate any relationship that would or could develop. You and I have both been around the block. Nicki is wise beyond her years and she isn't a kid, but her young adult life took an unusual path. I wonder sometimes if she realizes how it may have colored her outlook.

She's had a few flings...you know, one-night stands. It's almost like she hasn't been open to anything long-term." He continued before Val could respond.

"I care for you both, and I don't want to be in the middle of anything. I have expressed my concerns to her, and I'm telling you what I perceive. I don't need any sort of reply to what I've just said. Truly, I don't ever have to discuss this again with either of you, but that's how I see things, and I appreciate your listening."

"You know, JH, we had a heavy conversation with a similar tone the other night about how Nicki and I are at different stages of life. I don't want her to jump into something hastily. She was angry at first, but then she acknowledged that she needed processing time."

He nodded his head as if he agreed with what she had said to Nicki. He smiled back at Val as he rolled the window up.

On the crisp, manila envelope was a lined, light green sticky note, neatly taped on the top and bottom. Val recognized Nicki's handwriting.

Val. Enclosed is a very rough draft of the business plan—almost more of an outline. Note revisions on it as you see fit. Feel free to ask questions. I will turn in an outline of the draft to my professor only after I receive your input. Due 2/20/19 by 2100 hours. Thanks, Lucky. Lucky was underlined for additional emphasis. Val smiled as she tucked the envelope under her arm, and went into Bambi.

Her storage pod was due for delivery midday tomorrow. She would see how much headway she could make with the draft until it arrived. Perfect timing for a tome, since she had to sit here waiting. She had ten days to read and comment. She realized Nicki's project was a months-long endeavor. *The timeline should work, but man do we have to get cracking.*

After dinner and dishes, she sat down at the dinette with a pillow against the wall, and a glass of pinot noir. She leaned back on the pillow and pulled the stack of papers out of the envelope. She fanned through to the back page—eighty-five. *Well, well. Someone has been busy! Double spaced, but still...*

The first page was a class project title page. First line—"Amazing Grace:" Next line—"Innovation Dispersing Community Resources." Gaming was not mentioned on the page. Maybe that would mask the casino angle with any literature title searches in the near future. *Good. Especially at this stage.* "Jennifer N. Williams." She had forgotten Nicki was her middle name. *Jennifer? They must call her that in class.* Next line, "Capstone Project."

She turned to the next page and began reading the introduction: a brief history of nonprofit structures, tax codes, and other basics. The second section dealt with Georgia's history of chance games, lotteries, and raffles. This section dealt also with legislative efforts in Georgia, and successful efforts in other states to allow nonprofit casinos. The following sections seemed to incorporate a rough outline with comments and questions for Val. Maybe the timeframe was tighter than she thought.

Val fell asleep, but not because the topic was dry. She found it interesting, and she marveled at Nicki's succinct style and research. Val had hoped she'd be able to get through the lion's share of the plan itself before her belongings arrived, but she wanted to give the plan the consideration it deserved. After all, this would provide a case to Georgia legislators, the media, and the chamber of commerce.

***

Thursday was here. Val woke up early, excited. She looked at her phone with anticipation. Nothing, of course. It was six-thirty. Trucks might be on the road, but they weren't going to call her until they were thirty minutes away. She drank her coffee and ate a granola bar on the porch at Grace, as she had begun to call the tiny house.

Most of the utilities should be switched on within the next two days. If not then, by Monday's end...she hoped. She had arranged for pizza this evening to feed her guests. JH would pick them up from Peggy's when he left town in the afternoon. Nicki said she should arrive around three or four.

At eleven a.m., Val heard a car coming in. She looked out the front window of Grace, toward the road. The red truck. *Someone's early. Is this good or bad?* Val walked to the porch.

Nicki stepped out wearing a navy business suit. Classic cut with a white, princess-neck blouse. She was wearing her pearl necklace and matching earrings. She had on heels. *Heels!* In her left hand, she was carrying a paper shopping bag.

At the porch, Nicki reached forward to shake Val's hand, smiling.

"Ms. Scott. My name is Jennifer Williams. I'm working with an innovative nonprofit in Hancock County. I think you'll find it a perfect recipient for a Kelley grant."

"My god, Ms. Williams. Sold!" She chuckled, smiled, and shook her head in disbelief. "You look fantastic. And you've nailed your introduction." She paused a second as Nicki leaned in and kissed her cheek. "I mean, you've blown me away. Not that I wasn't impressed the first time I saw you..." she drifted off, still shaking her head and smiling.

"I just bought this at the la-de-da thrift store in Milledgeville. I told the lady what I was looking for, and she directed me to this," Nicki explained. "Even the heels!"

"She was dead on, girl. This is *perfect*, Nicki." Val felt the warmth of a blush as she admired Nicki's business look.

"She said it was a three-hundred-and-fifty-dollar suit when it was new. I paid twenty-five bucks...including the shoes."

"The way it is made, anyone in any sort of high position is going to recognize the quality. You will be a shoo-in for appointments, especially once you walk in." Val couldn't stop smiling. "I mean it. This is dynamite."

Nicki said she had her work clothes with coat hangers for the suit and blouse in the shopping bag. She wanted to show JH, but didn't want to sit around in the outfit that long.

"The reason I came early is not just the suit, though. It's been such fun hanging around Ashley—i.e., youth. She played me this fun song. I've been dancing around since I heard it."

"Change, and get back out here," Val ordered. "And, N-O, you cannot change right here. We have work to do. I can't be all tired out from you."

Nicki pursed her smiling lips and shook her head.

"Go on now. Git." Val laughed as Nicki strutted out of the room, having pulled the suit jacket off and thrown it across her shoulder.

When Nicki came dancing back in the room, she had in ear buds, was holding her phone, and mouthing lyrics. She was wearing a gray hoodie, jeans and sneakers. *Thank goodness. Clothes on. Still adorable, though. Nicki's new hair trim is a nice touch with the suit*, Val thought.

Val motioned for Nicki to give her the earbuds. Nicki put them in Val's ears and turned the blaring volume down a bit. She started the song from the beginning. Val was nodding her head with the beat. Nicki was pacing back and forth. She pulled one of the buds out of Val's ear.

"Can't we listen together?" Nicki whimpered. Val stepped to one of the stair cubbies and pulled out a splash-proof portable speaker. Nicki beamed, turned it on, and synced the speaker to her phone. The sound was ample for the tiny house, but Nicki increased the volume to as close to dance floor level as would be possible from such a tiny box.

"Ahyayaya," Nicki sang, mouthing the words to "Cake by the Ocean." Nicki smiled and pulled Val into the middle of the living space floor.

"I love this," she mouthed during the baseline, pointing at her ear. Within a few minutes they were dancing wildly. Val sure danced back in the day. Nicki had already shared how she loved to dance. At the end of the song, Nicki sought Val's approval.

"Risqué, for sure."

"That's what makes it fun. The first time I heard this I thought of you. Dancing with you. And eating that cake by the ocean...with you."

"Not sure those lyrics would make it on the radio," Val remarked. *And now I've solidified for her how old I am. Hmph.*

"Ashley said there's a clean version that plays on the radio."

"Hmm. Maybe I should listen to newer music playlists sometime." Val now had a new ear worm. It could accompany the other reminders of Nicki. *Just what I need. Imagining eating cake by the ocean with Nicki. With her in that black dress. Or a bikini, or cut-offs, or...Oh god. Save me. Please.*

"Why are you smiling, doll?" Nicki asked.

"Ha! I bet you can imagine. Thanks a bunch," Val said. *That damn devilish smile. Again. I'm doomed here. Or not.* She smiled at Nicki.

She managed to keep Nicki at arm's-length, albeit hesitantly, discussing the proposal. She had not been able to focus enough this morning, she told Nicki...she had been considering the placement of furniture.

"And me," Nicki added, smiling and winking, as if trying to find a chink in Val's armor. Val decided this song was one of the ways Nicki was showing that she was loving living life now. She loved seeing that Nicki wasn't too stressed by her current school and work obligations. She wondered if Nicki could be opening up to a longer-term relationship. *Am I though?*

Shortly after one, Val saw the truck pulling in.

"Let's head out to the spot JH roped off for the storage pod," Val said as they headed out the door. "He said this is the most efficient spot for access to the container and Grace. The truck will have the least amount of turns and maneuvering."

"That sounds just like something he would do."

"He's definitely one of the most remarkable people I've ever met."

"Ditto."

After a few hours, most things were out of the delivered container.

"Uh, boss. I'm not sure all of this is going to fit into Grace," Nicki said, hands on hips, looking back and forth between the items and the tiny house.

"Oh, ye of little faith," Val replied. "I worked closely with the tiny house folks who sold me Grace. They are very thorough when they tell you what to pare."

"But isn't this from all of your old places?"

"What's in the pod is all I have left after I moved back down, except what's inside Bambi....and a few things in Athens. I can always get rid of the things that won't fit. Someone in the area—maybe even Ashley—can benefit from household items."

"Yeah, I guess so, but you don't have much storage here."

"Luckily, skeptic, my extra loft provides storage for several large boxes."

"Okay. I'm a believer." She lightly punched Val on the arm.

"Hey, now." Val chuckled. *I'm a believer; I couldn't leave her. Oh shit. Cool it, Scott.*

They had just brought in the custom twin-plus frame and puzzled their way into the downstairs bedroom with it when Nicki looked at her.

"Uh. Isn't this a twin?"

Val looked up at her. "Uh, yes it is. One of me. Twin bed. Well, actually, it's a custom twin-plus."

Nicki hmphed.

"There's a queen in the loft," Val said, facing both palms at Nicki.

"Okay then."

After placing the memory foam mattress on the twin-plus, Nicki smiled her devilish smile.

"I think we should check just to make sure we both fit." Her long sweep of hair fell into her eyes. Val brushed Nicki's hair to the side.

"I don't think so, Not-so-Lucky. JH will be here soon. He's not going to find me lying down on the job."

"It was just going to be a test," Nicki grumbled. Val reached out and pulled Nicki to her, kissing her. "Finally! Some action," Nicki exclaimed.

Saved by the bell, Val thought as JH drove up. In uncharacteristic fashion, JH walked in, put the pizza boxes down, then held both arms up in the classic bicep reveal position.

"Here I am to save the day," JH sang in a beautiful baritone voice. Nicki squealed in delight, ran, and threw her arms around him. Val laughed and acknowledged his perfect pitch.

"Let's see what we have here. Looking good so far, Val," JH admitted as he looked around at the furniture and art Val had already placed.

The three were able to wrestle the queen mattress up into the loft, with JH pushing while Val and Nicki, up in the loft, pulled. Once they had it part of the way, JH climbed up a few steps, and pushed it the rest of the way. It worked. They brought in a small, upholstered reading chair and a lamp for the downstairs living space. The final upholstered chair would barely fit. Val decided to keep it inside until she saw if rearranging would help.

They used one of the chairs and the two stools to eat their pizzas. JH had brought two beers for them and a cola for himself. He asked Val how she was doing with that tome Nicki dropped off. Val laughed, and Nicki punched his arm. He just smiled.

"What I have read is great. I've read through the executive summary, but I still have to read the bulk of the outlined section," Val replied. "I was discussing this with Ms. Williams earlier. I was hoping she could join us this evening," Val said, hoping Nicki would take the hint to model her new suit.

Nicki excused herself, and Val related to JH her discussions with Frank the other day. He promised he would take a fishing trip next week. Nicki stepped out of the bedroom clearing her throat.

"Nicki! You look fantastic. That's so professional," JH exclaimed.

She reached to shake his hand as she had with Val.

"Mr. Evans, my name is Jennifer Williams. It's a pleasure to meet you."

"Jennifer. Hmm. Gonna go undahcovah on us, eh?" JH teased. "That'll be an appropriate outfit for the business world, Lucky." He nodded with satisfaction.

They discussed the thrift shop find, how she had never been a real girly-girl, but how she was oddly comfortable in the business attire. Val remarked that Nicki looked very comfortable in the heels, assuring her that it wasn't an easy task. Val wouldn't even attempt to pull off heels, but Nicki looked fantastic.

"I'd hire you! Oh wait, I already did." Val laughed. JH admitted he expected to see Nicki as a CEO one day, probably as his boss. Val nodded in agreement.

"You guys. Stop," Nicki demanded. She was blushing.

"Well, Lucky Williams. Have I ever seen you blush? Val, I think we've found a weak spot in Jennifer's armor," JH joked.

After they had finished dinner, JH excused himself for the night. Val settled up with JH for the pizza and walked him out to his van while JH ran through what he was working on for Amazing Grace.

"I'll be out here tomorrow. Hoping the power will be on tomorrow. Maybe you'll even have a well. Things are moving, Val. Let's hope Nicki can help shape the nonprofit we're looking for."

"Cheers to that. *Clink*. I've completed the online application with the state. That part is a piece of cake, but I'm looking at some grants. A friend in Athens said he'd go through my list and make some notes on what he thought would be the best bets for us. Thanks again, Mr. Evans. I couldn't have done this without y'all. Nice to know friends have your back," Val confessed. JH assured her she didn't have to worry.

***

Nicki was knee deep into the project—class discussions, gaming research, honing what she had turned in, reviewing Val's grant suggestions. She had all but given over the laundry to Ashley's supervision, but she definitely wasn't leaving Ashley high and dry. Three days a week, Nicki spent several hours doing online research at the laundry to increase her accessibility.

In quiet times, she wondered if Val would grow distant. Could whatever relationship they had wither because they couldn't spend as much quality time together? "Dinners are one thing, sex is another," Nicki said aloud to herself. *And god, do I miss that.* She did miss the closeness. Tender time. Feeling Val against her back as they slept. She acknowledged to herself the competing intensities of her project and a relationship. *How do I balance that?*

Chapter Seventeen

IT WAS MARCH, AND Val had been in Marshall for months already. Nicki's business outline was turned in and returned by her instructor with a few suggestions. One of these was to schedule a meeting with the county commission, a local government official, or a nonprofit organization leader.

"Hey, boss. Glad you could make it in." Nicki sat behind the desk that was actually Val's as the state's officer on record for her 501(c)(3) corporation. "You need to get in the desk?" They were using Bambi as a temporary office, and Nicki had set up Val's business laptop and stacked a few letter trays on the side of the dinette's top.

"No. Stay put. I'll sit here." Val dropped onto the side of the dinette across from Nicki. "You look quite at home in that spot."

"Ha. Just let me know if I start getting a big head." They both chuckled. "To what do I owe the honor?"

"Your email said you needed to meet with someone...needed the experience in making professional connections; I believe those are your words. I have some ideas."

"Great. I could always meet with one of the commissioners, but I'd prefer a non-profit person."

"A friend of mine, Tom Randolph, is a long-time nonprofit guy who's the executive director for a community-based nonprofit dedicated to supporting diversity and community partnerships that focus on family, however a family is composed. He's well known, well connected, and I know I can trust him to maintain confidentiality."

"Oh, Val. That sounds perfect. Can you shoot me his contact info? I'll give him a call."

"Well, here's the thing. I've already reached out and set up a meeting. I took the liberty of checking your calendar. It looks like the dates work."

"Do me a favor and send it to me as a meeting request. It'll sync with my phone so I won't miss anything. Should I go ahead and make the hotel reservations?"

"We can stay at my friend, Nancy's. I'll go too. Not just to visit my friends, but since I'm a Valiant Expeditions officer, it makes sense. I may not be there for everything, but I'd like us to have a brief meeting with Tom together. He can probably steer us toward some grant sources."

"Damn, Val. It'll be nice to meet some of your friends. It's exciting too...if I do get to attend some of his meetings. Okay if I call JH in here? He might have something to add."

"Don't see why not. The next thing I want to discuss is right up his alley." Nicki texted JH to ask him to join them.

"Well, hello ladies," JH said as he peered around the open door's frame.

"That was quick," Val said.

"Obviously. I was in the back of the van, looking over some schematics. What's up?"

"Nicki and I are going to Athens so she can have an observational experience with a long-time nonprofit leader who's friend of mine, but why I wanted you to join us is because of my friend, Nancy, who we'll be staying with while we're there.

"Her position is as a botanist. She'll be an excellent resource for researching the environmental impact of our compound. I hope to alert her of a potential consulting role and pick her brain regarding local flora."

"Certainly sounds like someone we know is very well connected, Ms. Williams." JH cocked his head to the side as his eyes turned toward Nicki.

"I fully support that opinion, Mr. Evans." Nicki and JH looked at one another with stony countenances. Val rolled her eyes at their teasing.

"Sorry to depart so soon, but I need to drive over to Milledgeville. I'll consider the information received and compile a list of concerns and questions for our project."

"Okay, okay. Y'all are too much." After a beat, she added, "Be safe out there, Mr. Evans."

"I'll draw up the notes of our meeting and place it in our shared folder," Nicki said as she waved goodbye.

"Don't think I've ever told you this, but Nancy has a small place at her house that she lets me use when I come to Athens. I have my own key. She said she's making reservations for the three of us at one of the wonderful restaurants in her neighborhood."

"No, you didn't tell me that. It all sounds so great. And a little unbelievable. You've got some nice friends."

"I've been lucky. Ha. Lucky." Val chuckled.

"Hokey, but yeah. Lucky."

What Nicki did not know, however, was that this Nancy was the friend who owned a cabin in Suches. Val had arranged to have the cabin for Nicki's upcoming birthday on St. Patrick's Day weekend. They would arrive in Athens on Thursday and have dinner with Nancy. Friday, they would spend the day with Tom, and then Friday evening, drive to Suches. Val hoped for a hike or two, since the cabin was close to the Appalachian Trail. *Is this going to be too intense? Full on mental engagement with the observation. Then an emotional encounter with grief about Trolly.* Val felt hesitant. She had not yet broached the subject, in part because she was not sure how Nicki might react to being in or around Suches. *You can't just spring this on her, Scott. You can't.*

***

Speak of the devil, Val thought as Nicki drove up. Val walked around from her patio project at Grace. "This is a nice surprise," Val said as she pulled off her garden gloves.

"I have a few things to do at the office, but I thought I'd see how things are going here first. And to ask you something." She paused. "Could I have a kiss?" Nicki pulled Val into a hug.

"That's your question? That's an easy one." Val leaned into Nicki's lips.

"Mm." Nicki pulled back enough to see Val's face. "That wasn't it, but I like the answer anyway."

"It's been busy for you, I know. I've enjoyed having riding time, but let me show you around. I started a little patio back here." Holding hands, the two walked to the back. "I have key herbs in these pots. I hope this makeshift greenhouse will protect them in case we have that late, hard frost."

Val turned to Nicki and held one hand up with fingers spread. "And now, in addition to the patio area, I have running water, electricity, septic, and internet." She counted off each item on her fingers.

"Impressive. And especially glad for that running water. Maybe a shower is in my future....with you."

"It could be arranged." Val narrowed her eyes as she smiled. Nicki pulled her into a hug again. "Glad you came by." She pecked Nicki on the cheek.

"JH told me you'd authorized the release of funds to start the community building."

"Yeah, and he secured the building permit, following the plans drawn previously by another one of my Athens friends. He, JH I mean, feels confident he can oversee this project. And I don't doubt him, but construction won't start until after our trip. I want to see that first ground-breaking for sure."

"Which brings me back to my question. I didn't want to ask on the phone," Nicki shared. "I need to drive up to Athens separately. It would be good to go on up Wednesday morning and do some research at the Richard B. Russell Library's Special Collections. Some of Zell Miller's papers may give me interesting perspectives on his work to get approval for the state lottery that funds the HOPE scholarship. If I go Wednesday, I can work several hours in the afternoon and most of the day Thursday."

"Can't think of any reason why I can't leave Wednesday. I'd like that. I can probably catch up with a few friends while I'm there, but if you specifically want to go alone—" Val started.

"Oh no, not that at all. I'm happy if you want to come. Especially if we can stay at Nancy's. That'll save on a hotel room. Not that I can't afford that or anything. It's just...free is better," Nicki explained. "I didn't want to assume. We haven't talked in a week, and I didn't know what plans you had made."

"Seems more like a month. It's been all business with us. And not monkey business either."

"I know. I've been so busy with school and the laundry."

"I know you have. I have to admit, I've been a little pissy about it. I mean, Valentine's Day. C'mon. A heart emoji that you're thinking of me with some more emojis. I was disappointed."

"I'm sorry. Your note was so sweet, too. And handwritten. I barely had time to read it."

"It's okay. I just miss you. You're doing more than the project would ever require of a student. Executive level stuff, Nicki. And another full time job."

Tears filled Nicki's eyes. Val retrieved a bandana from her back pocket and wiped Nicki's eyes.

"It's clean, I promise." Val kissed Nicki's cheek again.

"Maybe that change of scenery will do us both good. I could really use some cake by the ocean right now." Nicki's devilish smile spread across her face as she pulled the bandana from Val's hand. "Let's go look at the calendar and figure out when to leave Wednesday." She popped Val's butt with the bandana.

"If you have a few minutes, let's talk about what's been going on. I probably shouldn't be such an absent officer." They chuckled as they strolled over to Bambi, holding hands again. "I miss you," she said as they approached Bambi's door.

"God. Me too." Nicki opened the door and motioned for Val to sit. "Let me get my notes up here," she said as she booted the computer. "Here we go. I've been researching which legislators would be the best to lobby our proposal. I'll start with Marshall's, obviously, but I also want to talk with ones who were involved in early gaming discussions. I need to get a better read on which legislators might be sympathetic to that vocal, Christian gambling critic, Helen Pierce. She's the one who said the state was too good for casinos. She used situations of potential bankruptcy and, of course, the usual yada yada about a potential increase in crime, to justify her position. There weren't any successful bills that year, and she indicated she would continue her efforts against gambling."

"Right." Val slapped the table. "That's one of the main reasons I think we may have a chance. Amazing Grace's money won't go into the house's profits. It goes back into the community through things like courses that would help people *avoid* bankruptcy...and to develop community programs proven to lower crime rates. It will give community members solid, living wage jobs and benefits, and we'll look after their health through early-prevention initiatives."

"Preaching to the choir, but it's a difficult line for us to walk— holding back venture information regarding a potentially volatile topic, but needing to share the information with area leaders."

"I have to be able to address all concerns at all levels. And you know JH will have similar issues as he discusses the building projects." Val nodded in agreement.

"I need as much ammunition as I can muster to effectively support our position."

Val continued to be amazed by Nicki's sophistication in the business aspects of the project. That fueled Val's confidence that Nicki could handle any communication with aplomb.

"I'm deep into research...all the time. Following this trail or that trail."

"You are. I'm grateful for the work. I'll admit, though, I'm a wee bit jealous."

Nicki stood and stepped to Val's side of the dinette. She leaned in and kissed Val.

"I assure you, no one else is getting this kind of attention." Nicki kissed Val again. Val sank into Nicki's lips.

"I sure hope not." Val's voice caught as she replied. That attention she so desperately craved from Nicki was at odds with her thoughts, but Val reasoned it was time to discuss the potential trip to the mountains, if it was going to happen.

"It sure would be nice to move all of the stacks of papers from the bed right now, but can you sit down for a few more minutes? I want to discuss something with you."

"Uh-oh. That sounds heavy," Nicki said as she sat, again across from Val.

"I have an idea. I think I just need to put it out there. You have the right to process this. Please just listen and keep an open mind."

"God, Val. You're scaring me a little. What?"

"My friend Nancy is the one who owns the cabin in Suches," Val explained. Nicki stiffened and sat upright from her leaning-in position. The body language was not lost on Val. The Suches part of the trip had the potential to color their entire getaway, and not necessarily for the good.

"I'd love to take you to Nancy's cabin for your birthday weekend, but only if you're comfortable. It's totally up to you."

Nicki's eye movements indicated she was considering what Val had presented. Val could see the gears turning. She wondered if it was an unfair request. Val was aware that a birthday celebration may not logically be the time to relive the death of your daughter. Or husband.

"Nicki, I know this is pulling up all kinds of feelings in you right now. I can see it. I can feel it. I love Preachers Rock. And I want you to understand that it would mean the world to me to pay homage to Trolly, but it might not be the birthday celebration you were considering. And I want you to be ready to share that with me when you do. Think about it for a few days. No rush," Val added. "I want to be with you on your birthday, and celebrate you, if you're up for that. It doesn't have to be there."

Tears welled up in Nicki's eyes. Val felt as though someone was pushing a sharp knife into her own chest. She hated that she had triggered pain. "May I hold you?"

Nicki didn't nod. "It's a lot." Nicki put her face down and shook her head. "I don't mean *you* put me in a bad place, but I've talked more about Trolly with you than I've talked since those first times I opened up to John Henry and in group. I try to keep Trolly's life and death, and my life with Mike and his death, in separate little boxes. I might open the boxes to show someone, but I put the boxes away. Doing that, I don't have to see what's inside all the time. I don't know. Maybe I'm afraid all of those boxes will open at once. They might spill together with my life now, and I won't be able to put them back in."

"I mean, we haven't had much time for ourselves lately. Maybe it's too much. I'm really okay if it is." A few beats passed. "Do you think I'm in one of your boxes?" Val asked.

"I don't think so," Nicki said. "But I don't know, Val. I feel like you're outside of the boxes *with* me. That I can share what is in those boxes *with* you, but I don't need to *show* them to you because you see them through me, through *my* eyes. It's weird." Val could tell Nicki was trying to make sense of what she was saying. "I'm not sure this makes any sense to *me*. It's more what a dream would be. Surreal. Fluid."

"If they stay surreal or dream-like, they don't have to feel real?" Val asked.

"Maybe so. I just don't know," Nicki replied. "I need to think about it—on many levels. I'll try to let you know before we go to Athens."

"No hurry, and no pressure, Nicki," Val repeated. "We can wait until Friday if you want to. And if you decide yes, we're halfway there, and if you decide we need to turn around, we turn around."

Nicki stood and turned to leave. Val walked toward her, but Nicki didn't stop. She walked slowly out the door and back to her truck. Val followed quietly and stood next to Nicki as she reached the truck's door. Nicki pulled Val and guided her to rest against her body as she leaned her back on her truck door. Val wanted Nicki...needed her. She leaned in to kiss Nicki, but Nicki jerked Val's head back. The raw kiss was harder than Val had expected. Her moan escaped without warning. Nicki yanked Val's tee out of her jeans and drew her fingers firmly across Val's chest. If this was a punishment, Val welcomed the retribution for whatever pain Nicki felt.

"I want to stay." Nicki's raspy whisper filled Val's mouth. Val felt the *but* coming. "But I don't know that I'm not using this as a distraction." Nicki pressed her lips to Val's in a rough kiss.

"No hurry on the decision, you know," Val teased. "Stay. You can think later."

"Your consideration is noted." Nicki was smiling now as they kissed. She pressed her hand into Val's groin.

"If I stay, you have to promise this lovemaking stops right now," Nicki whispered again. She found Val's tongue. As they kissed, Val

117

reached into Nicki's jacket pocket and removed the keys. She put them in Nicki's hand.

"Bye, bye." Val didn't move her body away from Nicki's. Nicki tossed her keys up into one of the chairs on Val's porch. She turned Val around and pushed her toward the porch steps, picking up her keys as they walked by. Val locked the door behind them and followed Nicki to the bedroom.

Chapter Eighteen

BECAUSE THEY HAD ARRIVED in Athens a day early, once Val picked Nicki up from the library, they were able to catch a group of Val's friends who met regularly downtown for half-price wine night on Wednesdays.

When her friends piled into the chairs and booths, Val welcomed the hugs and kisses from her gang. In the shuffle, Nicki had become separated from her, and now they were at opposite ends of the table. At first Nicki seemed quieter than Val had expected, but she smiled and laughed. Val lamented the separation, but she was aware that Nicki was the type of person who never met a stranger. Still, Val didn't consider that Nicki might be somewhat overwhelmed by ten of Val's best, long-time friends, including Nancy. A later glance showed Nicki in an animated discussion, circling her hand in a large circle as if describing some process of one of the laundry's machines. She seemed to be holding her own.

During a friend's story, Val caught Nicki looking at her. Not just looking, but *watching* her. Val winked at Nicki when she could throw it in without her friends noticing—a secret thank you for putting up with the onslaught.

Her friends engaged Nicki, teasing her about the big night life in Marshall. One of her friends entertained Nicki with stories of men from Marshall that he and his partner had known from college back in the day.

"Now that was something," Nicki said afterward, as they walked to the car.

"Sorry I left you to the wolves. I forget how crazy it can get."

"It was okay." A beat passed. "You're lucky to still have such a big support system. Remaining close to so many people must be wonderful."

"I've known some of these friends since before you were born. I am lucky. Maybe I should adopt your nickname."

"Oh brother," Nicki replied as she rolled her eyes.

***

Val pulled up to the curb by the University's Russell Special Collections Building as planned, and Nicki jumped in. She slapped the side of her briefcase in her lap as Val pulled into the traffic lane.

"I'm beat."

"Good research then?"

"Yeah. I had an entirely new set of questions for Tom following the research yesterday afternoon. After today, I've added to that. Plus, I found some choice info on Miller's work on the lottery. It's pretty cool stuff, looking at his papers." Nicki reeled off interesting tidbits she had learned.

"Okay, okay," Val said after several minutes. "I know you're excited, but I don't think I can absorb all of that in a few short minutes. When you get your questions and notes together, I'd love to read through them, though."

"It is overwhelming, but it's so cool, Val."

"Hope you're ready for a nice walk up to the restaurant with us. You're not too overwhelmed, are you?"

"Maybe, but I'm hungry though....like usual, of course."

"It's only a twenty minute walk, and we have reservations. At least we don't have to wait. You're not too tired...or overloaded?"

"I'm all right. A walk will do me good. Sitting all day reading can be grueling."

Within fifteen minutes they were back at Nancy's and heading out for the restaurant. Val and Nancy chatted about the two houses that had been renovated on her street.

"Val tells me you own a laundromat in addition to being a full time grad student. I bet that's an experience," Nancy said, turning partially around to Nicki, a few steps behind them.

"I've been running on all cylinders, that's for sure."

"I bet. And you like living in Marshall?"

"Well, I've been there most of my life. My work is there. It's an okay place. Folks have been supportive. I sure could do worse."

At times, Val deflected by chiming in if she thought a subject was too intense. After Nancy seemed to sense Nicki's reticence, she changed to discussing her own work with plants.

By the end of dinner, Nicki was much more animated. She seemed to enjoy Nancy's knowledge of Lake Oconee and Lake Sinclair.

"Y'all still planning on going to the cabin?" Nancy asked on the walk home.

"We're going to see how the meeting goes tomorrow. She's liable to be exhausted after tomorrow's meetings," Val answered quickly, allowing an out for Nicki.

"Yeah. Playing it by ear at this point," Nicki added.

"Well, I arranged a delivery of seasoned wood. I just recently had the fireplace repaired. And last time I was there I left a brand new fire extinguisher...just in case!" They all laughed.

"The plan is to go, but we may need to skip the trip and get back anyway. Especially if Nicki's laundromat coverage falls apart."

Later, when they had made it to bed, Nicki snuggled up to Val's side.

"Thanks for bailing me out a few times. You knew I was tense, didn't you?"

"I couldn't tell if you were exhausted or processing. You just seemed...I don't know. Not distant. More like reticent maybe?" Val brushed her fingers across Nicki's forearm.

"Maybe all those things. Anyway, thanks. I was going to read a while, but I'm beat. Night." Nicki kissed Val's shoulder as she nuzzled in closer.

"Night."

***

Nicki wore her suit the next morning and carried a leather portfolio complete with legal pad and pen. Val wore khakis and a navy blazer— *her* typical business attire. Tom had Nicki accompany him to a board meeting to hear their discussions and learn about various nonprofit operational issues. This checked off one of her instructor's requirements. Tom seemed both honored and thrilled to have been asked to help in this way. Val read one of her copies of *The New Yorker* in Tom's office during the meeting. It might have been interesting, even helpful, for her to attend, but she wanted Nicki to have the experience she needed for her project.

Tom was a kind man. Val had worked with him years ago on a committee at the hospital that established a free or low-cost medication program. He was one of the community stakeholders, and he had provided valuable information. The project did not evolve into the program Val and her unit's social worker had hoped. However, the administration recognized the financial benefit to preventing readmissions through reduced-cost medications, so they had developed an alternative program.

With that project, Val learned to fully appreciate collaboration and compromise. It also provided her with experience speaking to large groups of administrators and community leaders.

Val would continue to hone those skills as she presented Amazing Grace's potential new programs and their results to various hospital departments. She hoped Nicki would continue to draw from her coursework and related experiences, and maintain an open mind about how Amazing Grace would develop. If Nicki grew to direct the non-profit, allowing her to fade from anything more than a board position, all the better. But she recognized public speaking and presentations were just around the corner for both of them.

Nicki seemed to thrive in Tom's environment. When Nicki excused herself to the restroom after the board meeting, Tom shared his awe of Nicki's contributions. Board members welcomed her and found many of her ideas refreshing. Evidently, she had spoken as frequently as any of the members. Tom assured Val that she was not overstepping. She was asked her perspectives as an outsider and a "younger" person. Most of the board members were closer to Tom and Val's ages. The few thirty- and forty-something individuals seemed thrilled with Nicki's presence and her ideas.

Their joint meeting with Tom proved to be wonderful—it was rich with information. Tom might not be an expert in running nonprofit casinos, but he was able to provide good nuts-and-bolts ideas, and suggested resources they could take advantage of throughout the state.

"Sounds like that was productive, eh?" Val said as they entered the car.

"Oh, Val. It was fantastic. I'm glad you suggested Tom. What a great guy."

"Let's go find some cabin in the woods, shall we?"

Nicki looked at Val as she fastened the seat belt. "I looked at the temp. We can check out that fireplace." She smiled and patted Val's thigh.

"If you're sure. Remember what I said about turning around, now. I mean it." Val glanced to see if she could read Nicki's expression.

"Yeah. I remember. But you know, sitting on the floor in front of a fire sounds mighty nice," Nicki said as they left town. Val noted Nicki's silence...the absence of meeting chatter that had accompanied most of the trip to Athens. Val assumed Nicki was keeping any thoughts of the hike to Preacher's Rock out of her mind and in its box.

As they drove up to Trahlyta's grave, Nicki was so distracted by the new traffic circle, she barely looked toward the rocks in the center. Then, as they drove past the grave, she turned her head away from Val and feigned looking out the window at the traffic circle's faux stone walls. Neither spoke for the rest of the drive. When they passed Woody Gap, Nicki turned toward the parking area on Val's side of the road. She assumed Nicki was avoiding looking at the start of the trail heading to Preacher's Rock.

The drive took an unheard of three hours with Friday afternoon traffic and a grocery drive-by, but they made it. It was dark as the sun dropped below the mountain and tree line. Val turned on the water and gas while Nicki tended to the fireplace.

Val sensed an uneasy calm in the air, even with wine, hors d'oeuvres, and a fire. They were sitting close enough to the hearth that their bolster pillows were quite hot.

"Dang. It's damn hot. I'm afraid these things are going to combust on us. Let's move back," Val suggested as she slid away from the hearth, dragging the pillow. Nicki nodded, and crawled to follow Val.

"If it looks good tomorrow, let's take that hike to Preachers Rock," Nicki offered. "I haven't hiked more than three feet recently. Hopefully I won't have a heart attack on you."

"Well, well. Lucky for you, I know CPR," Val replied, staring straight ahead. "I see you're smiling...even if you're not laughing."

"Hokey," Nicki whispered.

"Now, really. If you think the hike is going to be too much, we can always go for a walk around the lake. Or there's a shorter hike to Lance Creek."

"Oh yeah! I know that hike," Nicki said excitedly. "One of the hills on that walk is filled with wildflowers in the spring. I love that hike." Val showed Nicki the collection of wildflower books on Nancy's shelf. "Hmm. That would be cool sometime, but let's stick to the plan."

They decided on arriving at the trailhead to Preacher's Rock at seven a.m. to beat day hiker traffic. Val assumed Nicki would not want scores of people to see her sobbing on the rock. They may not make the sunrise, but that was okay.

Noticing that Val was heading into the bedroom, Nicki softly asked, "Would you be okay if I sleep alone tonight?"

"Of course. Whatever you need." She made the bed for Nicki and turned the covers so Nicki could slip in when she was ready.

"Your room is ready, ma'am," Val announced, smiling.

"I'm going to sit by the fire a little longer...maybe until it fades." Nicki reached out to Val. She took Nicki's hand in hers, leaned over, and kissed her.

"Night." Val brushed her hand across Nicki's head.

Val pushed the door to her room shut, turned the light off, and second-guessed if the trip was a good idea. She acknowledged to herself how much Nicki was processing right now. *Downtime—and separate downtime—is good. You know that, Scott.* Val had just drifted off when she heard the bedroom door hinge squeak. Nicki tiptoed in and leaned to kiss Val's cheek. She tiptoed back out, and Val heard the sounds of Nicki preparing for bed.

***

Luckily, they were fog-free in the morning. A blessing.

"Happy birthday. I'm glad you've come into my life," Val said to Nicki. Nicki nodded, but barely smiled as she sipped her coffee. On the drive to the trailhead, the only thing Nicki said was how she had forgotten the extreme curves in this area of Georgia. The parking lot wasn't crowded yet, though vehicles were already parked on both sides of the road. They set out on the trail, Val leading the way. Nicki didn't complain, but her occasional ugh or dang let Val know, as Nicki predicted, that she wasn't in hiking shape. When they arrived at Preacher's Rock, Nicki held her arm out to keep Val from stepping off-trail.

"Can I have a minute?" Nicki asked.

"Of course. I'll wait for you to call or come get me." Val squeezed Nicki's hand as Nicki turned to the short trail access. Five minutes had passed, Val figured, when Nicki reappeared. She took Val's hand and led her in and onto the Rock. The bald rock outcrop allowed a view of multiple mountains and hilltops. In between many of the hills, banks of clouds looked like white lakes.

"It's so beautiful," Val acknowledged. The sun's position made them both squint, and added to the difficulty of seeing the expansive view. Their hands at their brows blocked the light. Tears streamed down Nicki's cheeks. Val put her arm around Nicki's shoulders and pulled her close as they continued admiring the view from the overlook.

"Hello, baby girl," Nicki muttered. "I love you. Your daddy loved you, too. I know you're happy and dancing." Softly Nicki half-sang, half-cried, a few lyrics from "Unwritten." Nicki turned around to walk out. She took a few steps, turned her head to look back.

"Bye, baby girl." Val followed her out. They hiked back to the truck in silence. When her hands and arms weren't steadying her balance or pushing back brush, she held Nicki's hand. Nicki stopped once at another clearing, and Val pressed into Nicki's back. Nicki took Val's hand and pulled it around her waist in a hug. Nicki released her hand, and Val wiped a tear from her own eye.

When they arrived back at the cabin, Nicki said she wanted to shower. After her shower, she went back into her room and shut the door. In a couple of hours, she emerged.

"Thank you for this gift. I feel better." She reached her hand out to Val, and Val held it as Nicki sat beside her on the arm of the sofa.

"Sorry I deserted you. Just needed some time."

"I didn't feel deserted," Val said as she kissed Nicki's hand. "I walked around the circle a few times to help rid my legs of some of that lactic acid. I may cycle every other day and work out, but nothing compares to scuttling up and down rocks and trying to maneuver on that uneven terrain."

"Where's my cake?" Nicki joked. "I'm starving." *Devilish smile.*

Val shook her head, groaning aloud. She lit the five different colored candles on the chocolate cake she had made the day before in Athens.

"One for you. One for me. And for those who are here in spirit: Trolly, Mike, and your aunt. Happy birthday. And this isn't 'Survivor.' We aren't out of the game when you blow out the candles! Make a wish," Val added quickly. Nicki smiled, stopped a second, nodded, and blew. Val cut two slices, and she and Nicki sat across from one another at the table.

"Wow! This is good," Nicki said with a mouthful.

"Don't sound so surprised! I do know how to cook, you know," Val replied. In the best singing voice Val could muster, she started, "Happy birthday to you—"

Nicki stopped her. "You don't need to sing that. And it's not your voice. It's just...you know?"

Val mustered up some courage and tried singing, "But I keep on hoping..." Nicki beamed. She walked to Val, reached down to Val's cake, picked up a big glob of icing with her finger and put it in her own mouth.

She leaned into Val's face and kissed her, icing and all, both of them laughing.

Val and Nicki made the most of the remainder of the weekend. Nicki drove them around several old haunts, including onto the property where she and Mike had lived with Trolly.

"Hate to say it, but I'm glad no one was around. Way some folks are up here, I was a little afraid we might get shot at."

"Swell." Val turned her head to the side and looked out the window. "Now you tell me."

Nancy's fireplace certainly received a proper workout. They spent lots of time on makeshift pallets of quilts and blankets, even sleeping on them Saturday night. Sunday night, Nicki made her way into Val's bed. Val was relieved Nicki had relaxed. Nicki seemed to have let Val back in emotionally. She loved opening her eyes in the morning and seeing Nicki's face next to hers on the pillow.

Chapter Nineteen

ALL THE WAY HOME, the work ahead dominated Nicki's chatter. She encouraged Val to consider updating the incorporation now to include local officers instead of only her friends. She stated firmly that she was prepared to make her recommendations.

"I haven't spoken with JH yet," Val said, "but I think he should hold an office. The three of us...at least until we have others on deck. How about me as president and treasurer, you as secretary, and JH as a non-officer board member? Just for now, you know."

"If you think that will fly legally."

"No reason it shouldn't. I'm more concerned with filling the board of directors' seats. It's really not too difficult to change officers. I think it's important, though, to have names on letterheads, brochures, and proposals. And things will look legit if the names are right," Val explained. "You need those props to make visits to other local leaders and legislators."

Val was somewhat relieved when she dropped Nicki off. She was exhausted by Nicki's endless energy...once she engaged. Val assured Nicki that, no, she did not need any more cake. In Nicki's house, in hers, *or* by the ocean. At least tonight. She knew Nicki could persuade her, but she was grateful that this evening, she didn't.

***

Two months passed. Nicki met with each commissioner separately, asking for discretion and support. Each one had agreed, though each expressed that anything even resembling a casino would encounter skepticism, if not resistance. She was pleased with her first big foray into the action part of her project.

Val and Nicki met with Sandy Ann, filling her in on the full details of the project. They asked for her confidentiality until their first press release. Her excitement was obvious.

"Lord knows people around here need a break. We don't have such a high unemployment rate because business is booming in Hancock County!" Sandy Ann said. Val and Nicki both agreed Sandy Ann was a natural for the board, and she accepted.

Nicki's next stop was her aunt's preacher, Donny McDuffie. She and Val agreed they needed one more respected community member to weigh in before moving on to legislators. She had emailed Val the suggestion, but hadn't heard back. She didn't feel it would be risky. They had seen eye-to-eye so far.

***

"Little ol' Lucky!" he boomed as he saw Nicki walk through the office. "You need to come here to see us a little more often, like *Sun*days," he greeted her.

"How's your mamma-n-em?" she asked in her best Southern, country accent.

"At ninety-six, she's doing fairly well, and Nan and the kids are great. They're not kids, of course. They have their own. And everybody's well." He chuckled. "That aunt of yours, though. I sure do miss her."

He regaled her with oft-told stories of her Aunt Mae, recounting how Nicki had sold a few acres of land and donated to the church's building fund in Mae's name. Nicki avoided saying she would come back on Sundays, but confessed that she needed his input as a community leader. She laid out the elevator speech and gave him her card and a brochure.

"Jennifer N. Williams. Not going by Harris or Nicole, huh? Operations Intern. Valiant Expeditions, Doing-Business-As Amazing Grace Delivered. Hmm. Anything that has Amazing Grace in the title can't be all bad, but I don't know, Nicki...a casino? You know, they always say the mob comes in." He seemed skeptical, and Nicki voiced her appreciation for his perspective.

She explained that the way a nonprofit is structured, it would be difficult for it to allow an organized crime syndicate to flourish.

"You know, Reverend Donny," Nicki said, "I've always respected you. Your dedication to the community's poor, the way you welcome those who don't have white skin, and your sermons on unconditional love. I'd be honored if, after hearing more organizational details, you'd agree to serve on the board. You know the name Reverend Donny McDuffie on the board would be a boon to our mission."

"Oh Nicki. Are you working on an MBA or a Masters of Bull Crap? I am sufficiently buttered up, but—" he started. Nicki joined him right on cue, and together they said, "All the glory should go to God." They both laughed aloud.

"That's my little Lucky!" he boomed through his laugher. Nicki was surprised how comfortable she was with him even now, but she wondered what he would think if he knew she was seeing a woman. If he knew, he didn't let on, and he didn't seem at all uncomfortable with her. It seemed everyone else in her old circle knew. How could he not?

"Whadaya say, preacher man?" Nicki asked. She flashed him her devilish smile.

"I can't say you're not hard to resist, Lucky Harris...I mean...Williams. But if I agree to this, you have to know I'm going to speak my mind. And you may not approve." Nicki assured him she wanted nothing less.

"Just keep in mind, your name on the letterhead as a board member might make you a target," Nicki warned.

"Well, that won't be the first time," the reverend recounted. "You have to remember when we pulled out of the Southern Baptist Convention. You've surprised me here, I have to say. This idea is interesting. If it goes as you hope, it will be a real gift to folks around here. By the way, you look quite grown up." He motioned to her suit. "I'm right proud of you. Your aunt would be, too." Nicki blushed.

***

When Nicki returned to the car, she thumbed through emails on her phone. Distracted, she thought back to her conversation with Reverend Donny. "Amazing is right," she said aloud. She thought he must know, or have heard, about her seeing Val. It seemed like everyone must know, but she hadn't encountered any sort of negativity. Had the town really changed that much?

She remembered when the only gay person was the florist. He was pretty closeted, and he provided the arrangements for Donny's church every Sunday. And there were the softball women. Surely everyone knew about them. There was certainly plenty of gossip. Seemed like everyone had always lived together pretty peacefully, though.

An email from Val's attorney friend, John Elbert, broke her daydreaming. He was confirming with Val that he would be honored to serve. That completed their board. She was anxious to share the news with Val and decided to head that way.

Nicki swung by the laundromat to check in with Ashley. Ashley had a nice baby bump going now, and that made Nicki smile to herself.

"Hello, Miss Nicki," Ashley said.

"Ashley, Ashley. Just Nicki...*please*," Nicki said, smiling. "How's it going? Anything I need to know?"

"A couple things. Aunt Peggy told me Daddy would be getting out next week, so please give a heads up to your friend on that one. Maybe to you, too." Ashley looked above her glasses and pursed her lips. Nicki rolled her eyes to the ceiling, remembering her earlier thoughts.

"The other thing, and I hope you don't mind. I should've called you, I know. I talked with Mr. Simmons at the dry cleaners. He doesn't like doing regular washing anymore, so we're going to be drop-off locations for one another. He'll deliver washing to us, and we'll deliver dry cleaning to him. That way, people can have one stop for both services. I've already worked out the books angle, so don't worry. We're not doing a mark-up, because we're both going to benefit. At least, that's what we think right now. We'll see."

"Dang, girl. You don't need me at all, do you?" Nicki smiled at Ashley. "I'm proud of you, Ashley. You're a lifesaver for me. A gift right now." Ashley blushed.

"Let's just agree to say we have a mutual admiration society," Ashley said, smiling.

"Agreed, but are you worried your dad will cause any trouble?" Nicki asked.

"Hopefully he's dried out. If he's not having to pay for me, maybe he'll leave me alone. I know that may only be wishful thinking."

"We can hope, though, can't we? Okay, then. You know how to find me, my dear," Nicki said as she walked out of the door. Nicki noticed a professionally-printed sign on the outside wall, near the door. "Simmons Dry Cleaning, Official Drop Off Location." Nicki waved to Ashley to get her attention, pointed at the sign, smiled broadly, and gave Ashley a double thumbs up. Nicki thought how proud she was to see Ashley becoming her own businesswoman.

***

Ashley's playlist was blaring in Nicki's truck as she drove out to the property, Nicki dancing in her seat the whole way. She parked beside Val's truck and danced her way up the steps. When Val answered the door, Nicki continued dancing, and took Val's hand to dance around with her. Nicki continued dancing and motioned with the other hand to the building that was now being constructed at the end of the drive.

Nicki was still dressed in her suit, and she felt elated from her meeting with Reverend Donny and Mr. Elbert's email.

"Hey, doll," Nicki sang to the tune of "Cake by the Ocean," her favorite song. "Wanted you to know we got a board now, board now..."

"Don't quit your day job," Val teased. "What do you mean?"

"Haven't read your emails today, have you?" Nicki read Mr. Elbert's email. She explained how Rev. Donny had agreed to serve as well.

"That *Baptist* church! Are you crazy?" Val said harshly.

Nicki explained the church's withdrawal from the Southern Baptist Convention, their social conscience, their support of women as preachers, and their welcoming mission. She further explained that having the name Marshall Baptist Church on the letterhead would be a real boon to the effort.

"You look nice, by the way. *And* good job. You're right, I had no idea," Val replied. "Sort of dropped off my radar, I guess. Too much retirement. Not enough focus. I'll do better." She chuckled. "But you're not focusing on me now, are you?"

Nicki was looking over at the building, her mind's wheels turning. "JH's van is at the building," she said. "Is he busy? Can I go over and look even if the guys are working?" The usual Nicki Williams bubbly stream of consciousness. It was a good thing it was okay, because Nicki had already made her way, heels and all. Val hurried after her.

JH placed a hard hat on Nicki's head, then one on Val's.

"No hat, no entry," he said seriously. He looked down at Nicki's heels.

"Really? You're going to wear those here?"

"I didn't know I was going to be touring in the dirt. I thought I was coming to see this lady," she said, pointing her thumb at Val.

"Since we're all here, though, Ashley told me today that Ben Linton's being released next week. She thinks since he's dried out, he may leave everyone alone, as long as he doesn't start drinking again."

"Yeah, I heard about that...and the terms of his release. I'll go ahead and talk with Sheriff Jenkins to make sure Linton's making his mandated AA meetings. Sure hope he doesn't act up again. Val, you and Nicki both need to stay alert."

Nicki shared the good news of the board taking shape. They discussed her upcoming trip to meet with the state legislators at their regional offices, since she had missed the legislative session this year. Waiting until next January would definitely make keeping a secret difficult. Nicki offered that if someone was going to spill the beans on this project, it was likely going to be from the county commission. She suggested getting the press release out now. They agreed it would be prudent.

"Can't keep it a secret forever, can we?" Val added.

"Too many people know already," JH said, nodding.

He suggested adding someone in the education field, such as the retired high school principal, to the board. Or someone who had served on the area's council on aging. Val looked at Nicki.

"Great ideas, Mr. Evans. I'll get on that and press releases next week," Nicki said. "See? We just completed our first officers' meeting. We'll put the minutes in our corporate binder." Val nodded, and commented on how well they worked as a team.

Starting on the main buildings would require additional funding. Val had used some money to finance the initial phase of the project— the community building currently going up. JH had browbeat a couple of his construction friends to donate some laborers and some materials into that, knowing they would get a nice tax write-off and some good press. The community building was now estimated at half-cost.

JH continued to refuse one dime in payment. He only asked for expenses to be reimbursed. Having a free contractor was a major factor in keeping costs low. With his hands-on ethic, they probably saved on the labor of at least two workers. Even with Grace's benefaction, fundraising had to commence soon, and would need to be coordinated with press releases.

Nicki's MBA project was on track for completion. The capstone would consist of the completed business plan and corresponding minutes from meetings, tied together with explanations of the processes. It was a huge big picture project. Her professor had already recommended she continue the project into PhD work. It was exciting to consider, but she was now invested in seeing the entire project through, if Val agreed.

For the MBA, she had opted for the nonprofit management and leadership track of study. Val had already secured new cards for Nicki: "Jennifer N. Williams, MBA. Secretary. Valiant Expeditions d/b/a Amazing Grace Delivered." She was using the new business mobile listed on the card. Nicki had obtained two other suits, this time matching skirts and jackets, in black and gray.

Nicki had sent letters to two legislators who had supported Georgia gaming, asking them if they would meet with her for advice. She enclosed brochures, business cards, and the rendering of the completed community building. She used official letterhead that included the names of the six board members. Nicki reflected on Val's comment about her business acumen. How Val said she had come to expect it as natural. It was a good feeling, and she knew it bolstered her self-confidence.

Nicki and JH had completed dual presentations to a few civic organizations and area churches. Press releases were sent out regarding efforts to fund a new area nonprofit designed to provide community engagement, jobs, and a better quality of life for greater Hancock County.

***

Because Nicki was spending so much time in the community at meetings, working at Val's desk in the community building, or from her home, Val typically saw Nicki in passing. They had met for dinner only a few times in the past two months, but Nicki typically ate and ran so she could attend community meetings.

Val had researched several grants, and using Nicki's previous proposals, had mailed off a couple of applications with tight deadlines. There were more to do.

The nights they spent together, Nicki fell asleep quickly or came in late, leaving no time for hanky-panky. Val had suspected, even worried, that their life stage differences might lead to their growing apart. She hoped it wasn't happening, but how could she hold it against Nicki? Nicki was swamped.

Val missed her, though. Not just Nicki's body, but her energy. *Where is my devilish smile? That luscious mouth?* Val felt a familiar longing as she remembered Nicki's kiss. Their lovemaking. *Jump on the bike, girl. Focus on something else for now.*

Val's newly-found free time enabled her to take longer and longer day rides. She saw herself training for a bucket list bike tour—perhaps Maine to Florida. That was a list she was actively working through, taking advantage of every opportunity. Val signed up for a couple of two- to four-day training rides, one of them being the Athens to the Coast ride in two weeks. She invited Nicki to join her on Tybee Island at the end of the ride. Nicki said she thought she could swing that.

Chapter Twenty

VAL'S PHONE ALERTED HER to a text message. She had been asleep since ten-thirty. Her phone displayed two-thirty a.m. *Nicki. Geez.*

"U wake?" the text read.

"No," she replied.

"(Wink emoji) U R now." Val jumped off the bed with a tap on the bedroom window. *U R right—Shit.* She wished she could send such a message.

"Jesus Christ, Nicki! What the hell?" Val spewed as she opened the door.

"I'm not sorry," Nicki said. "But I know it was rude. I wanted to see you."

"See me you did. Good night." Val pushed to close the door. Nicki put her hand in quickly, preventing its closure, then followed with her body. *Haven't seen you in what seems like weeks, and you decide the middle of the night is a good time. Thanks a lot.*

"Let me in, Val. Please." Nicki seemed serious as she pushed. Val let the door swing open as Nicki pushed through.

"What!" Val said curtly, as she plopped into her chair, hands folded across her chest. Nicki waved a letter. "So?"

"It's from the Janus Federation. They've funded us a $250,000 grant."

"What? No way! Did you send them something?"

"Of *course*, I did. I sent applications for what seems like a hundred different grants! Well, maybe it was just five, but what do you think I *do* all day?" Nicki yelled excitedly. "And Janus also agreed to match up to $100,000 during our first 'Fishes and Loaves' campaign."

Val remembered that, while she was out of town on a bike ride, the board had agreed to search for a matching donor for an annual fundraiser.

"Nicki. That's super. I'm speechless. And not only because you just scared the shit out of me. It's incredible news." Val shook her head in disbelief. "I mean, I thought I'd never get done with three grants...and that was using your proposals for the most part."

"So why, then, wouldn't I want to tell you?" Nicki asked. "I had already gone home and forgot I hadn't checked our post office box today. I have been so obsessed checking it every day. I got up out of the bed, dressed and went back out. Between that and Ashley, there was no way I could go to sleep." Nicki was animated.

"What about Ashley? Is she okay?" Val was now concerned.

"She's wonderful. Did you know she brought in her cousin, Peggy's son—he's gay—and trained him at the laundromat? Ashley is a natural born businesswoman. As soon as the baby is born, she's going to begin college classes. I made her promise me. Of course, I'll ride her ass until she does." Nicki sounded snippy with that pronouncement. "If I hadn't told you already, I've had Mr. Elbert draw up a bill of sale and contract for the laundromat."

"What?" Val shouted. "Are you going somewhere? You are just full of surprises tonight."

"Well, I hope not. Going somewhere, I mean. I hope you'll hire me *here* full-time. A real, paying job. Of course, I'd rather it be paying with benefits, but Ashley needs a job. Something that will allow her to raise her baby. I'm selling the laundry to her."

"How can she afford that? Is Peggy going to help her?" Val asked. "And by the way, I hoped you'd be interested in staying on...yes, with pay and benefits. It's not like I'm a harsh taskmaster, you know."

"Ha, funny you are. Anyway, she only has to pay me a thousand dollars," Nicki said. She smiled. "I want her to have to pay something— to have her be invested. The contract says she has to pay fifty bucks a month for twenty months. It's more like a no-interest loan. Do you realize she's already had to order two new machines? She's thinking of a new location for the laundromat, but she doesn't want to do anything until the baby is a couple of years old," Nicki said.

"You must be as proud of her as I am of you," Val admitted. Nicki smiled, looking at Val in a way she hadn't seen before. *Is she irritated with my saying that?*

"Proud? Huh? What *do* you think I do all day?" Nicki asked in an irritated tone.

"Avoid *me*, mostly," Val replied.

"Oh, no you didn't!" Nicki pushed Val's shoulders as a bully might do. Val stood up to protect herself. *I think she's teasing me.*

Nicki pushed Val onto the love seat. She kneeled in a way so that one knee was between Val's legs. Nicki positioned her knee against Val's crotch.

"That...is...not...true. I go *crazy* sometimes. I want to see you. Be with you, but I have so much to do and not enough time," Nicki said.

"I forgive you, if that's what you're looking for," Val snarked. *Ooh. That was mean. Ha. Ha. Ha.*

"You are asking for it. I swear." Nicki shook her head. She pushed Val's head gently, so it rested on the sofa back. She leaned in and moved her lips just above Val's. Val tried to lift her head to meet Nicki's lips, but Nicki gently held Val's head in place.

"I'm sorry to have scared you, but I'm not sorry I'm here," Nicki whispered, lightly brushing Val's lips.

Val pulled Nicki on top of her. They slid to the floor, kissing.

"I have a bed back there, if you want to get a little more comfortable."

Nicki rocked slowly against Val.

"I thought you wanted me to go," Nicki teased softly.

"That was then. Since you've apologized though—" Nicki's deep kiss stopped Val's taunt. "I wanted you to go, but now I think it would be nice if you came," Val whispered.

"Hokey," Nicki whispered, smiling. Nicki stopped rocking, stood up, and helped Val stand. Nicki led Val to the bedroom. She undressed Val slowly and pushed her softly onto the bed. She straddled Val, and softly caressed her nipples with her lips. Val arched, and guided Nicki's mouth back to her lips.

"That mouth," Val whispered into Nicki's mouth. "I have missed your mouth. You."

"Oh, jeez." Nicki sighed as Val positioned her head between Nicki's legs. She kissed Nicki softly until she moaned and arched her back.

Hours later, Val noticed the sky beginning to lighten.

"Should we sleep now?" Val asked softly.

"You decide," Nicki whispered as she gently caressed between Val's legs. Val moaned softly into Nicki's mouth.

***

Two days passed before either Val or Nicki emerged from Grace. JH had noticed Nicki's truck, but neither Nicki nor Val answered their phones. Nicki did return a text to JH at one point to say they were both quite fine after he threatened to come in or call Sheriff Jenkins. Later, as Nicki was leaving to prepare for her week, she kissed Val goodbye.

"Don't let me wait so long next time. Rescue me."

"Sure. I don't want to invade your space or interrupt a process. Hope you understand that."

"I do, Val. I don't want us to drift apart, though. I've added your bike trip to my calendar. Nothing would prevent my meeting you in Tybee. Let me know when and where to go, okay?"

"Ms. Williams, I'm so glad you *came*." Val kissed her fingertips as if to kiss Nicki.

"Not half as glad as I am, Ms. Scott."

Devilish smile. Oh my. You cannot do that right now. We have to get some work done.

"The press release regarding the grant will go out later."

Val suspected Nicki had already shifted back into work mode.

***

After her ride, Val checked her texts. She had heard a couple of buzzes. Nicki had been out to see her and saw the bike was gone. She asked for Val to run by.

Nicki seemed all business when Val arrived, as if yesterday had never happened.

"I want you to look at this website before I present it to the board," Nicki said as she opened up her laptop and motioned for Val to come around her desk. "Josh Crisp, Ashley's cousin, developed a sample website that would serve as a funding page site."

"He's a kid, right? Graduated with Ashley?" Val was impressed, given they were both practically kids. Val had always worked, but she had believed Ashley and Josh were of a different generation—one that expected others to do things for them. She clucked her tongue at her own prejudices.

She continued looking around the website and discovered the "levels of giving" section. This was fleshed out into potential categories. Anywhere he was unsure, he had substituted the *lorem ipsum* text she recognized from a position she'd had years ago at a copy and print shop.

The giving levels, in dollars, were: Good Samaritan, one hundred dollars; Open Hand, fifty; Tabitha's Act, twenty-five; and Rising Light, ten. Under each entry was a small gibberish line. The last entry included a line for "Other" donations with an open dollar field.

"We'll be able to get this page, when it's up of course, out on social media. If all of us have our friends push it out to others, it should generate some interest, and hopefully, some money," Nicki explained.

She showed Val another proposed page of Amazing Grace casino's site. She explained how she had sent a few files from the architectural renderings to Josh. These pictures would be replaced with photographs as buildings were completed. The completed community building's photo was already dropped in. Nicki suggested website approval at the next board meeting.

"We need to secure a net address as soon as possible," Nicki said.

"I say, let's go for it," Val answered. "And please, compensate Josh for his work. Whatever you think is appropriate. If JH isn't around to sign a check, let me know. I'd like to make sure I'm at that meeting. This is great stuff."

Nicki repositioned herself on the edge of the desk and pulled Val—sweaty clothes and all—between her spread legs. Nicki's arms slipped around Val's waist.

"I know I can't keep doing this. I don't want to wait so long to see you. I know I'll see you at the end of the Tybee ride, but I mean in general. After the ride, I want to discuss what *this* is—what *we're* doing," Nicki said as she pointed back and forth between them.

"Okay. Let's talk now, but after I take off these sweaty clothes. We don't have to wait till Tybee. Let me go home and shower."

***

As Val showered, she considered their relationship. *What are we doing? What is this? I know I like it, but I'm not sure I can do the couple thing right now. Especially with someone that much younger, but we're doing everything a courting couple would do, except moving in.* She wondered if Nicki would begin to grow tired of their relationship. *Oh no. I'm even thinking relationship as in a couple relationship. Who am I fooling, though? Anyone on the outside would see us as a couple. As a dating couple. Should we see ourselves that way? All I know is I haven't been this happy in a long time.* Nor had she so *craved* being with anyone in years. Val put her hand to her face, but the shower had washed away any vestige of Nicki. *Is it just lust?*

Val walked out of the bathroom, towel drying her hair. She looked around at her space. *Too small for two. Her place is nice, though. Hm. Don't get ahead of yourself, remember?* As Val was dressing, she heard a text from her phone. Nicki.

"Come 2 dinner. Let's talk," the message said.

Requisite "K" from Val, and she added "6pm unless I hear otherwise."

***

Nicki was now the key face of Amazing Grace. The board agreed she should be hired in an administrative position as soon as she had her MBA in hand. In the meantime, she would draw a small salary as secretary of the corporation.

In the near future, Nicki would be away for weeks at a time, especially in January when the legislature re-opened. The board had agreed to begin construction of the thousand-seat performance venue, and its construction was due to be completed by September. Since the high school auditorium was the largest of any such space, they hoped the performance hall would complement community needs now and in the future.

The community building was in its final stages, and now Val had an office set up there, but in function, it was Nicki's office. They would finish the shell of the second building in the next four months. It would house security and facilities operations. One unique feature of that building was the presence of ten dorm-style rooms and a kitchen. On-duty security personnel, coming off-duty security or work staff, or board members, who became ill while on the clock, would have a place to crash before they left, exhausted, or before someone could come pick them up.

She looked forward to the time the Amazing Grace casino building would be completed, but they knew it was crazy to begin building before a legislative thumbs-up. The hotel would complete the project's current timeline, but that was not expected for several years.

Nicki and JH had convinced the board that the complex would have a lower environmental impact if they utilized green construction principles. They would be using recycled hot mix asphalt throughout their vast parking lots. All lights would use Dark-Sky Approved fixtures to minimize light pollution. Plans for the solar panel farm were completed with the power company's input. That would roll out with the performance building.

JH had suggested, and the board had approved, a one-mile, two-lane path to allow community members and visitors to have a safe place to walk. The path, now completed, was constructed with porous concrete. It started at the Community Building, wound around the pond near the front entrance, and outlined much of the property.

The path was nicely landscaped with Sheriff Jenkins' help. He had, with Nicki's official proposal, presented the idea to the District Attorney and Department of Corrections. They agreed to a collaboration utilizing laborers from work-release and community service sentences.

JH and Val had continually marveled at Nicki's leadership. Her long view was spot on, every single time. Nicki's ability to harness local individuals for ideas and projects was awe inspiring. JH and Val both agreed it was all Nicki's instilling this sense of accomplishment and self-worth in people. So crucial, and *appropriate*, for their mission. Nicki had high expectations of people, and she communicated complete trust in their abilities. That led to outstanding performances.

Val chuckled to herself. *Oh yeah. Not just amazing, but hot.*

***

Nicki had prepared a nice pasta dinner: angel hair *aglio e olio*, salad, and wine. Girl Scout cookies, bought from one of the laundry's families, would serve as dessert—an assortment of Thin Mints, Tagalongs, and Trefoils. Simple and delicious. Val sat in the living room as she waited for Nicki to finish dinner preparations. Nicki brought her a glass of wine and they toasted.

"Let's eat first. It's still warm," Nicki said. Val nodded and headed to the table.

As they ate, Val related details of her upcoming trip—the room she had secured, the restaurants she had looked at, and her memories of other rides in the area. Nicki listened, but a little too quietly, Val thought. After Nicki cleared the table, she brought the plate of cookies out in one hand and the bottle of wine in the other.

"Grab the napkins and your glass, doll." Nicki nodded toward the living room.

They sat facing one another on the sofa, sitting cross-legged.

"You know we've been seeing one another now for six months," Nicki started. Val nodded, smiling at her. Nicki did not return a smile.

"I wasn't expecting to feel this way. And I don't know what you're thinking about us, but I know for me, I don't want you to see other people. And—"

"I'm not interested in anyone else right now, either," Val replied. "I enjoy my life right now. I love it—the riding, the project, *and* you."

"That's sort of the thing, though, Val. I want to be a little more to you, I think, than just one of your interests." Nicki looked into her glass. She seemed angry.

"No. I don't mean it that way, Nicki," Val explained. "You're a huge part of why I love my life."

"Val, I'm just going to say it. I wasn't going to, yet, but I am—"

"Nicki. Don't. Don't say anything you or I may regret. I don't want to mess up this thing."

"Well, then...fuck you, Val. I love you!" Nicki blurted angrily. She stood, crossing her arms in front of her. "I do. I'm not ashamed of that. I am in love with you. And if that fucking messes up your good life...Fuck you." She was not yelling, but she certainly was not calm.

Val stood up, put her arms around Nicki, and held her.

"Don't think I'm not in love with you. I am." Nicki's face was turned as far away from Val as it could be in an embrace. Nicki didn't move away, but she was as stiff as a board.

"By now...by now, you know me well enough...I need to process what you're saying. More like what you aren't saying. I need a day...or a week. I don't know. I mean, I guess I want a commitment you don't want to give me," Nicki said.

"I'm not going away, Nicki," Val whispered. "I'm going to still be here. Maybe you'll have processed all this by the time you pick me up in Tybee," They were still in a hug, but Nicki tried to pull away. Val held her tightly and guided Nicki's face to her. Val looked at Nicki's closed eyes.

"Please open your eyes and look at me, Nicki," Val requested. Nicki opened her tear-filled eyes. "You are remarkable, Nicki. I love how I feel when I'm with you. When I'm not with you, I'm thinking about you."

"I know, I know. But you're so much older, and know how tenuous new relationships are, and you..." Nicki grumbled. She reached for Val's phone, handed it to her, and pushed her gently. "Go home. I'll see you in a day or two. Maybe I'll have forgiven you for not saying what I want to hear."

Val leaned in to kiss Nicki, but Nicki moved her face, so Val kissed Nicki's cheek.

"You're lucky you're so hot," Val teased as she walked out the door. "Even when you're mad." Nicki did not smile.

Chapter Twenty-One

VAL HAD BARELY TURNED onto the main road when her phone started popping off. Text. Another text. Another text. *Dang. What is going on? Nicki must be yelling at me.* Val had the phone safely in her pocket. She considered accidents as preventable injuries. She was not going to be one of those texting statistics. The alerts and tones continued all the way to her house. When she pulled up to Grace, she grabbed the phone out of her pocket.

"What!" she yelled at the phone.

Ashley. Josh. Ashley again. Josh again. JH. Four email notifications on the screen. *O-M-G.* Nicki had handed Val her own phone by mistake. Their phones and cases were identical, and Nicki didn't notice. Val rediscovered Nicki had the lock screen enabled. Val could answer Nicki's calls or place an emergency call, but she felt trapped. *I don't want to drive back. If she wants her phone, she can come get it!* Before Val could close the door behind her, Nicki's phone rang with the ringtone "Cake by the Ocean." *Oh no. What a nut!*

"Naomi, here. What can I do for you, Diddy?" Val said with a smile. Nicki laughed out loud.

"Cute. Real cute," Nicki said. Val was glad she heard a smile. Nicki told her tomorrow she would be working from home in the morning and at the laundromat with Ashley in the afternoon.

"Can you just bring it by on one of your *rides*?" Nicki sounded jealous.

"I'm going to switch the sound button off, and I'll drop it off at the laundry around three tomorrow, okay? You know, you're quite a popular person."

"No worries. I'll just catch everybody on my computer," Nicki said confidently and with a condescending tone. "I'm still mad at you, though."

Val was anxious to return Nicki's phone, but not necessarily as a ruse to see Nicki. More because she was afraid Nicki would be missing important information. Val knew she wouldn't be receiving anything important. *Nicki, Nicki.*

"How do you solve a problem like Jen Williams?" Val sang the *Sound of Music* tune in her head. *But I am certainly no nun!* Val laughed aloud at the absurdity of the vision.

***

When Val arrived at the laundromat the next afternoon, she found both Ashley and Nicki in the office. Ashley was folding clothes, and Nicki, with her feet up on the desk, was leaning back in the desk chair, sporting earbuds. Nicki was holding Val's phone up, looking at it, as she nodded her head. Ashley tapped Nicki on the arm and pointed at the office door.

"Hi, Val," Ashley said.

Nicki quickly sat up and dropped both feet to the floor. She tapped the phone's face to stop the current tune.

"I hoped you wouln't mind. We've been listening to your playlist. *I've* been listening and sharing anything I thought Ashley might want to hear," she admitted, guiltily. "I mean, I've told you before to lock the screen if you don't want anyone in your phone," she continued, as if to justify herself.

"I don't mind your listening to my music. Either one of you," Val said.

"But I should have asked you if it was okay," Nicki admitted.

"It really is okay, Nicki. I don't mind."

"Your collection is interesting and varied. Ashley's happy you added the DNCE tune," Nicki said. She then began her own critique of Val's tunes. "What do you see in some of those songs? I like a couple of the Beatles songs. Those are ones Trolly liked. We'd dance and sing to them. I'm going to add a few to my own, like that Cure cover and the Aimee Mann song, but, some of them are sort of hokey, doll," Nicki said. Val frowned at her. "Who listens to Jim Neighbors' 'Misty' besides you?"

"You don't have to listen to them. Just because I like the songs, doesn't mean you have to like them," Val replied. "May I?" She reached for her phone as she stretched out her other hand with Nicki's phone.

"Y'all need to make up if you're having some sort of spat," Ashley said with a smile.

"We're not fighting," they answered in unison.

"I may be younger than you two, but I'm no dummy. I know y'all have been fighting," Ashley said. "None of my business, but it's obvious." She took the clothes she was folding and walked out of the office door to the laundromat floor.

Val looked into Nicki's eyes and smiled. *A couple. Hmmm.* Ashley had confirmed Val's suspicions about how the two of them looked together. Nicki had told her about what her thoughts were after Reverend Donny's visit. Val had noticed Athens certainly seemed to embrace the LGBTQIA community, but Marshall was deeply surrounded by a conservative rural landscape. It was nothing like Athens. Young adults, like Ashley, certainly were open. Josh was gay, and Peggy was supportive. Was her view skewed? And Ashley had been dating an African American guy. That was known to raise an eyebrow or two, even still, but Ashley seemed to be respected by many in the community. She was well liked. Her acceptance of different lifestyles would be noticed. *A couple, eh? Yeah, a couple.*

She excused herself and left. Nicki smiled but didn't say anything. *Guess she's still mad.*

***

Val's ride to the coast was just what she needed. The getaway. The long days of thinking. The nighttime hotel lobby get-togethers. Val met an attractive woman on the ride. They rode at a similar pace. On the second day of the ride, their chats revealed that indeed, Lee Floyd, was a lesbian. And she was single. Lee was taller than Val by a couple of inches, and she had long, muscular legs, chiseled features and short, gray hair.

Several people on the ride and in shops along the way asked if they were sisters. They would laugh.

"Well, yes we are," they'd say, thinking, *Sister Friends* as they said it. They had had a lot of fun on the ride, and it was nice to have a few heady conversations with someone her age.

Lee lived in Tybee, on the Georgia coast—the closest beach to Savannah at the ride's end, just under two hundred miles from Marshall. Her place was just down the street from Dot's Restaurant, a spot Val knew.

"So where are you staying when we get there?" Lee asked.

"You know those rooms Dot has...just down the block from yours, if it's where I think it is?"

"That's a great place to stay. Convenient. And you know...a lot of sister-friends frequent Dot's."

"Oh yeah." Val nodded and said she had noticed that on previous visits.

Later that night, Val texted Nicki.

"Don't bring fancy duds. Going out low key @ beach. Met sister-friend on ride. Havin' great time. Hope all's well. See U Sat. (Mwah emoji)"

No reply. Val resisted thinking the worst. She emailed Nicki the ride end map showing parking areas.

***

As Val and Lee rode into the lot at the Savannah Civic Center, Val spotted Nicki standing against Val's pickup in the adjacent parking lot. Nicki was wearing a short khaki skirt, flip flops, and a white Oxford shirt, opened to reveal her cleavage.

"Lucky Williams!" Val yelled. Nicki, wearing her Usher shades, looked up from her phone. *Oh my, my, my.* Nicki smiled and waved, though Val sensed it was guardedly. Val and Lee rode across into the lot, and Val jumped off. Lee straddled her bike and watched as Val greeted Nicki. She didn't want to dirty Nicki's white shirt, so she pecked Nicki on the cheek.

"Nicki. Meet our new friend, Lee Floyd," Val said, nodding her helmet in Lee's direction. Val rested her hand on Nicki's shoulder.

"Lee, Nicki 'Lucky' Williams."

"It's nice to meet you after hearing so much about you. I'd shake your hand, but you just don't have any idea where these gloves have been." Lee laughed. "Later, though."

Lee was referring to the way riders wipe their noses on their gloves when nothing else is handy. Val guessed Nicki assumed something else, based on her expression.

"Later works," Nicki replied without emotion.

"Look. I need to hit the head. I'll be right back, then Lee and I have to check in at that tent over there," Val explained. "When we check in, they give us an armband for a meal. Nicki, I can pay for a meal for you, if you'd like. It's barbecue, but there'll be potato salad, chips, and soda. Of course, there's also a celebratory cake at the end of the ride."

"Nah, I had a big breakfast. Nothing for me," Nicki replied. Val nodded and headed toward the line of toilets at the other end of the parking lot.

"Val has told me a lot about you. She's crazy for you. I hope you know that," Lee said, smiling.

"We're giving you a ride, right?" Nicki offered, having mustered a modicum of civility. Lee explained she had planned to call a buddy who could come pick her up, but she'd gladly take a ride.

Val approached. "Let's go check in and grab that end-of-the-road food they promised," she said. "Nicki, you want to walk with us?"

"I'll wait here. I told Lee we would give her a ride," Nicki said.

"Great. That's nice. We're going right by her house, so why not?" Val said, smiling at Nicki. *Maybe she's not so mad after all.* "Lee, I don't care so much for the barbecue and slaw, but I'd love some of that cake," Val said. She glanced at Nicki, knowing she was riling her. Nicki didn't respond, and her sunglasses denied Val any real satisfaction. She realized it wasn't a nice thing to do, and hoped she hadn't pushed her luck.

Nicki was quiet on the road to the beach. Val let Lee drive since she knew back streets to navigate out of the city and onto the road to Tybee. Val sat next to Lee in the middle of the truck, so Nicki could look out the window. Lee and Val exchanged high fives as they dropped Lee off.

"See you at six. I'll call the gals and make sure they save a table for us," Lee said.

Val drove the block to the apartment and into the small off-street parking lot behind the building.

"Did you have one of those flats again?" Nicki asked once their bags were safely behind closed doors. Val confirmed she had.

"It didn't take as long though, since Lee was there to help out," Val replied.

"That Lee is just what you needed," Nicki snarked.

"If I weren't so greasy, I'd grab you right now. Tempted to do it anyway," Val chided. "Let me get cleaned up so I can properly greet you. And I mean *properly*. You look fantastic by the way." Nicki had slipped her glasses to rest on top of her head. *Oh Lord, please help me.* By this point, Val craved Nicki. "I mean it. Fantastic."

"I'm going to walk to the beach while you're cleaning up. I'll be back by dinner, though. I don't want Lee to think I'm rude."

When Val was finished with her shower, she looked out the window. She saw Nicki sitting in one of the double swings at the edge of the beach. She debated whether to give Nicki time. *Shit. She's had almost a week. My cake comment probably didn't help anything.*

"Come inside please," Val texted Nicki. Nicki responded with a thinking emoji. Val texted back, "No emoji for what I'm thinkin bout."

Nicki stood and turned around. Val saw Nicki was walking back to the apartment. She hoped.

"So, what *are* you thinking?" Nicki asked as she entered the room. Val pulled Nicki toward her and pressed her firmly against her body, but she left her robe closed. Nicki didn't move away. She slipped her arms around Val's robed shoulder and upper back.

"I missed you. But you know, I didn't appreciate what you said—"

"Nicki, I know. I'm sorry about that cake thing," Val interrupted. "You were obviously jealous. It seemed silly. That wasn't a fair thing to say, though."

"It wasn't," Nicki agreed as she brushed her lips across Val's.

"I'm glad to see you," Val whispered into Nicki's mouth. They kissed. Nicki pushed Val back onto the bed, and as she straddled Val's legs, Nicki pulled her skirt up. They continued kissing and rediscovering one another.

"Val, I downloaded Kat Edmonson's cover of 'Just Like Heaven' by The Cure. I don't want to experience another loss. I don't want to wake up to being forever without you."

"I honestly don't see myself just leaving. And I don't see myself pushing you away. I do know people drift apart, though. That happened in Maine with my ex. I don't want to see it this time...or ever again, frankly."

"Is your interest in cycling and those trips, meeting new people...is that going to contribute to our drifting apart? I was jealous, Val. When I saw you and Lee ride up...I mean, she's good looking. Y'all obviously have hit it off."

"Nicki, I'm sorry you were jealous. We had just had that disagreement before I left. You said you wanted time. Texts aren't the way to have a discussion, but I didn't feel right not communicating at all. I mean, we have to be able to meet new people. Feel comfortable with that, right?"

"Should I worry at all the new people you're meeting? Men *and* women. Intense discussions in lounges, hotel lobbies, and government buildings. You're gorgeous, intelligent, confident, and engaging. Should I be worried?"

"You know your Indigo Girl's song, 'Crazy Game?'" Nicki asked. "Just listen to that song when you're worried. I'm going to be there for you. Have you thought anymore about our discussion? The disagreement we had before your ride?"

"I have, but I don't have any better understanding than I did before about your concern. At this point, we're certainly acting like a couple. I've always remained monogamous. No reason for me to look elsewhere. Is that what you mean?" Val asked, hoping she was explaining in a way Nicki understood.

"I'm in love with you. I want to know where that's headed. I think being worried about another loss pushed me to anger. I mean, you just don't seem to want to commit. I don't want you to have to say 'partner' or 'girlfriend' when I'm introduced, but I can't help it. I do want you to think that way. And maybe that's not fair right now," Nicki said. "Just please don't get tired of this. Fuss at me. Make me think about it. Just talk to me, please. Don't let me lose you."

"I don't see that happening. Maybe I can't see things the same way you do. You're right, though. We should both think about it. And talk about it."

Val let her robe open, and she pulled Nicki's head onto her chest and held her. Val drifted off into a nap, feeling Nicki's leg against her. When Val woke up, Nicki was sitting in one of the chairs looking at her. Nicki smiled at her with that much-missed devilish smile.

"I hope you're not chilly. I didn't want to wake you by covering you up," Nicki said. Val smiled as she dressed for dinner.

They strolled to the restaurant holding hands. As they walked in, Lee waved them to her booth.

"Here they are! You ladies come here!" she shouted. The server smiled at them, escorted them to Lee's booth, and took their drink orders.

Nicki had warmed up to Lee by the end of the night. At one point, Lee leaned into the table and looked at Val.

"Damn, girl. If you ever get tired of this one—" Lee said, pointing at Nicki. Val pushed Lee's hand away.

"Hands off. She's not going anywhere, Lee. I'll make sure of that."

Nicki smiled at Val. It was a different smile than Val had seen Nicki give before. Val wanted to take Nicki down to the beach right then and there. *Later.* Val chuckled to herself. She had saved a wrapped piece of cake in her ride's swag bag. *Later.*

After dinner and goodbyes with Lee, Val and Nicki walked along the beach. The moon was bright, and the tide left enough sand for a long walk. Val had brought a small messenger bag, ostensibly for her water bottle. When they had reached a relatively unpopulated section, Val pulled out a bedsheet. She and Nicki spread it out. She took Nicki's hand and guided her down to the sheet. Val pulled the cake out of the bag. Nicki laughed and swiped some icing with her finger. She put it in Val's mouth. They laughed and kissed.

"That isn't what I was hoping for," Nicki explained.

"We'd have quite the audience, don't you think?" Val asked. Nicki nodded, pushed Val down and rolled on top of her. She gently rocked between Val's legs.

After a few more kisses, Nicki rolled, pulling Val on top of her.

"Come with me. Let's go back, but *come* with me," Nicki whispered. Val was warm, aching.

Chapter Twenty-Two

ANOTHER SWEET MORNING WITH Nicki's face next to hers on the pillow. *I could get used to this, I fear. Why would I fear it?* She considered the significance of her mind's word choice. Was she hesitant to commit for fear of being hurt or because she feared a loss of freedom? She was aware that she had never admitted to Nicki that she feared commitment. She had pressured Nicki to admit it, but Val hadn't yet admitted it to herself. She kissed Nicki. Nicki opened her eyes and smiled, pulling Val close.

"I need to tell you something, Nicki," Val said.

"Anything, doll."

"You say that now." Val smiled. "I've decided to do a bike ride from Maine to Key West."

"Wow! That sounds cool. And it's right up your alley. How long? When?"

"I'd like to start in September. It'll be getting cool up north. Hopefully, I make it to Florida by the time it's starting to cool. I figure it's going to take about three months, though."

"Do you think September will be the best time? I mean, because of the project. And three months? That seems like a long time to be gone."

"Nicki, I figured you'd be heavy into construction details and fundraising. I won't see you that often anyway. You're totally capable of handling it, don't you think?" Val decided she would reveal the second, and the most potentially contentious, part of her plan for the ride.

"The rest of the story is that Lee is going to join me on the ride," Val said. Nicki sat up.

"That shouldn't bother me, Val. It shouldn't, but it does. I need time to think!" Nicki snapped.

"I worried about what you'd think, but at least you've spent some time with Lee now. And I thought I noticed your comfort last night when I told Lee in no uncertain terms that we were together." Nicki turned onto her back. She pushed her fists into the bed.

"Argh."

"What more can I do to prove to you...to prove to you..." Val hesitated. Nicki turned quickly to face Val again.

"You can't even say you'll commit to me, Val. Every time I think I can relax with you, with us—" Nicki sounded livid. "I am *not* going back with you today. You drive yourself. I'll fly to Augusta and have a friend pick me up. Or take a bus. Fuck you, Val. Fuck you."

"Nicki. I'm sorry. Listen to me," Val pleaded. "I'm sorry. I am so scared of losing you. Of you moving on. I haven't ever said it, I know," Val continued. "That I'm hesitant to commit, because I'm afraid of losing you."

"What have I said, Val? What have I told you? Why can't you trust me? I love you," Nicki said, holding Val's shoulders firmly. "But I can't be with you if you can't trust me," she said.

"Exactly!" Val shouted. "Trust *me*!" She softly repeated, "Trust me." She wiped her eyes. "Please."

"You're right. This situation is crazy," Nicki admitted. "But still. Thank you for admitting it wasn't just on me."

"It wasn't just you. And it wasn't fair of me—letting you think it was all you, but I'm not even sure I knew that. Let's go home, okay? Together." Val put her hand on Nicki's cheek. Nicki took Val's hand and kissed her palm. She then put Val's palm back onto her cheek.

"Okay. I don't want this argument to be what I'm going to remember," Nicki admitted.

"Nicki. Don't worry. I still feel you. Still," Val said softly. "I know what I'll remember." She and Nicki kissed. "Let's not have this argument again, okay?" She kissed Nicki, finding her tongue. Nicki sighed as they kissed.

***

The ride home was uneventful, except for Nicki trying to distract Val by leaning out of her seatbelt to put her head on Val's breast. *Preventable injury. No way.*

Val dropped Nicki off at her home. Nicki walked around the truck, and Val lowered the window. Nicki leaned inside the window, put her hand around the back of Val's head, and kissed her firmly.

"You only have to ask me, doll," Nicki said softly. "I would love to come finish that cake."

"Get ready for work tomorrow, Ms. Williams," Val said as she pushed Nicki's head beyond the door, rolling the window up. "That's an order!" was what Nicki heard from the shut window. Nicki pulled out her phone and texted Val a pouty emoji, a mwah, and heart emojis in separate texts.

The next morning when Val checked her email, she saw Nicki had sent an email telling Val and JH she was working from home to try and answer some of the fifty emails she had received during the trip.

"Got your email. (Thumbs up emoji) (Heart emoji)," Val texted her.

Val caught up on errands and took a load of clothes to the laundry for drop-off. Cute little Josh greeted her.

"Hi, Miss Val. Ashley's legs were swollen, so her doctor said to stay off them today. She's at Mom's. They say swelling's normal, and that as long as her blood pressure stays normal, she'll be okay."

"Oh, good. I'm glad to hear that. And how are you?"

"I'm ready. Nervous, but ready. I'm pretty sure I can handle this whole thing on my own." He circled both arms around, indicating the laundry's operation.

Josh was a tall, thin, young man, Ashley's age, with curly, dark hair. He was hoping to study computer science and programming in college. Nicki had relayed Peggy's version of Josh's story. He had known he was gay since middle school. Peggy did not want to accept that he was homosexual when he first came out, but she loved her son. Now, she wanted him to be happy, find love with a wonderful partner—man or woman—and lead a successful life.

"Are you going to see Miss Nicki today?" he asked. "I want to run something by her. I don't want to bother Ashley, even though she said to call." She told him she wasn't sure, but he could always call her.

He shared that he and Ashley had discussed the potential of having a dance club. Not dance club as in a business, but rather as an informal social organization. A group of their friends who would come and learn some fun dances. He acknowledged the community had no place for open LGBTQ community members to take ballroom or any other dance classes. He wanted to ask Nicki directly about doing it at the laundromat, even though she had said it was Ashley's place.

"Would I be able to come dance, too?" Val asked.

"That would be so cool. I mean, you don't have to take classes. I would love it if y'all would come as a couple," he answered, beaming. *Couple. There it is.*

***

Weeks had passed. Nicki had been back in her non-stop schedule since the day she arrived home. There had been an occasional quick make-out session in Val's office. A few late-night phone calls. A couple of quick walks on the path. But they mostly traded texts or emails back and forth. Today, Val had seen Nicki at the Pizza Joint with Josh. They invited Val, but she was going home after a ride. She had another hour on her ride to go, and wanted to keep her momentum. She put some of Peggy's famous cheesy breadsticks in her water reservoir pack and continued her ride. She told herself she shouldn't feel jealous that Nicki was spending time with Josh but not with her.

I live within yards of her workplace, but she still doesn't come over. Hm, Val thought on her ride home.

Val heard a text alert on her phone while she was riding. When she pulled up at Grace, she pulled the phone out of her pack.

"Calling goes 2 ways. Don't sulk," read the text from Nicki. Val could feel Nicki's devilish smile.

"K. Come C me, then," Val texted back.

Val had time to shower and eat a couple of cheesy bread pieces. With a quart of water, it was dinner. Nicki drove up an hour later. Val opened the door, and as had become Nicki's typical greeting, she pushed Val inside and onto the chair. She inserted her knee between Val's legs and firmly against her crotch. This time she pushed Val's head onto the back of the chair and leaned into her mouth with her lips. Nicki gently sucked them and found Val's tongue.

"We gotta go," Nicki said, jumping up and pulling Val's arm. "Dance club at the laundry tonight. We're going. Just ol' freeform dancing to some fun music tonight."

"Sure!" Val smiled, even though she admitted to herself that she was disappointed.

"No alcohol." Nicki took the six pack out of Val's hand. "We have to set a good example for the eighteen-year-olds." *Of course we do. Frowny face.*

Josh and Ashley were the music suppliers, and Ashley had brought a Bluetooth speaker. Six high school kids showed up. Ashley introduced them to Nicki and Val. The six seemed to know each other pretty well. They mostly danced in two pairs of a guy and a girl, and one pair of two girls, but occasionally, the guys would go outside, and the girls would pair up or dance without a partner.

Everyone danced across from the office and onto the floor in the rows between the machines and tables. Laundry patrons were invited to join them, but they seemed perfectly happy to watch and weave through the dancers with their baskets. Everyone took at least one turn dancing with a seated, dance-forbidden Ashley. She would practically fall out of the chair, moving as much as she could without standing. She served as the DJ. It seemed as if the group was in deep need of release. Everyone hugged one another as they filed out at the end of the night. Ashley and Josh were on cloud nine at the turnout and the excitement in the room. Nicki commented that she hoped they didn't have to turn people away next week.

Val suggested the community building's largest room could accommodate the group. Since the laundromat office closed at five p.m., everyone could meet at the center at six or seven and dance until nine, whatever everyone wanted. They decided that would work nicely. Josh would get the word out to the group.

Nicki drove Val back to Grace. They sat on the porch talking about how fun it was to see the kids have a good time. Just being themselves.

"I enjoyed being on a date with the woman I love without having to worry what anyone else thinks," Val admitted. Nicki beamed at Val and grabbed her into a big hug.

"You know that's the first time you've said that?" Nicki said, still holding Val.

"Said what? No it isn't. I've told you." Val thought a moment. *Haven't I?* "Surely."

"Uh-uh. Nope. But I'll take it where I can get it," Nicki said, then blew out a raspberry at Val. "Look. I gotta crash. Okay to stay with you tonight?" Nicki asked. Val nodded with a smirk.

"You don't have to ask me that, you know," Val said.

"I'm not going to make those kinds of assumptions, doll," Nicki said. "We have our own places, our own spaces, but I love that you said that. I mean, both things are nice to hear."

Val smiled at Nicki. *Damn. I'm crazy for this woman.* They moved to the bed and snuggled. Both of them were asleep within minutes.

***

JH was out of sight the past few months, except at board meetings. He was constantly working on the site, directing workers while meeting with subcontractors or placing orders. He had reluctantly agreed to a small salary when Val had reminded him of the organization's mission.

154

Val decided she and Nicki should have JH to Nicki's house for supper next week.

"It's time," Nicki agreed. "To do that together, right?"

"Yeah...together. You're right. And if anybody deserves a thank-you meal, it's JH. I'll ask him tomorrow."

When Val called JH, she insisted they wanted to cook for *him*. She was almost surprised when he agreed, and they settled on the date and time.

When JH arrived at Nicki's place, he handed her a plate of homemade brownies.

"You have to share, Lucky." He smiled. "I know you and my brownies. And since you're both hosting, you both get brownies." He made sure to repeat it to Val, washing up a few dishes. He leaned and pecked her cheek.

When she put the bowl into the drainer, she dried her hands, turned around, and gave JH a big hug.

"I'm so glad you agreed to take a break and have an evening with us." Nicki put the brownies down and stepped to get *her* hug from JH. She lingered in the hug, with her head on his chest. He looked down at her head, smiling.

Nicki repeated the pasta dish she had made for Val. Val made the salad.

It was their first time cooking as a couple for someone. Val considered how her perspective had changed. She did consider them a couple. She could tell Nicki was elated Val that had agreed to doing that, even if it was for someone who clearly loved and supported them.

Val remembered JH's suspicions about Nicki's feelings. Here they were, in a situation JH predicted. What Val hadn't counted on, though, was that she, too, would be in love.

The three thoroughly enjoyed one another's company. There was so much to discuss and catch up on. They agreed that they should do this at least once a month. Nicki brought up Val's ride with her new friend in September. JH knew better than to be pulled into that one, but he mentioned how much safer it would be with a riding partner. Val clarified it wasn't only with Lee, but that it was with eleven others in a large organized group ride. Nicki glared at Val.

"What! You never said that. You let me—"

"You never gave me a chance to talk." Val smiled, pulling Nicki into a hug. "Shush." Nicki shocked Val by planting her mouth directly on

Val's lips. Not just a peck, but a luxurious, *From Here to Eternity* kiss. JH just laughed.

"I think I'll step out of the room on that note, ladies," he said. They turned around and both laughed. The three of them alternated bending at the waist laughing, then arching back and continuing to laugh. They were caught in one of those bouts of laughter that one cannot seem to control.

"Lucky," JH was able to get out between laughs. "You have met your match." He continued laughing, but managed to take control enough to say, "Val here is not going to let you get away with that foolishness." He leaned and braced on his knee, getting his breath between laughs. "And Val, I don't know if you have any idea what has hit you, but I love you two. I had my doubts, but I love you together, too. You two will find a way, I think." He resumed laughing.

As Nicki walked away from Val, she grabbed the dishtowel, popped Nicki on the butt with it, and ran. Nicki chased her out the front door. JH sat down at the table to recover from the laughter. He reached from the chair and pulled a brownie off the plate on the counter and ate it, watching Val and Nicki.

When Nicki caught Val, she pushed Val against the pickup and kissed her. They exchanged another long, luxurious kiss.

"We probably shouldn't leave our guest alone any longer," Val said, smiling. They held hands and walked back in, shoulders pushing against one another.

Chapter Twenty-Three

THE REMAINDER OF THE summer passed too quickly. Ashley delivered a baby girl August fifth, a week early. Nicole Antonia Polk, named after Nicki and the baby's father, Tony Ronald Polk. Baby and mother were both doing fine. Val, having just returned from her September bicycle trip, met Ashley for lunch at the pizza place.

"Who's keeping the little one?" Val asked as they headed to the table in the far corner of the restaurant. "I was hoping to catch a little glimpse."

"You and everyone else in town. It's Peggy's day off." Ashley said as she took the water glasses off of the tray and slid it to the side. "It was nice of her to give me a break."

"What's been happening here? Give me the gossip."

"Well, Josh and I kept up with the dance club until I went into labor. He seems to be doing just fine with the laundromat and keeping up with his programming courses. He has one class at the university, and goes to Athens overnight once a week."

"Yeah. Nicki said that my friend Nancy has been letting him stay in my little place when he's there. I'm so glad that works out for him."

"And we trained a single young mom, Traci Hart, to oversee the laundromat when Josh is there. Traci has a three year old. She told me she's been helping Nicki with the shelter program and was in her grief and loss group. I'm so glad we can give to her like Nicki provided for me."

"One of the wonderful things about the community here, Ash. It's really cool. And so handy for all of y'all...you know, the 'it takes a village thing.'"

"Exactly. Don't know if Nicki's told you, but Josh met a super nice guy, Zach, at one of the Athens' clubs. We've all met him. You'll love him, Miss Val."

"I look forward to it. I can see how Josh has really blossomed. He seems so much more confident...interested, you know. In the laundromat. In school. And in all of the things he does for Amazing Grace." Val heard her name called from the counter. "I'll go." She returned with the pizza, with plates and silverware on top of the box.

"I'm glad things are working out so well for everyone," Val said as she pulled a piece of pizza onto her plate. Ashley followed suit.

"Nicki said she's been busy."

"She has been. Fundraising. Community meetings. We don't see one another quite as often as I'd like." The conversation lulled as they ate.

"Then you were gone on the bicycle trip, right? What happened with that? I thought you'd be gone until November." Ashley added after wiping her mouth.

"I was. My friend, Lee, and I started, but that hurricane almost caught up with us. When forecasters indicated the likelihood for dangerous winds and rain, the company had to cancel the trip early so everyone could get home safely. They gave us all credit towards a multi-day trip. Lee and I rode a few days on our own, but by Richmond, Virginia, it was clear it was safer to go home and finish up on our own another time."

"I know you were disappointed. You had been looking forward to it. And the training. You'd been riding so much. Will you have to retrain?"

"As long as I keep up with at least one long ride a week, I should be okay. And yes, it was disappointing, but not much we can do about that. And this way, at least I have a fighting chance of seeing Nicki. Facing three months of not seeing her was daunting, I have to admit."

"I guess it would be." Ashley looked at her phone. "I guess Peggy doesn't need me. I just feel so funny being away."

"That's natural, for sure. I can't wait to meet her, Ashley." Val tidied the table as they stood to leave.

"Oh, Miss Val. I can't wait to show her off. She's so sweet. Let's all get together soon, if we can." After hugs, they each headed their own ways.

***

November brought another birthday for Val. She was now on the downhill slope toward her sixties. She felt no older, but she questioned again how their relationship could stand. Val looked at Nicki not only as a lover, but also as a remarkable businesswoman. She continued to recognize Nicki's different stage of life. Val worried she couldn't maintain the energy Nicki generated. She tried not to think of the future, but she considered it a self-imposed burden.

However, every one of Nicki's texts or calls or visits were accompanied, even still, with a stomach flip, the same as the one she experienced that first night Nicki opened the laundromat to her.

Nicki surprised her with a birthday trip to Asheville, North Carolina. Val was relieved to know Nicki was still enthusiastic about their relationship. Nicki had booked a large, three-room suite with a fireplace at the city's oldest historic inn. For the night they arrived, Nicki arranged a private session in an outdoor, warm tub the size of a small pool. This was followed by a couples' treatment consisting of an exfoliation herb wrap and massage.

The next night, Nicki arranged for a limousine that would take them up to Lookout Observatory. The inn had prepared a special hors d'oeuvres picnic basket. Nicki had also arranged for Val's friends in Washington to send a bottle of Val's favorite Willamette pinot noir.

Nicki was wearing a vivid red, shirred, mid-thigh dress, diamond-like dangle earrings, a matching necklace, and black patent leather heels. The dress was the same style as her black one, and it hugged her curves the same way. When Nicki had walked out of the dressing closet earlier, Val's knees quivered.

"Holy crap. Where are we going?" Val asked. "You know exactly what you're doing to me."

"Oh, hush," Nicki answered as she pressed her body against Val. "C'mon. Let's go. Our car awaits," she whispered in Val's ear, nibbling lightly. *Oh somebody, please help me.* Val could barely refocus on walking.

Their driver was obviously used to similar arrangements. Once they were inside the car, he raised the privacy glass between them and did not open it when they arrived. The shock of the limousine was enough to bring Val back to earth. They enjoyed their picnic and wine, their newly soft skin, and the relaxed state of body and mind that massages bring.

Nicki and Val stepped out of the limo to see one of the most beautiful night views either of them had ever experienced—dark and remarkably clear. The Milky Way, Orion, and even some meteors associated with the Leonids were visible. They could also see specks of twinkling lights spread across the city below, and beyond to the distant hills. Nicki spread a sheet so they could look up from their backs. After a minute or two, Nicki rolled on top of Val.

"Let's get back to where we were just before we left the room," Nicki whispered as she nibbled Val's ear again. She pressed her groin into Val's, and pressed her lips to Val's. They kissed deeply.

"I can't see the sky, but I am seeing stars," Val whispered.

"You are still so *hokey*," Nicki whispered as she unbuttoned Val's coat. She pushed the coat open on one side, and moved her mouth to Val's right breast, on top of her blouse.

"Oops. It's a good thing the inn has a laundry service," Nicki apologized softly.

"If the shirt were off, you wouldn't have to worry about lipstick stains," Val replied.

Nicki helped Val back up, grabbed the sheet, and they stepped back into the limo. Nicki guided Val onto one of the long stretches of seating. She removed Val's coat and her blouse.

"Are you sure there aren't any cameras in here?"

"Cameras would be nice," Nicki replied softly. "I can watch the video when you are off on one of those cycling trips." Val shook her head in disapproval. Nicki removed Val's bra and slipped off her slacks and panties.

"What about you?" Val asked as she arched her back to find Nicki's groin. "I want to feel you."

"In good time," Nicki whispered as she leaned her head down to kiss Val again. "If I'm too close, I can't see your whole body. I need *this* right now," Nicki said as she looked at Val.

Val kept trying to pull Nicki closer. Nicki kept raising her body in movements of slow, controlled push-ups. When Val lowered herself back down, Nicki would follow her and just barely touch Val.

"Oh god, Nicki," Val managed to whisper with ragged breath. "You're killing me."

"That's my goal," she whispered back, smiling.

Nicki slid down Val's body, brushing her lips across Val's abdomen, from one side of the belly to the iliac crest, and then to her mons. Softly, she kissed Val, then nibbled. Val raised her hips in response, and Nicki backed away, holding that same light pressure. Val moaned and lifted in anticipation. Nicki caressed Val's breasts with her free hand and lightly fingered Val's nipple. Val could no longer think, hear, or see. She could only feel. Her gyrations met Nicki's teasing mouth, but never fully. The long sweep of Nicki's hair tickled. Val's moans became whimpers. Her hands were in fists against the leather seat. The throbbing ache for Nicki was painful.

"I need for you to make me come...please," Val whispered.

Nicki slid up to Val's breasts, allowing her tongue to circle her nipples and kiss them. Nicki's mouth continued its exploration of Val's breasts and then returned to her mouth. They kissed deeply, but softly, with Val's attempts to feel more of Nicki's body. Nicki's fully clothed body raised just above Val.

"Nicki. Please," Val cried softly.

Nicki slid the entire length of Val's body, rocking gently with the full pressure of her body until her mouth reached Val's slit. Nicki kissed Val as she had kissed her mouth. Val sought more pressure from Nicki's mouth. Nicki again backed off the pressure. Val was unable to hold back. She took both hands and pushed Nicki between her legs, trying to hold her head. Nicki pulled one of Val's hands off and pulled herself off Val.

"Oh no, doll. This is a birthday present I want you to remember. I paid a fortune to have this limo and driver for the entire night. And I'm going to make it last as long as I can." Nicki teased softly, resuming her tongue's exploration of Val's sex.

Val was breathing in through her teeth and out with a soft moan. She knew she was going to come.

"Please let me hold you, Nicki, please," Val begged as she softly whimpered.

Nicki sucked deeply before moving quickly back to Val's mouth. They resumed the deep, soft, luxurious kissing. Nicki pressed against Val's body, fingers resting in Val's slit. As Val shuddered, violently, she moaned guttural *ohs* into Nicki's mouth.

As Val's orgasm subsided, Nicki delivered another deep kiss. Val felt Nicki's dress and legs slide across her as Nicki changed position. Val began arching her back to feel Nicki against her mons and labia. Her breathing quickened again. Her elbow was bent, and her arm rested on her forehead as if to block bright light out of her eyes. Her whimper was as deep as a moan.

"Nicki, please," Val whispered.

"Should I stop?" Nicki asked as she pulled herself up, double-checking.

"Please do *not* stop...do not stop. Oh god...don't stop," she said as Nicki's mouth found its way back down Val's body. Nicki spent time caressing Val's inner thighs and giving Val's slit light nibbles and strokes of the tongue. Val arched her back to increase the pressure. Again, Nicki rose, not allowing Val to escape the teasing motion.

The increased tempo of Val's hip movement signaled the nearing of another orgasm. Nicki slid her tongue inside Val. Val gasped as Nicki's tongue plunged deep and slid out to lightly suck her clit. When Nicki's fingers moved to Val's mouth, Val sucked on two of them, moving her tongue around them. Nicki's tongue again slid into Val, this time with her wet fingers. Val cried out with a loud moan. She shuddered and pulsed in Nicki's mouth. Nicki held Val in her mouth until the pulsations slowed. She moved back to Val's mouth with her own, kissed her softly, and fell back onto her side, pulling Val to her.

Nicki pulled a down comforter off the seat and covered them. She used a remote to turn off the lights. Val drifted off to sleep with Nicki holding her, Nicki's leg draped between Val's. Nicki drifted off, Val's damp warmth against her.

***

Nicki reluctantly woke Val at three o'clock and told her she needed to pee. She tapped on the privacy window—the high sign for the driver to return them to the inn. On the ride home, Nicki helped Val dress so they could jump out as soon as they arrived.

After they returned, they briefly cleaned up. Nicki slid into bed, still in her dress. Val pulled Nicki's back against her front, and Nicki could feel Val's warm groin. Val slid Nicki's dress up to her waist. Again, Nicki was not wearing panties. As Val's hands slid around Nicki's front, one went between Nicki's legs. The other moved up to Nicki's breast. Nicki was still aroused from their previous lovemaking session. Her hips rocked with Val's caress. As Val lightly pinched and stroked Nicki's breasts, Nicki sighed. Her hips continued to rock, deeper and harder against Val's groin.

Val's fingers teased Nicki with rhythmic caresses. She slid her fingers into Nicki's slit and along her clitoris. Nicki placed her hand on top of Val's and guided her hand and fingers to increase her own pleasure. Nicki also put her other hand on Val's hand that was caressing the breast. As she felt a deep, pulsing ache, Nicki took the hand from her breast and slid it around to Val's bottom. Nicki massaged Val's cheek as she pulled Val forward. Nicki shuddered, and she held Val's hand still for her orgasm. They continued a slow rock together. Nicki moaned and guided Val's hand again to gently and slowly allow a continued orgasmic pulse. Nicki felt Val climax, and she guided Val to face her. They fell asleep again, legs intertwined.

***

The Indigo Girls were playing at a small Asheville venue that night, Val's actual birthday. Nicki did not tell Val where they were going, but she asked Val to dress nicely—business casual. Nicki wore one of her suits—slacks, jacket, and pearls.

"Where are we going? You look so business-like. Nice. An art opening? To the theater?"

"It's a surprise, silly," Nicki replied and clucked her tongue.

Nicki had obtained VIP tickets for the performance that included a meet and greet backstage, complete with hors d'oeuvres. She knew Val would have never guessed that. Nor could any gift make Val happier. She was thrilled by how her plans had been received so far. She had never felt closer to Val than she did tonight. And she was sure Val felt the same.

Nicki had sent Amazing Grace information to the Girls' booking agent when she began working on a performance hall concert calendar. To her great surprise, her VIP ticket purchase had alerted the agent's staff to make a connection between Nicki and a potential Amazing Grace performance for the Girls. He thought this concert could be an opportunity to catch up on project progress.

As the car service dropped them outside of the hall, Val looked up at the marquee.

"What! You're so...Oh, shit. You're kidding, right?" She grabbed Nicki and hugged her. She was acting like a television guest on Ellen who had just been given a ten thousand dollar check. Nicki guided Val inside by putting her hand on the small of Val's back. Once in the door and identified as VIPs, hall staff whisked them backstage to a side room where a large group of people were mingling. Nicki worked the crowd, introducing herself and Val to key people, mostly city and state government officials, but also to the booking agent's staff. Once they made it through to meet the Girls, Nicki was surprised by Val's timidity, how she looked like a dumbstruck teenager running into her idols. Luckily, Val did not need to speak much, because this was Nicki's milieu. Nicki was gracious in having the opportunity to share their excitement about this Georgia nonprofit.

A brief discussion regarding the new Georgia governor's alleged efforts to suppress Black voter turnout in several counties—one of which was theirs—followed. The story of his election had made national news, and it was still a topic of conversation among political types. Everyone backstage empathized with Nicki's account of the race from her small county's perspective.

"You're amazing, Nicki. I'm not surprised, you know, but wow. So adept. I mean, your effectiveness in building alliances. Just amazing." She pulled on Nicki's hand, squeezing it. Nicki forced back tears, overcome by Val's acknowledgements. She had been working so hard. It wasn't like she didn't know Val appreciated that, but she had never expressed it so strongly. *Never so much right from her heart*, Nicki thought.

The concert was energizing and inspiring. She was into so many of the songs, even some she hadn't heard from Val's playlist or the university's radio station.

Val leaned over and shouted, "Now you see what I mean!" Nicki nodded and kissed Val.

Afterward, Nicki had one other request for Val.

"Hey, will you come with me to one of the dance clubs now?"

"Nicki, I'm exhausted, but even if it's *my* birthday, I couldn't disappoint you after all you've arranged this weekend. Let's go." Nicki squealed and ordered the car service.

When they arrived at the club, they could hear and feel the music, especially the bass lines. Eighties music blared. Nicki knew that was Val's favorite. When Val smiled, Nicki shouted a "happy birthday," headed straight to the bar, and ordered two champagnes. She led Val by the hand, snaking through the crowd as each held her flute. When Nicki found her perfect spot, she started dancing, toasted with Val, and Val joined her in the dance.

Nicki squealed and beamed as Josh and Zach danced up next to them. They also had champagne flutes with bubbly, and leaned and kissed both Nicki and Val without missing a beat. Both of them shouted "happy birthday" to Val, who was now shaking her head at Nicki's ploy. The four of them danced for an hour and a half without stopping, except for runs to the bar for a refill and waters for the group. At two-thirty a.m., Val and Nicki called it a night, and the guys walked them out.

"Guys. I can't thank y'all enough. I thought this one was sneaky," Val said as she pointed her head at Nicki. "But y'all are right there with her. It really made my night extra special."

"This was our first big trip together, so we're thrilled. Look, we're staying at a friend's, not far from your inn. We'll give you a ride," Josh offered. On the way, Val entertained them with stories of Nicki's business prowess backstage before the concert.

Back at the Inn, Val admitted her exhaustion. Nicki pouted, but she slid naked against Val in between the sheets on the deep, pillow-top mattress and under the heavy feather-bed-style comforter.

"Nicki, this is the most incredible birthday celebration I have ever had. You are amazing. Thank you," Val whispered into Nicki's mouth as they kissed goodnight.

"I don't want any reason for your forgetting me...ever," Nicki replied softly. "Night." After a few minutes of snuggling, Nicki turned to spoon her back into Val. Val pulled her arm to cradle Nicki.

"I love you," Nicki whispered.

"Oh babe. I love you, too. I don't say it enough, I know. But I do." Val kissed Nicki's shoulder.

Nicki felt tears fill her eyes. She was glad Val wouldn't see the tears. She thought back to her feelings earlier. All the doubts she had about Val's commitment in the past. How she felt that now she could be comfortable with their relationship. She wiped her eyes, settled into Val's hold, and drifted into sleep.

Chapter Twenty-Four

JANUARY MARKED THE ONE-YEAR anniversary of Val in Marshall, of many friendships, and particularly of her relationship with Nicki. Val could not believe how things were progressing with the project. January also marked the beginning of a new legislative session.

Nicki spent close to the legislature's full forty days in Atlanta with occasional weekends home. She met with Governor Long to present tentative results of a robust community investment. With the community center staff reaching out, to hosting, facilitating and leading education workshops in group facilitation, at least ten community groups were regularly using the facility. This included JH and Nicki's grief support group, JH's veteran support groups, Alcoholics Anonymous, and the unofficial Dance Club. The Dance Club had now grown to weekly participation of at least fifty—mostly teens, but a few adults.

Per Sheriff Jenkins, petty theft had decreased in the past year. Sandy Ann's husband, the principal, said truancy and the high school drop-out rate had decreased. The decreases may not have been huge yet, but Val hoped these may solidify into a more stable trend over time.

Nicki shared these anecdotes, and also presented historical data related to nonprofit casinos in New York, Iowa, and Nevada. She painted a potential picture of Governor Long as the new Zell Miller, bringing hope of a different sort, as the savvy, progressive governor who worked to bring a sensible gaming plan to the state. He seemed interested and positive. And appropriately flattered, Nicki had told Val.

Val used her time to initiate the first programs of the newly launched Screening and Community Kidney Education Delivered—SACKED. The project aimed to prevent and delay progression of kidney disease in the surrounding area's residents. Val had begun work on this in the months prior to her big bike trip. She had submitted it to Tom for his suggestions just before she left, giving him ample time to review and make suggestions. While Nicki had been in Atlanta, Val had been able to complete her tasks related to its initiation. One of those tasks had been identifying a SACKED program director. Val interviewed several individuals before hiring a half-time family nurse practitioner, Fran Worth, to help with development and logistics.

Fran Worth had worked as a medical-surgical floor nurse for ten years before her back injury at the hands of a confused patient. After six months with outpatient rehab, it was determined floor nursing was physically unsuitable for her. This led Fran to pursue the Family Nurse Practitioner master's degree and license, a move she saw increasing her options.

Val had met Fran on a cycling trip and kept in touch. Fran rode a recumbent, which she touted as less painful for her back and helped keep her healthy. Val encouraged Fran to apply, which she did. The interview proved what Val knew. Fran was the one.

Fran proved invaluable with the planning and setup of the program. This was a win for Fran as the establishment of the program was one of her graduate administration class's community health projects. Fran, too, had seen the same need for early education and intervention and prevention, especially for those with diabetes and hypertension.

Nicki had procured a donation from the area car dealer for a retired cargo van in stellar condition. Josh worked with the local technical school to have the existing bins re-arranged, to have a small desk and some file cabinets installed, and to have the van painted, complete with signage. The dealer donated the cost of an awning mounted on the van's side. The end result was a professional-looking, highly functional, mobile education and screening van.

Fran and Val presented healthy snacking and bicycle safety programs to each elementary and middle school class in the county. They had arranged for two health screenings to be held in the big box store's parking lot—one in winter, and one in late spring. The local nursing schools had already agreed to have the screenings become one of their students' required community health clinical experiences. Fran had written a proposal for two part-time student intern positions to help with screening referrals and follow-ups during the year. Fran would also serve as a clinician for the casino's sick child daycare area when it was operational.

The trajectory of SACKED was on course. Val and her friends in healthcare were well aware that almost everyone in their community knew someone on or close to beginning dialysis. These were people who would never travel to a larger city for these services because they may not have had access to transportation for the hour-plus trip.

Building health resources close to home fulfilled the goals of Val's initial mission.

JH had continued his VA group in Milledgeville, thirty miles away, once a week, but he was also holding one at Amazing Grace's Community Center. George and Frank came regularly now that Pops had passed on and Noodle was settled safely in an Augusta group home.

***

The Amazing Grace campus was buzzing with activity. In addition to the security and facilities building, where administrative offices resided, the performance hall structure, Rock of Ages, was now complete. The sound system was in, as well as all electrical and plumbing. The finishing touches, signage, and state and local inspections would be completed by early September. With the main casino building solidly underway, JH had predicted that if pro-gaming efforts were successful this session, and if the weather cooperated as it had last year, the Casino could open by next December.

The Amazing Grace payroll had grown: two part-time security guards, a part-time public relations and IT position held by Josh, two full-time facilities staff members, one full-time landscaper who coordinated with Sheriff Jenkins for assistance from community service individuals, and Fran as the family nurse practitioner. Once the casino opened, there would be potentially two hundred additional twenty-four hour part-time positions, all with health insurance, making project positions desirable and providing community coverage needs.

Val and Lee were on target to begin the second half of their previously-aborted trip down the east coast. They would pick up in Richmond mid-September to avoid vacation crowds. There was one huge difference in Val's life plans though. She would have nowhere to live. She was selling the tiny home and Josh would be living in Bambi.

Ashley's labor and subsequent bundle of joy put a damper on her for a week or two, but she picked right back up on the business aspects while living at Peggy's. Josh was staying in the laundromat office—at least until Ashley vacated his bedroom at home. She would move the beautiful crib and changing table Nicki and Val had given her into the laundromat or her next home. When Josh was able, he would move into Bambi while Val was gone, and let their new worker live in the office if needed.

It made Val happy to think of Josh in her Bambi. She fondly remembered a friend who lived in a small camper in college. Their group used to laugh when they would visit him there, but they all thought it was super cool. Knowing a wonderful, young gay man would be living in it flooded her with memories.

***

Ashley had begun seeing her high school sweetheart, the father of her baby, again. Tony Ronald, T-Ron, or Tron, as he was called, had gone by the laundromat to talk to Ashley. He told her that her dad had come by and apologized to him. It was part of Ben Linton's twelve-step recovery process. Tron now felt safe to resume seeing Ashley, if she would have him.

Ashley always thought he was a good guy. He had been a star basketball player and a pretty good student. Ashley had heard Tron was taking courses at the technical school, and was considering signing up with the Sheriff's Department. Tron was convinced he wanted to be present for their child, and even if Ashley didn't want to pursue the relationship, he wanted baby Toni to know her father. Ashley agreed to begin seeing him again, and to let him see Toni on a regular basis. Once Ashley and Tron had resumed dating, they began looking for a place to live together.

Ashley would begin her advanced accounting college coursework soon. Peggy, Val, Nicki, Josh, and even JH were involved in Toni's care, and Ashley knew how much better it would be to have a steady home supplemented with help from loving friends—the village concept, Ashley called it.

Tron and Ashley talked with Val about the costs of a tiny house. Val loved Ashley and her pluck. She offered to sell her tiny house to Ashley, owner financed.

Val's bike ride was soon going to take her away for a month or two. While she was gone, Ashley would rent with a purchase option, the rent going toward the down payment. Living in the tiny house would help Ashley determine if the three of them could make a go of it in such tight quarters.

"But where will you live when you come home? You've given up all of your places. I don't think that's such a good idea, Val," Nicki said on one of their visits.

"Josh'll have his own place by then. He'll have been looking for something while I'm gone. So, I can go back to Bambi."

"Sounds like you're okay if it doesn't," Nicki replied curtly.

"Oh ye of little faith," Val said. "Nicki. Don't things usually work out as they're meant to? Everything's been going so well. It's going to be all right."

They had never seriously discussed moving in together, and Val wasn't sure she was ready for it. It had crossed her mind, and she was pretty sure it had crossed Nicki's as well, but when Nicki didn't offer to share her home with Val now, she wondered if their having separate spaces would continue to be a necessary component of their relationship.

Ashley and Val sat down and drew up paperwork making it official that Ashley would move into Grace after Val left for her trip this coming September. That evening, Val had dinner at Nicki's house.

"Let's toast to Ashley, the homeowner-to-be," Val suggested, raising her glass.

Nicki stiffened up, but she raised and clinked her glass.

"Are you sure you're not taking Bambi and moving to Savannah?" Nicki snarked.

"No, ma'am, I don't plan to," Val replied.

"But without a home, you won't have any particular reason to return," Nicki said. "You'll have pretty much reached your goals here, it seems to me."

"Nicki. I am beyond thrilled with what has happened with this project. I love this community now. And I—" Val started.

"But..." Nicki said. "I know there's a *but* coming."

"As I was saying," Val continued, "And I love you. Why would I leave without discussing things with you anyway? And we still have the casino to finish, and then the hotel project. I think there's a good bit to go yet."

Nicki looked away, distressed. Serious.

"Nicki. Please stop inventing scenarios that aren't helpful. This is our hang-up. We've had this discussion multiple times. Please, let's not have it anymore. I'm not going anywhere. I'm not."

"You're right." This time Nicki looked down. "Let me go think about it a minute. You know I just shoot off. Just give me a minute." Nicki walked into another room. After fifteen minutes, she returned. She rested a hand on Val's shoulder and looked into her eyes.

"I'm so sorry, doll. I really am. I don't know what gets into me...how those thoughts grip me. I don't understand, though, how you can be so fancy-free about the future."

"I know. I appreciate your honesty. I have fears. I do, but I think we love each other enough to work out any issues. Right?" Val feared, though, that she would see this discussion again sometime. And she wondered if she should suggest their moving in together. *It's her house. It has to be her decision. Right?*

Before she left for the night, and knowing Nicki had an early morning, Val kissed Nicki goodnight. As Val was pulling away from the hug, she ran her fingers between Nicki's legs.

"Think about me tonight. I'll certainly be thinking about you," Val whispered. Nicki smiled as Val shut the door.

"Meanie," Nicki whispered, smiling. *Devilish smile.*

***

The next day, Val was riding her usual twenty-four-miler. She stopped briefly at a local quick-stop for a ride snack. As she was pulling her leaning bike away from the quick-stop's wall, a familiar, dreaded blue pickup pulled in next to her. Before she could mount and ride away, the driver, Ben Linton, stepped out quickly.

"Miss Scott." Val was taken aback and somewhat nervous. "If you would give me two minutes, I would appreciate it," he continued.

"I'm not sure it's a good idea," Val replied tentatively.

"Miss Scott. *Please.* I only want to apologize," he said, facing the ground. He raised his head up and looked at her. "Miss Scott. What me and those boys did to you was my fault. I know that was wrong. It is important to let you know I regret what I did that day. My influence led the boys to act that way."

"I appreciate your saying that," Val admitted. "Thank you." Val knew recovery was a hard road.

"I would never ask you to forgive me for that. What I did to so many people...I am a drunk. Always was. What I did to you and to Ashley...that was bad. I lost her. And I hurt someone...two people...that she cares for—both the boy and you," he said. "Anyway, I do want to pay you for the window I broke. I talked to the dealer. That window I broke would be close to a thousand bucks, installed. I know your insurance probably paid for it. I can send them the money, or I can give it to you. I don't care which. But I need to make amends."

Val extended her hand to him and they shook.

"Mr. Linton, I know this wasn't easy. I appreciate that you're on the right path. I tell you what, though. You make that check out to Amazing Grace Delivered or Valiant Expeditions," she said as she handed him a business card from her under-seat bag.

"We allow space for Al-Anon and other good community organizations. We're always fundraising. This is a nice gesture. You can even donate in someone's memory or honor. I'll thank you for the donation, then we'll be square."

"I'll do that, Miss Scott. Thank you for your understanding. I see why everybody is so grateful to you and all y'all are doing." He drove away. Val waited for him to vanish from sight before she resumed her ride. *Amazing Grace. Amazing.*

Chapter Twenty-Five

VAL CONTINUED HER TRAINING, occasionally on weekend rides with Lee. Val felt like Nicki trusted her, but she worried if that would wane after two months on the road. She and Nicki had continued their conversation, in general terms, as to whether they considered themselves officially a couple. They had not made any sort of formal commitment. Val had admitted, again, that two months apart seemed long. However, Val's brush with death years ago solidified her determination to accomplish her long-held dreams. She was finishing the ride.

At this point, the nonprofit casino laws appeared to be on track for a January passage, based on information from political pundits Nicki had worked with. Even though nonprofit casinos weren't a new idea, the necessary lobbying was still formidable. Val continued to trust that Nicki was capable of coordinating these efforts.

Months ago, Ashley and Josh had convinced Val, JH, and Nicki that they should have an initiation event for the building—a community *thank you* celebration in the form of a Karaoke Night on the Friday following Labor Day. The board thought it was a splendid idea. They appointed Ashley point person, with help from Mr. Troup, the high school drama teacher and chorus director. Josh would handle social media, flyers, and programs. Nicki would handle press releases. Mr. Troup would emcee.

Karaoke proved to be a wildly popular idea in Hancock County. Mr. Troup advised Ashley and Josh that he was going to have to hold auditions if people didn't quit signing up. Troup had estimated time for only twenty performance slots.

He and Ashley had released guidelines to prospective participants. Nothing was to be allowed that wasn't positive, hopeful, or kind.

Several people in the Dance Club had opted to perform a number. Mr. Troup's class, which he fashioned as *Glee* performers, were including at least two numbers, and board members were encouraged to perform.

Val had never sung publicly. Still, she was grateful they were doing some karaoke at Dance Club and wanted to be a part of the launch event. A crowd of people she wasn't sure about, but if other board members could do it, so could she. It honored the community, and helping this community was something she had hoped for since her first few years in nursing.

***

The Amazing Grace Karaoke Community Celebration was only two weeks away. JH assured them that everything would be ready in time for the dress rehearsal, although construction issues were delaying the opening until September.

Val was concerned the building wouldn't be finished in time. She was scheduled to leave for Virginia and the bike trip the Saturday following Friday's performance. With all of the prep work for the show, Val and Nicki seemed to have no time for what either considered proper goodbyes.

The entire community, donors, and area government leaders were invited to attend. The event would be free, but it was agreed that tickets would be issued to estimate the head count. Ashley, Josh, and Mr. Troup would be the only ones who knew until performance night exactly who was performing, and what would be performed.

Val and Nicki were working together and separately on their performances. They were to sing "Who Says You Can't Go Home," with Nicki taking Bon Jovi's part and Val in the Jennifer Nettles role. They had performed it in karaoke once at Dance Club. The Club attendees' enthusiasm had settled it.

Two numbers appeared on the program as "Special Guest Performance," generating quite a buzz. These performances were not included in the dress rehearsal, so even the performers were excited. Val and Nicki overheard comments such as, "Who is it?" and "I'll bet it's Tricia Yearwood!"

Peggy was in the sound-proof control room with a window to the stage she could see the performance as she minded Toni. She could hear over the room's speakers.

Mr. Troup's high school students passed out programs and exchanged them for the entrants' tickets. It turned out that almost five hundred were picked up early, and that included the thirty performers. A few more were given out at the ticket window just before the show. Everyone was pleased, though. This was a good community turnout for karaoke by anyone's standards.

JH flashed the lights, and Rev. Donny walked out onto the stage.

"Let us pray." His brief message was that he hoped the Amazing Grace project would bring as much support into the community as the Board of Directors had hoped. He prayed for God's blessing on all of those making the entire project possible, and he prayed for God's blessing on each and every person attending. The Marshall Baptist choir filed onto the stage and sang "Amazing Grace." JH joined the choir for this number, and several audience members sang from their seats.

Next, Mr. Troup introduced himself. He asked Nicki, as the organization's front person, to come say a few words.

When Nicki walked out onto the stage among incredible applause, she nodded to the audience. Val's jaw dropped. Nicki had been in the dressing room, and Val had not yet seen her. Zach had come up for the performance and evidently had worked his magic on Nicki's hairdo. The Sharon Stone's super short cut pixie feigned a mussed look, but it was obviously extremely controlled. She was wearing her black shirred dress. Nicki looked fantastic! *Damn. That is one hot woman.*

"Thank y'all for coming. You know how hard we've all worked for this moment. Tonight is not about the Board, though. It's about you!" She swept her arm toward the room.

"Please enjoy yourselves tonight, and feel free to sing along. You've probably noticed our jumbotrons along the walls. Everyone should be able to see them, so you can sing along with any song, if you feel so moved. It's okay if you're not a singer. Enjoy yourselves. We know *we* will!" She smiled and nodded her head to the crowd as they clapped.

Mr. Troup came back out and introduced his high school chorus class, who would be singing "I Gotta Feeling," by the Black Eyed Peas.

"Wow," Val mouthed when Nicki approached Val backstage. She puckered her lips in an air kiss for Nicki. During the performance, Val stood next to Nicki, shoulder to shoulder so their arms would touch. Josh and Ashley were also standing on that side of the stage. Val tapped Nicki's arm and nodded toward the back. Frank and George were dressed in black twill pants and gray twill shirts with *Security* patches on the sleeves, and metal name tags high and to the right on their shirts. They had black baseball caps with a security patch as well.

"I didn't know," Val whispered in Nicki's ear.

"JH, of course," Nicki whispered back. They smiled and nodded.

A few community members sang an uplifting hymn, and Aretha Franklin's "Respect." Nicki was invited back on stage in the spot of the "Special Guest Performance." Ashley looked at Josh, now shoulder to shoulder, pressing against her, and he smiled. Katy Perry's "Firework" started. Ashley stood agape as Nicki belted the song. Josh nudged Ashley into the spotlight's edge. Nicki turned to Ashley and sang to her. Occasionally, Nicki would motion to the audience, including them in her salute. Josh was clapping softly as he sang with Nicki, but away from any microphone. Tears ran down Ashley's face, and several board and community members started singing. When Nicki ended, Ashley ran and hugged her. The audience stood and applauded. Most everyone knew what Ashley had suffered, and they saw how she had come back swinging. From the control room, Peggy wiped tears from her eyes.

A group of Mr. Troup's dance students did a nicely choreographed instrumental version of "Cake by the Ocean."

Sandy Ann came out strutting in fancy Western wear to "Man! I Feel like a Woman." The crowd hooted and hollered, obviously enjoying the performance.

Next up was Nicki and Val's duet. Val was wearing her black jeans and a black silk T-shirt, so the two of them made quite a pair. The audience would shout and raise their fists when they said "S'all right." Nicki played a mean air guitar. They received a standing ovation.

Nicki walked off the stage, but Val stayed behind as the second *special guest*. The Bruno Mars song, "Just the Way You Are," started. Nicki swung around backstage when she heard Val's voice and realized Val had not followed her off the stage. Nicki stood wide-eyed and blushing intensely. Val smiled as she sang and glanced at Nicki. Val knew the crowd had little doubt about who she had in mind while she was singing. Val had become comfortable with the community, and with the apparent knowledge they were a couple. She also hoped this may solidify for Nicki that she didn't mind others knowing they were a couple. Nicki put her face in her hands. She was standing off-stage, but she was definitely on display. Josh was pretending to jump up and down, clapping softly and beaming. Ashley was weeping again, but she was smiling and clapping. Val received a standing ovation led by the Dance Club group. She bowed and walked off stage.

After a few other numbers, the executive board filed on stage led by Ashley and Josh. The program read, "Perfect." Ashley started the solo of Pink's song, and Josh provided back-up. The executive board joined them onstage during the last few verses, and several members of the choir and chorus filed onstage. At the end, everyone in the room was singing. The audience was standing and clapping, and the performers were singing with outstretched arms. Both the audience and performers were crying, smiling, and hugging one another. Val felt this served as a version of "passing the peace" for her and Nicki.

The night was a huge success. Everyone was talking to one another on the way out—this song or that, what they loved, how much fun it was. Val believed Amazing Grace's message of hope was embraced by the community.

The students, Nicki, JH, and the security guys would return for clean-up Saturday, but right then, Nicki and Val had a date for some goodbyes. They slipped out to head to Grace. Val's truck was packed and ready to go.

***

Nicki's eyes welled up as the two sat in Grace's living space. Val repositioned herself on the floor between Nicki's legs, and she put her head on Nicki's chest.

"That was fun, but I'm glad it's done," Val said hoarsely.

Nicki stood, pulling Val to stand also.

"I will miss you," Nicki said, kissing Val. "You're sweet, you know. I can't believe you sang that song. It was beautiful. You blew me away. You did. I still can't believe it."

"This sounds hokey, but I mean it. You are the best thing that has ever happened to me, Jennifer Nicole Williams. I love you." Nicki pulled Val's face to hers. They kissed. "I want you to pick me up in Key West. Please. I want you to come," Val said softly.

"I have work to do here. You come back *here* when you're finished," Nicki replied. "I'm still a little pissed, you know."

"I know that, but I think you understand why I'm going."

Nicki nodded and shifted her eyes from Val's. She had heard from Val so many times about her bucket list. She understood, but that didn't mean she had to like her being away.

"Don't do this now," Val said. "We don't have much time. I don't want us to fight tonight. I'm doing this ride, Nicki."

Nicki sunk onto the floor and cried softly. She was again torn by what she feared was Val's lack of commitment. She knew Val loved her. She had heard Val profess it to the community tonight. She had no reason to doubt it. So why did it hurt so much?

"Nicki." Val pulled Nicki's face up. "Come be with me now. Let's go to bed." Nicki got up and walked back to the bedroom as if she were a child heading to do a dreaded chore.

"I'm going to ask again. Stay with me tonight, but only do it if you can *be* with me."

"I'm not sure, Val. This is tearing me up. I'm not sure why," Nicki admitted.

"Will you be here when I come back, Nicki?" Val asked. "I'm not leaving. I'm going on a bike ride. Yeah, it's a long one, but I'm coming back. I'm coming back to *you*."

"That's your plan," Nicki said. "But now that you've given up your home and your trailer—"

"It is my plan. Just as your plan is to stay here. I have friends now, right? Maybe someone will put me up for a while." She tapped her index finger on Nicki's chest. "Remember, we're going to trust one another, right?" Val said. She leaned and tried again to kiss Nicki. Nicki responded this time. Was Val saying she would live with her?

"You do have friends. Good friends...very good friends," Nicki replied, smiling as they kissed.

Val slipped her hand under Nicki's dress and slid it around to her bottom. Nicki pulled Val into her and arched her back to feel Val between her legs. Val threw her arms around Nicki's neck and dropped them to her shoulders, down to the small of her back and around front to between her legs. Nicki sighed into Val's mouth, and they kissed softly. Nicki ached for Val. They made love until first light arrived.

Val left Nicki in the bed, kissed her lips once more, dressed, and Nicki heard the truck drive away.

Nicki rose slowly. She smiled to herself, knowing she had left a little note in Val's suitcase as a surprise. She wasn't sure she had made peace with Val's departure, but she was proud of herself for that coup.

The short, handwritten note displayed several words from the 'Til Tuesday song on Val's playlist, "Coming Up Close." She knew Val would hear Aimee Mann in her head when she read the song's final stanza. She hoped Val would understand coming home meant she wanted them to live together.

"Come on home," Nicki whispered, as she thought of the note.

***

What Nicki didn't know was that Val, too, had a surprise. For her. With JH, Val had plotted with the Board during Nicki's most recent business trip. Nicki was so busy following up from her Atlanta meetings and preparing for the show, she had not thought twice when Val hadn't added the Board meeting minutes to the corporate record. Nicki had known every agenda item, and she knew those items would sail through.

The next day, when Nicki walked past Val's office in the administrative suite, she noticed the new door plaque read: "Jennifer N. Williams, MBA." Next line: "Chief Executive Officer." Nicki squeaked, quickly unlocked the door and flung it open. Val's things were gone. The desk was neat and empty except for a new stack of business cards. They read: "Jennifer N. Williams, MBA. Chief Executive Officer." She shook her head, smiling.

Under the cards was an envelope that read "Nicki" in Val's handwriting. Nicki opened the envelope and pulled out the small note. Obviously printed on a computer were the last three lines of the refrain of Natasha Bedingfield's "Unwritten." Nicki recognized that Val remembered Mike's note to her. Her eyes filled with tears of sadness, joy, and release. She felt so relieved to feel Val's empathy and love. Yes, and commitment.

Following, in small cursive handwriting, Val had added the last two lines of "Cake by the Ocean." She held the note to her chest.

Chapter Twenty-Six

NINE MONTHS LATER

"HEY, CAN YOU COME in and taste this?" Val called from the open kitchen window. She rinsed her tasting spoon and waited to hear Nicki's reply.

Val saw Nicki's head pop up from the flower bed below the window.

"Be right there," Nicki answered as she stood. "I still can't believe you're here...so many months later," Nicki said as she washed her hands. She dried them and reached for the spoon.

"God, that's good. You're right, the crab was a good addition."

Val wrapped her arms around Nicki's waist and pressed her against the counter.

"I'm glad you invited me. I love being here. It's a good life, you know. And I agree about the gumbo, too. That roux is what really makes it, though. Thanks to Aurora for the special instruction." She returned the spoon to its rest.

"Toni still napping?" Nicki asked.

"She is, as far as I know. Glad Ashley and T-Ron were able to steal a long weekend. It's fun having a baby here. As nervous as I was about you getting sad, it's been the exact opposite. And she's so good."

"Yeah. I think it helps to know we're just godparents, though. She's all Peggy's tomorrow!" They both laughed at Nicki's pronouncement.

"You got that right. I look forward to our little Bambi trip next week. I can't believe you have a week off. Beach and biking here we come!" Val smiled.

"Val, are you thinking that since it's fun having a baby here that you want us to have one?" Nicki's head tilted as she asked.

"Uh. No. Are you?" Val grimaced, baring her teeth in fear.

"No. I think about it sometimes, but it just doesn't seem to fit into our lives."

"Whew. You know I love you more than anything, but a child? No, Nicki. Not up for that."

At that moment, a little cry wafted from the hallway. They looked at each other and laughed.

"Uh-uh. Nope. Not in the middle of the night. I'll go," Nicki said, chuckling as she walked to the bedroom.

"Nit-nit! Nit-nit!" Toni said, holding her arms straight up for Nicki, opening and closing her fingers. Nicki pulled Toni into her arms, kissed her cheek, settled her onto her hip, and returned to the kitchen.

"Look who I found," Nicki said to Val, who leaned and kissed Toni's cheek.

"Bam-bee?" Toni said, pointing toward the screen door, where Bambi was parked outside. Nicki put Toni down, and Toni pattered to the door. She looked intently at Bambi, and then turned to Val.

"Bam-bee." This time she pointed and slapped the screen lightly.

"She really likes that Bambi," Nicki said, smiling.

"Good taste if you ask me," Val replied. "Should I give her another tour?"

"Nah. I'm hungry. Smelling this gumbo is making my stomach growl. I never had lunch."

"Well, let's eat," Val said, placing Toni into the highchair. "I might as well just put the bib on myself. She gets more on me than she does on herself. You eat first. I'll feed her. Then you can clean her up and play while I eat and clean the kitchen."

"Fair enough." Nicki leaned and kissed Val's cheek. "God, I'm glad you came home to me."

"Never thought of doing anything else, Ms. Williams."

The End

Appreciation:

"Cake by the Ocean"
Joseph Jonas / Justin Tranter / Mattias Per Larsson / Robin Lennart Fredriksson
Cake by the Ocean lyrics © Warner/Chappell Music, Inc, Universal Music Publishing Group

"Coming Up Close"
A. Mann
Coming Up Close lyrics © 'Til Tunes Associates

"Unwritten"
Danielle A. Brisebois / Natasha Anne Bedingfield / Wayne Steven Jr Rodrigues
Unwritten lyrics © Sony/ATV Music Publishing LLC

"Crazy for You"
John Bettis / John Lind
Crazy for You lyrics © Universal Music Publishing Group

"I'm a Believer"
Neil Diamond
I'm a Believer lyrics © Sony/ATV Music Publishing LLC, Universal Music Publishing Group

About Ann Tonnell

Ann Tonnell is a retired RN, having worked in management most of her nursing career. However, her first career was typesetting and composition. It was not until retirement that she found inspiration to capture stories in writing. She lives with her wife in a small community in the North Georgia mountains just yards from the Appalachian Trail. She is a DIY dabbler and avid cloud admirer.

Email
Website https://anntonnell.com/
Facebook https://www.facebook.com/ann.tonnell/
Instagram https://www.instagram.com/anntonnell/
Twitter https://twitter.com/anntonnell

Note to Readers:

Thank you for reading a book from Desert Palm Press. We appreciate you as a reader and want to ensure you enjoy the reading process. We would like you to consider posting a review on your preferred media sites and/or your blog or website.

For more information on upcoming releases, author interviews, contest, giveaways and more, please sign up for our newsletter and visit us as at Desert Palm Press: www.desertpalmpress.com and "Like" us on Facebook: Desert Palm Press.

Bright Blessings

Made in the USA
Middletown, DE
17 June 2022